Some Comments on Books by Ned Conquest

The Gun and Glory of Granite Hendley

" . . . [The book] must have been fun to write. And with or without a knowledge of its Scottish background, it is certainly fun to read."
— Carlos Baker, *Princeton Alumni Weekly,*
"Good Reading" Supplement, 24 November, 1970

"While . . . put out as a Western, . . . [the book] should be more justly regarded as a novel that happens to take place in the pioneer West.
" . . . [T]he characters . . . stay with you despite the brevity of the story and the unavoidable paucity of descriptive and atmospheric passages."
— Carter B. Jones, *The Sunday Star,*
Washington, D.C., 15 March 1970

Achilles and Company

"Ned Conquest has created — created is the word, not merely written — an intriguing book for all readers . . . . The plays are a delight to read and imagine . . . . But they are also serious and adventuresome works of literature about major figures in our cultural heritage."
— John Funari, *The American Oxonian*, Spring 1990

" . . . An unsuspecting layman could possibly mistake the tragedies for long-lost originals."
— Heller McAlpin, *Princeton Alumni Weekly,*
21 December 1988

Virginia, the Gray and the Green

" . . . [S]plendid short story collection . . . . It is the internal battles that rage within each character's soul that will attract readers."
— Bruce Simon, *Richmond Times-Dispatch,*
23 December 1990

" . . . [S]ix short stories that haunt like elegies and leave the reader pondering the permanent maiming of the human spirit by war."
— John Funari, *The American Oxonian*, Spring 1991

The Way of
the Eagle

by

Ned Conquest

SUNSTONE
PRESS

SANTA FE

These stories are a work of fiction. Except for the historic persons specifically named in this book, no likeness to any person or persons, living or dead, is intended; and none should be inferred. Any similarity is purely coincidental.

Artwork by Patrick O'Brien

Sunstone books may be purchased for educational, business, or sales promotional use. For information please write:
Special Markets Department, Sunstone Press,
P.O. Box 2321, Santa Fe, New Mexico 87504-2321.

Library of Congress Cataloging-in-Publication Data:

Conquest, Ned.
    The way of the eagle / by Ned Conquest.
        p. cm.
    Contents: A woman, a dog, and a hanging tree—The death of Granite Hendley—Author's afterword.
    ISBN: 0-86534-398-5 (softcover)
        1. Southwest, New—Fiction. I. Title.

PS3553.O5147W39 2003
813'.54—dc21   2003054385

Published in SUNSTONE PRESS
Post Office Box 2321
Santa Fe, NM 87504-2321 / USA
(505) 988-4418 / *orders only* (800) 243-5644
FAX (505) 988-1025
www.sunstonepress.com

The Way of the Eagle

The Way of the Eagle includes two short novels and an Author's Afterword on their composition. The action of both novels takes place in the "sun-baked, rattle-snaked Southwest" of the 1870's. A small town called Paco serves as their common setting; and both stories are told in the first person by a Paco townsman, one Sam McCallum. A number of the town's characters appear in both tales, and the struggle to achieve some viable sense of community justice underlies the action of each. However, each story is independent of the other and moves to its own particular rhythm.

The first novel, *A Woman, a Dog, and a Hanging Tree* deals with a capital crime and its effects on the people of Paco. The second novel, *The Death of Granite Hendley*, tells of a peace officer whose rough but efficient ways incur the hatred of the town he serves.

Little Paco — an isolated, almost negligible way station on America's westward march — experiences in its growing pains some of the problems which have, and which always will, beset the human community. And here, in a *milieu* usually thought to be dominated by men, each of the Paco novels features a distinct female character who, in her own way, could teach the angels (if not the men around her) a lesson in love and courage.

"When I caught sight of Sadie and him, they were driving in from the other direction. The street we were on ran the length of Paco. Across it housefronts faced each other like cards in a giant poker game. Sadie and he looked slivery small as they came along between — human chips in a game whose rules we could only guess."

A Woman, a Dog, and a Hanging Tree – page 34

The Way of the Eagle

A Woman, a Dog, and a Hanging Tree

The Death of Granite Hendley

Author's Afterword

A Woman, a Dog, and a Hanging Tree

To the memory of my grandmother,

EUGENIA BASKERVILLE TENNANT
(MRS. HENRY FAIRFAX)

9 January 1873 – 30 September 1966

" . . . steadfast, unmovable, always
abounding in the work of the Lord . . . "

1 Corinthians 15, 58

"A dog, a woman, an' a walnut tree,
Th' more yeh beat 'em, th' better they be!"

— Stephen Crane, *The Red Badge of Courage*

1
New Hand and Sore Thumb

ONLY ON LOOKING BACK can a man begin to understand. It may be reason enough for growing old. And though the understanding, when it comes, may be as much a dream as whatever went before, we take it because it's all we have. We can't believe we gave so much so long ago for nothing — or that the passing years could drive the same hard bargain. We take the "all we have" and call it friend, and leave the rest to do its worst when come the dreams that feed on sleep.

I never knew her as well as she knew me; but she it was who made me hope some day to understand.

A legal hanging was an unknown thing in the town of Paco then. It turned out old and walking young for a hundred miles around. Some who came believed it wouldn't happen — prayed it wouldn't, those who knew the use of prayer. It took us every one by something grimmer than surprise, though it all began a good long year before.

I was riding foreman then for a Paco rancher by the name of Casskel Cramer. Paco seemed to be where I stopped when I left Virginia in '65. The town itself wasn't worse than most in the southwest territory then. Cass Cramer (who must have thought he was hell-bound) used to say, when he liked a thing, that it suited him down to the ground "if not to a damned sight lower." I felt that way about Paco. Its desert of rock-ribbed ranch made the war and the wreck of home seem more than a world away. To judge from its sorry present, Paco had to have a future — which was more than some who came there felt *they* had.

Cramer owned the Coupled C, a fair-sized spread some seven miles northwest of town. His herd kept me and eight or nine punchers busy. If six of them put in a good day's work, I could get along. Even with five I managed. But it wasn't easy to hold six men who would put in a good month's worth of anything. So Cramer kept some spares. I guess it wasn't bad policy. When work got heavy, somebody always took down sick — snakebite, gunshot, DT's, or the like. Or somebody took to the road — quit or got run out by the Paco fathers.

Cramer wasn't the ideal boss. Thin, moody old man he was, with salt-and-pepper hair and a nose that sometimes got too big for its handkerchief. His assets included an ill-tempered wife, a no-good son, and some of the finest grazing land around. He liked my work; I liked his pay. We said no more to each other than we had to. I kept clear of his family, too. His wife didn't care for my manners, and I'd had to slap his boy down once when I caught him spying on me.

Maybe what I liked least about Cramer was his way of hiring hands without a word to me. If he happened to be in town when a parcel of drifters showed, one of them, like as not, would be drawing pay by sundown. It was a cinch and a sin, too, he never asked me before he hired Giff Lothers.

I came in from a day's work and there was Lothers, laying out blanket and chaps in the bunkhouse. On the way to my own room I caught sight of him through one of the open windows. I went in to convince myself I was wrong. His thick shoulders and heavy back were unmistakable, though. When he stooped, his back looked like the neck of a full-grown bull.

"You!" I said to his back.

Charlie, Oscar, Gilson, Harl — the rest in the bunkhouse looked around when they heard my voice. He didn't. He played with gloves and gear on his bunk like they were chops on a griddle.

"You — *new* man!" I said louder.

He turned around like he had all the time in this world and the next.

"Where'd *you* come from?" I asked.

He found room in the top of his pants for all four fingers of each hand.

"Hell!" he said through stubby teeth. "Does it matter?"

His little eyes and mouth looked school-kid young of a sudden. The eyes giggled from under a black sweat ring of matted hair.

"I asked you a question," I said.

He licked at the corner of his mouth as if he liked the taste of sweat.

"Let's leave it at Abilene," he said.

I stared at him hard a moment and went. Leave it at Abilene! I kicked at a rusty can as I made for the ranch house.

That Abilene roping contest had happened a year or two ago — before I made it to Paco. I wouldn't forget it if I woke up dead tomorrow. The big prize went for bulldogging; and for cutting out and throwing beef, my mare and I were as good as any. I didn't enter the rough-riding contest. He did. All the town's youngsters entered. And Lothers won — stayed on a wild steer almost till the beast got tired of bucking. I saved my strength, like all the old hands. And I beat him — beat them all — fair and free by the word of the judges. He didn't take their word, though. I saw him eyeing me, looking surly, as soon as they named me winner. It wasn't till I had the prize in my hand that he hit me. He was right beside me in the ring, and I must have seen it coming. I had time to turn and take his blow in my hair. I remember thinking that the little sack of gold I held would help when I could get to him.

His second punch came before I recovered, this one to my chest. I struck up under his third swing — caught him below the chin. I got one into his stomach next and flattened him with a blow to the head. I was so damned mad I dropped on top of him, pounding away. Next thing I knew, two fellows rammed me in the gut with a fence rail. When I was on my back, they used it to hold me down. Nobody had to hold him. They told me later they thought i'd meant to kill him.

The kitchen door stood wide to the night. Inside, Cramer's wife was setting the table where we ate. I didn't even look her way. Cramer usually primed for supper with a pull or three at the parlor jug. I found him in his favorite chair between the jug and a kerosene lamp, reading the Paco paper.

"Did you hire that son of a bitch in the bunkhouse?" I nodded over my shoulder.

I didn't barge in unless I had something on my mind, and Cramer knew it. His wife got mad as hell when I stalked through the house; but Cass, to nettle her (or me), ignored it when it happened.

"Every one of 'em, including you," he said across his paper.

"You know the one I mean."

I'd heard it back in Abilene, but now I couldn't call Lothers' name.

"Since I do the hiring, I must have hired him," Cramer muttered.

"What the hell for?"

"Twenty-five dollars and found — same as the rest."

I took a deep breath. Cramer looked back to the *Paco Gazette*.

"Get rid of him," I said. "He's not the same as the rest."

"I want him here. He'll stay."

"You've got eight men and me already," I told him. "How the hell many men do you need?"

"Somebody might kill you," Cramer remarked.

I laid my hand on the butt of the Colt I always wore.

"That'll be a harder day's work than was ever done on *this* ranch," I said.

"You're not working 'em like you should!" Cramer shook his head and looked back to the *Gazette*.

"He's no good, Cass," I said as calmly as I could. "Get rid of him."

Cramer folded his paper and laid it on the table next to him.

"Lothers'll stay the month," he said. "if at the end of that time you want to fire him, go ahead. I saw him make a few throws with a rope: I think he'll prove a good hand. I hired him and he'll stay his month. I don't want to hear any more about it."

I turned abruptly and left. On the way I almost walked over Cramer's wife, who'd sneaked to the door behind me.

Things turned out not quite as I'd expected. Lothers did good work — at least while I was looking. And he didn't talk back, or not to me. His "month" stretched into three or four. I said no more to Cramer.

From the first, Lothers got along with the men about like a bitch in a beehive. He set too much by himself, as the Bible puts it — made them feel he thought he was better than they.

After supper he never joined in with a salty song or story. Instead, he liked to read or practice throwing a lariat. I can't say what he got from books, but he knew more tricks with a rope than a monkey on a hundred feet of vine.

The only one he hit it off with had to be Cass's wife. Martha Cramer, who seemed on the wrong side of most things, *was* on the wrong side of middle age. He acted more than polite around her. And Martha swallowed it like the "grande dame" she wasn't. We figured Lothers must have a way with women. We were all to learn that women sure as hell had a way with him.

To me, he was one more straw for the camel's back — maybe a couple short of the last. I was getting used to him (so I thought) till the Saturday night in June we ran into Momma Skyfoot. I've said how it all began for me. Most in Paco felt it began for him that night.

I don't think Lothers had ever seen her before. He knew of her, though. We all did. Old Indian woman she was, with a face to scare a ghost. Gutted and crossed with age, it looked like a washed-out hill. Apache, Cheyenne — none of us knew her stock or tongue. She skinned a living out of her one-eyed mule and the humans fool enough to deal with her. To other Indians she traded roots and herbs for the feathers and trash she sold us whites.

I left her alone myself. People said she could tell the future; and since what she told was mostly bad, it had a way of coming true. I figured I heard enough bad news from *friends*.

On Saturdays most of us headed for Paco to wet down the week. We often saw the old woman camped along the way. She knew the white men made their journey every seventh day — in a better mood and more money than during the rest of the week. Up until "Lothers' Saturday night" she always camped on the same little knoll two miles west of town. From way off we could see her tepee jutting out of the brush like a rusty funnel. Her mule would be staked down close by; and she herself sat next to the tent, hunched under a filthy blanket. To kill the smell of that blanket, she always smoked a pipe of the strongest shag this side of a buffalo's bottom.

No one had seen her for weeks before that sorry Saturday. We figured she'd given the devil his due — his *overdue*, as Cramer put it. But there she was in her usual spot, stump-ugly and full of fleas as ever.

I was ahead of our bunch when I saw her. I kept on past till I heard Lothers holler "Hold up!" I reined in as he waved the men down.

"Hey, you old sow!" he called to Momma Skyfoot. "What the hell are you doin'?"

She stirred the ash of her little fire. Without looking at him, she answered in halting English:

"I wait — for you."

Lothers dismounted, grinning.

"Well, get out the best you got," he said and started toward her.

"Quite a woman you found yourself."

"Paco won't see *you* tonight.!"

The men made cracks as he stopped and stood in front of her. She never glanced his way — just laid a coal to her pipe and sat there spouting smoke through two black nostrils.

Lothers squatted facing her. The talk he started went on for what seemed minutes. I got tired waiting.

"See you in town," I told Charlie Currus, whose horse was next to mine. "It has a couple of things I'd rather watch than this."

I was back on the road when a cry from behind turned me. Lothers had leaped at the old woman and had a hand on her throat.

I was down in a minute and the men with me.

"Let her go!" I yelled as I ran for him.

Lothers had both hands on her now. He shook her as if he would snap the eyeballs out of her head.

Charlie reached them first. He grabbed one of Lothers' wrists and I, the other. Together we flung him off. We hadn't meant to, but we'd flung him toward the fire. He screamed as he rolled through it. The fire was more alive than that old woman. It left a scar on his shoulder which people afterward spoke of as "Momma Skyfoot's Mark."

By the time he got to his feet, four of us stood between Lothers and the woman. She lay in a knot on her stomach, legs around to one side. Now and again she heaved her back to gasp.

"Are you all right?" I asked her. "Can I help?"

"White man — no help!" she got out finally.

"We better leave her," Charlie said.

I nodded and turned to Lothers.

"What the hell's the matter?" I asked. "You out of what little mind you got?"

"She told me I had blood on my hand!" he almost whispered.

I felt like calling him the damnedest fool God ever let live.

"I asked, '*Whose* blood?'" he went on quickly. "She wouldn't tell. She looked back at that pipe of hers and ordered me off like I was dirt. I said, 'As well *yours* as another's!' and jumped her. Hell, I didn't hurt her. I just wanted to scare her — make her tell me what she meant."

I shook my head. I was so damned mad I couldn't do a thing but spit.

"*White* blood!" came a cat-like hiss behind me.

The old woman's voice stiffened the hair on my neck. She'd crawled back close to the fire by now and huddled there, staring into the embers.

"White blood!" she repeated, rocking slowly back and forth: "Not Indian."

Lothers moved to go after her. I shoved him back.

"Mount up!" I said. "You've done enough. — And she's done enough to you."

He lurched away from me, called her a name, and started for his horse.

"Oscar, Charlie —," I motioned the rest, "get going. I'll join you in a minute."

I wish now I'd gone with them, instead of staying to make our peace with that black stump of a totem pole. I reached in my left front pocket and felt the five dollar gold piece I'd put there when we left the ranch. Momma Skyfoot looked like she didn't know I was there.

I swore to myself — at her, Lothers, the whole damned mess. It would mean beer instead of whiskey for me tonight, but I tossed over the coin. What was left of the fire caught it in a shiny arc as it fell. It landed less than a foot from her knee.

"I'm sorry about what happened," I told her.

She said nothing — made no move for the gold. I began to be sorry I'd thrown it away. She was goat-gut tough, that woman. It would take the devil to strangle her, and I didn't envy *him* the job. I was ready to grab my coin back when her voice came, low and threatening:

"You have — in your hand — to wipe white blood away. — But you will not."

Only her lips had moved. The words cut me like a whip. I turned and saw that the men were on their horses. Charlie was holding mine. They were all watching, but they couldn't have heard. I wondered a moment if I could have.

"What?" I asked, and turned again to face her. My damp shirt felt cold as a shroud on my back.

"Did you hear me?" I said when she made no sound. "Speak!"

Out of her wrap came a single trembling hand. She waved it like a queen dismissing her lowest subject.

"Go," she said. "I speak no more."

For a moment I thought of forcing her. And then I laughed at myself. I breathed deep and let my right hand feel the butt of my Colt. I wondered what could have scared me about that blanket of bones.

She gathered her hand back into herself and sat as she had, not moving — not even breathing, I hoped. I left her and went for my horse.

As we rode to town, I couldn't join in on the talk of the Indian woman. I remembered what she told me, though. It was the calf that, as they say, grows fat under its owner's eye.

2
Song and Dance

I THOUGHT THE BRANDING of Lothers was the worst this Saturday night could hold. So, I guess, did Lothers. But he and the night were young.

We all seemed headed for the Spinning Wheel — a bar with dancing women (if not girls) and a roulette wheel that took what liquor left of our pay. Lothers seemed in a hell of a hurry to get there. He wouldn't wait to see Doc Hobbs — claimed all he needed was a coat of lard and another shirt to top it. The only place you could buy both was Abe Dalt's general store. Dalt had long since boarded up, but he let us in for an extra dollar.

I laid out Lothers, sunny side down, across the big front counter. He groaned a time or two, but I got him greased like a new axle. His old shirt went for bandages: I tied them on with strips torn out of the sleeves. Binding the wound was *his* idea.

"That burn should breathe," I told him. "You want to let the air get to you."

"I want to let the liquor get to me," was all he said.

Well, it was "skin off his own damn' back," as one of the men remarked. Gilson said the burn must have made Lothers hot in the 'hind legs, too. Lothers let it pass. When he got himself dressed, we all took off together.

A moustachioed Mex called Frisco ran the Spinning Wheel. He was oily as his hair; but his whiskey wouldn't blind you, and he didn't water the beer on Saturday night. As we tied up across from his place, some of the boys dropped raw remarks about what they were going to do with Frisco's girls. Gilson laughed:

"Any one of them women could cook you *all* — like a mess of second-hand chicken necks!"

"Any but Sadie!" Lothers snapped. "Mind your God-damn' tongue!"

It surprised me more than it did the rest. I heard a snicker as Lothers spoke.

"I guess it *don't* go for Sadie," Gilson said. "Some women — like that Indian witch — can fry a guy with his clothes still on."

I stepped between them and caught Lothers' wrist on the way up.

"Hold it!" I said. "You're in no shape for a fight. Gil — the rest of you — beat up somebody else's hand. Come Monday, I mean to get work out of this one."

They all laughed but Lothers. I stayed next to him as we crossed the street.

"I didn't know you were seeing *her*," I told him. I guess I hoped it wasn't true. He came back hard:

"There's a hell of a lot you don't know, McCallum."

We were on the verandah then. I stopped. He and the others went on in.

I walked back to the steps and tried to think. In spite of the noise and the crowd inside, I *might* get a word with Sadie. I didn't ask if I had the right — or whether she would listen. I guess I hoped a warning now might make up part of the good I'd never done her.

I turned and hit the swinging doors. Things inside looked just the same: female pictures, dusty mirrors, wormy woodwork back of the bar. Every lamp in the house was lit — along with most of the customers. Paco was a lot rougher then. Towns, like people, feel their oats before they feel much else.

Sadie would be in the roulette room: I couldn't talk to her there. I camped down at the front-room bar with the sawdust, sweat, and stale beer. That room was like the liquor Frisco served: for drinking, not for smelling.

I hailed Jukes, the bartender. He slid me a bottle. I slid it back.

"Beer," I said.

Jukes blinked:

"You sick?"

"Maybe — of your whiskey."

Jukes knew not to believe me; but Frisco, who was standing near, turned to put in his two pesos' worth. His eyes hopped like a couple of jumping beans above his skinny moustache. He had on his usual pin-stripe coat, which I knew concealed at least one throwing knife. (Frisco claimed he was faster with a knife than with a gun.) I don't trust a man who carries weapons I can't see — but he and I got along, I guess.

"Allow me!" he said, and laid a hand on my shoulder. "For my friend, a drink of the best!"

He mentioned a brand I'd only heard of. I don't know whether I resented more his hand or calling me friend. But he took his hand off quick enough, and for a free drink I've been called worse.

Jukes set me up. It was Saturday night whiskey — no mistake. I swallowed twice and felt hot down to my boots. When I opened my eyes, I would rather have looked at Sadie McGrath. But there was Frisco, holding his bottle, smug as a skunk in the henhouse.

"Was good?" he asked.

"Damned good!" I chased it with the hair on my hand.

"Am glad you like!" He shoved the bottle to Jukes. "Now you know what to ask for!"

Frisco could have sold a stove to the devil in hell. I hoped he soon might have the chance.

"Now I know."

"Enjoy yourself!"

And he moved off, giving me a last little greasy grin. Jukes still held that bottle of run-walk-and-lie-down. When he looked at me, I shook my head:

"Beer."

He shook his own head back, but drew me a glass.

"You're gonna want something stronger," he said. "Sadie's got a new dress!"

I kept quiet. Sadie made her own clothes and made them well. If a woman sings in a place like Frisco's, I guess the cut of her crinoline counts as news. But I hated hearing it across the bar — for *her* sake, I told myself.

Jukes shrugged and moved away. I drank alone till a cheer from the back room roused me. I turned as Sadie came in to do a song.

She had a new dress, all right. It rose straight off the floor in a gush the color of copper. Black fur rimmed the top where the cloth gave out on the way to her throat. And the whole thing shone like it was dripping wet.

As she walked in, even Frisco's croupier followed her. The big front room picked up the cheer till the yelling made the candles flicker.

She moved to the inside end of the bar, where Frisco had built a stage. Lothers came with the rest of the back-room bunch. He wasn't yelling, though. He watched like a man who'd just seen the face of God. I figured he must be drunk already.

I glanced at the others around the room — youngsters virgin to the razor, old men gray at chin and brow. They watched as if they owned her, this woman blessing a damned snakes' nest with the frail perfume of music. She was like the upright Frisco had — a piano come around Cape Horn to remind us of a better life. Only *she* didn't sound any worse for the trip.

Sadie was big, and her face was not her fortune. Too much guts showed in it — eyes too deep, nose too big. When she got mad, she threw that nose up at you like a double-barrelled shotgun. But she had a neck of living marble; and what God didn't give her above it, he made up for below. If you watched any of her but her face when she sang, you'd think you were hearing the Queen of Sheba.

I don't recall her song that night, but it ended all too soon. The place uproared. Gray hair and green whiskey howled like wolves in heat. They wanted Sadie to dance. And she *could* dance any fiddler weak in the wrist. But her boss wanted her back by the roulette wheel, where her draw did more for the house. She left the stage to Frisco's "fancy family," as we called the other girls.

I stuck with the beer at the bar. I was almost feeling myself again when Doc Hobbs ambled up. Sometimes he and I drank together, though he never took very much — claimed he didn't know when somebody might have a fight or a baby or both. His hair was yellow as sand, and he had some sand (and sense, too) inside him. Why he'd settled for Paco, I could never understand. "Because there wasn't a doctor here," he always used to tell me. And I would drink "to the next doctor: may he stay the hell home!" And Hobbs would drink "to the next

patient: may he not die till I do!" I would throw mine down
and he would sip, and the night and life would go on.

We called each other a name or two and swapped the usual
lies. He looked down at my glass.

"I'm glad you're drinking light," he said. "Your man back
there with the burn —"

He jerked his head toward the gambling room.

" — he's getting done even browner in a game of stud."

"So?"

"Gonna want looking after," he nodded.

"I'm not his father."

Hobbs laughed.

"He's too good-looking for that!"

I grunted:

"He won't *let* anybody look after him."

"They're the kind that need it most."

I turned on him suddenly.

"Why the hell are you telling *me* this?"

Hobbs shrugged:

"I should tell Sadie?"

And he sidled off to join some others.

I ordered one more beer. Meanwhile Sadie came back for
another song. The yelling and the stomping made me wince.
This time Lothers followed her drunk on his feet, shouting
and waving a pack of cards. Later I'd heard he'd won the last
two hands. When every one else knocked off for the song, he
hollered at Sadie to wait. Frisco told her to sing.

I don't know why, but I moved and moved fast to head
Lothers off. Every bad word I knew got hollered in my ears. I
pushed for the farther side of the stage. Sadie was already
there, climbing the steps. Frisco and two of his men were
heading that way, too.

Lothers stopped when he reached the steps.

"Come down, woman!" I heard him holler.

Sadie was already on the stage.

"You come up here!" she answered.

I was just ahead of Frisco. If Lothers had tried to go on up, he might have made it. Instead he reached for the end of her dress. Sadie stepped back and I was able to grab his arm. He turned and swung with the other hand. I ducked: the punch caught Frisco in the mouth. Carl Riper, one of Frisco's henchmen, struck at Lothers and missed.

The crowd surged forward, pinning us all against the stage.

"Help me get him out back!" I yelled in Frisco's ear, "or you'll see a fight that'll tear this place apart."

Frisco came alive. Cursing in Spanish and English both, he flailed away at Riper. Carl turned and shoved Joe Grale (Frisco's other flunkey). The three of them beat the mob apart.

While I still had my back to the stage, I glanced around at Sadie. She was white with rage, shame — I don't know which. A tiny metal object gleamed in her good right hand. She tried to hide it in a fold of her dress — but I knew a Derringer when I saw it. She must have had it in a hidden pocket — a pocket she'd put in that skirt herself.

The pistol disappeared so fast I wondered if I'd seen it. I didn't have long to wonder. The kid on the piano plunged into Sadie's song. The crowd began to get helpful.

In my left hand I held Lothers' right with enough of a twist to make him behave. I'd gotten his gun in my other hand. He squirmed like bait on a fish-hook as I shoved him along. We followed Frisco and his men through the back room and thence to "outhouse alley."

I didn't get him out fast enough to save him a kick in the haunch from Frisco. Lothers was on the stoop by then, and I let him go when Frisco connected. He hit the ground, rolled on his side, and started laughing.

Riper and Grale stood with their boss on the stoop. Frisco looked from one to the other and nodded down at Lothers. By now I was on the ground beside him.

"Leave him be," I said, when Riper and Grale came off the stoop. I still had Lothers' pistol out.

"I owe him one in the mouth," Frisco muttered.

"These two don't."

"Then I come pay him myself!"

Frisco started down the steps, taking his coat off as he came.

"Not tonight," I told him.

His men had stopped when I raised the gun. Frisco stopped when I cocked it. Lothers meanwhile called the Mex and his mangy mother a couple of dogs.

"Shut up, you hear?" Frisco shouted.

Lothers shut up. I was glad he did.

"Let's go," I said, and shoved a boot in his ribs.

"He don't come in my place again!" Frisco said, breathing hard. "He come in again, you break his back. You hear me Carl? Joe?"

"We hear you," one of them answered.

Frisco turned and walked back into the building. The other two followed, slamming the door against us.

I stared down at the sorry soul who'd made me nothing but trouble. I wonder what I might have done if I'd known the trouble he was *going* to make.

"Get up!" I said, and kicked him again.

He didn't move. I swore aloud. I could *hear* what was the matter. He'd passed out cold and started to snore there in the dirt where he lay.

3
Memories and More

I GOT LOTHERS onto my shoulder and hefted him 'round to where we'd left the horses. I laid him over his saddle jack-knife style and brought him home bent damned near double. He snored through it all like a fast freight and never even got sick.

Sunday at the Coupled C was a day for getting over Saturday. So, sometimes, was Monday. *This* Monday, all were up but Lothers, though few were up to much. I set the men to patching fence and took off on my mare to survey rain damage to the road through Cramer's front forty.

I was on foot, dodging rattlesnakes up a wash off the road to town, when I saw a two-horse rig approaching. The horses were poorly matched, and the buggy yawed like a goose.

I walked back out to the road and waited. A woman was holding the reins. What I'd thought was a child on the seat beside her turned out to be an old friend. Sadie Magrath was driving, and beside her sat the yellow feist I'd given her months before. I spotted the dog one day on the range, whence he followed me home. I gave him part of my supper that night: he stuck to me afterward as if I owed him money. But Cass's wife didn't care for dogs, and one day Cass said either I or the mutt would have to go.

"Looking for some one?" I asked, as Sadie pulled up.

"I reckon."

She had on a plain brown skirt and blouse I liked a lot better than what she'd worn two nights ago. The dog began to strain at the strap that held him to the seat. Sadie just sat and stared like she was counting the lines in my face.

"Blink seems to think it's me," I nodded at the dog. I'd named him "Blink" because of the way he batted one eye when he got excited.

"It wouldn't be the first mistake he's made."

She seemed in a feisty mood herself.

"You're a long way out of town," I said, "for a sassy female."

"I'm protected."

She reached down into the boot and lifted the muzzle of a Winchester.

"You know how to use that thing?" I asked, as she let it drop at her feet.

"I know how to use what I have to."

"You do!" I admitted. "I just didn't know you owned a rifle."

"I don't — or a buckboard, either. The rifle came with the rig I borrowed."

I nodded.

"Do you own that Derringer you were carrying Saturday night?"

I thought she almost blushed.

"I didn't know you'd noticed!" She glanced away and started scratching Blink behind the ears.

"I notice most things about you."

"*Do* you?" She kept on petting Blink.

"The Derringer was a last gift from my uncle," she said, not looking back at me. "He raised me — after my parents died. He gave me the pistol just before I came west. 'It's not an honorable weapon,' he said, 'but where you're going, there aren't many honorable men.'"

I chewed on that for a second.

"You have it with you now?" I asked.

"Of course!" She turned her head and let those hazel eyes burn mine.

"Did you have it with you all the time you and I were together?"

"All the time we had our clothes on."

I guess she saw my forehead sprout sweat.

"Do I shock you?" she asked.

"No, but you sure as hell try."

She laughed. "I don't think I will much longer!"

I let it pass.

"*Why?*" I asked. "Why did you have that damned thing with you while you and I were together?"

She bared her teeth in what should have been a smile.

"Somebody might have killed *you*, Sam. *Then* where would I have been?"

I didn't take much to the joke. I moved over next to her near-side horse. One of the traces was twisted.

"I'm thinking your uncle was right," I said, as I busied myself with the harness.

"About there not being honorable men out here?"

"About a *Derringer* not being honorable!" I looked up at her hard. "It's like a knife up your sleeve."

She shook her head and smiled.

"Still trying to convince me I shouldn't be working for Frisco!"

"I didn't say a word about him."

"No, but you were thinking it. — He's always treated me well, you know."

"That's no sign he always will."

"It's no sign *anyone* always will," she said softly.

Her words came from a long way back. Some things I remembered made me wince.

"Sadie, I —!"

But my mind was years away. I remembered the wife and farm I had in the Shenandoah Valley before the war. It seemed forever ago — blue hills and shining water and fields yellow with wheat.

"— you never told me about your uncle," I said without looking at her. I could almost smell the corn growing — feel the plough in my hands, the reins around my neck.

"I never thought you wanted to hear!" Her face and the tense white sky behind her seemed to relax a bit.

I saw gray uniforms as she spoke. I hadn't been married a year when I left to fight to keep my farm and the Valley the way they'd always been. — The worst of it was that even before Appomattox I knew it could never be.

She was telling me something about him — her uncle. I looked away. My wife was nothing like Sadie, but Sadie made me think of her. She was small, almost frail, my wife — gold hair and a freckle or two and eyes green as clover. I didn't want to remember . . . .

I'd walked home from Appomattox. I was weak and had no boots and only the food I could beg. It took me more than a month. It didn't matter. Sheridan had already been there. The Valley looked like the floor of hell — everything burned — houses, fences, woods, fields. I had trouble finding my farm — or where my farm had been. It looked like God himself forgot it. My chink-log house was dirt and ashes. A few burnt stalks were all that remained of the oak grove over the well. And there wasn't a trace of Glenna — my wife. She was gone from the face of the earth, like four years' worth of strength and dreams.

"He must have been a fine man," I said when Sadie paused.

She went on but I didn't hear. — The day after reaching home, I heard about Glenna. She'd died in the arms of a sister of hers three days after Sheridan's raid — died with what might have been my son. She'd carried it since my last home leave, while the army lay at Petersburg. Seeing the Valley, I was almost thankful the child had never lived.

Sadie finished. I felt her eye me hard.

"But you came here to see *Lothers*!" I said in a fury of unbelief.

My tone made her jump. — I wish I knew what *I'd* come here to see, I remember thinking. I'd left Virginia forever, begging food when I couldn't work; borrowing, paying, trying to save; pushing west for open land and fewer people.

"I came to see *him*," she said at last. "I made some ointment like what Uncle Grig used once on me — when I burnt my arm as a child."

She reached under the seat and picked up a jar of whitish stuff with a newspaper over the top.

"I don't know whether it got me well, but it took the soreness out," she said.

"You might try some of that stuff on his *head*," I nodded at the jar.

She took a deep breath.

"Sam, he's asked me to marry him!"

I must have looked like *I* could have used that ointment. She let me have the worst.

"Which is more than any one else has done."

I took a step back. There'd been other women since I left Virginia, but I knew there would be no wife. Glenna was a child when we married: a thing of beauty more than a full-fleshed woman. Sadie — and the others — were more women than things of beauty. And that's not something you tell them. Anyway, I never told Sadie. The most I can say is I never tried to deceive her.

"You think he's worth having?" I asked, not knowing what else to say.

"I would tell *him* before I told any one else."

"Sadie, you can't be serious? You don't even know him. He's —"

"He's selfish and a bully," she cut me off. "He gets blind drunk at least once a week. He gambles and picks fights and can't keep a civil tongue in his head for ten whole minutes together."

"You know all that and you still want —?" I shrugged and flapped my hands.

"I know, too, that he works hard — that he reads and tries to improve himself — that he's been true to me since we met, and that he loves me."

I shook my head. I didn't think he could love anything but himself. I wanted to say so much I couldn't get out a word. I stood and swallowed and stared at the hole I'd dug in Cramer's road with the heel of my boot.

"Sadie," I began finally, "I don't know what you want —"

"Don't you?" she smiled.

I tried to go on:

" — and I don't know what he wants. But I know that women are rare out here — and a decent one is rarer still."

"So are men — *real* men!"

"Rarer than you think," I nodded soberly. I guess I'd never considered Lothers a man.

She adjusted her gloves and straightened the reins to drive.

"Thanks for fixing the harness," she said. "One other thing about him, before I go. He wants to make a name for himself — maybe represent this place in the legislature, if the territory ever becomes a state."

I couldn't help laughing:

"He expects to live that long?"

"And last," she went on, "something he and I have in common — though I've never told him so! He feels some admiration for you."

I almost choked.

"He must have been sick-drunk when he told you that!"

"Not at all," she said in a level tone. "He admires a person he thinks is better than he is. He hates any one he thinks is worse."

Blink could have knocked me down with his tail.

"He thinks I'm *better* —?"

"He thinks you've proved it to him. He never told me when. Not that he doesn't think some day he'll prove he's better than you. So watch your step. He may try to do it when you're least prepared."

I shook my head again.

"I know something else about him that you for damned sure don't. You're too good for *him*!"

She sat a moment in thought.

"Nobody's too good for any one else," she said. "At any given time some one might not be *bad* enough — but nobody is too good."

With a little laugh she flapped the reins and went. I stood and watched till she disappeared, dragging dust that made me think of a bridal veil.

When the dust settled, I pulled my hat off suddenly and threw it down. I must have sworn, and I guess I kicked at it, too. Anyway, I scared my mare. (She was standing close when I did it.) She bolted after the wagon, and I had to walk all the way back to the ranch. If I wasn't mad when I started, I sure as hell was when I arrived. I took it out on two of the men I found asleep behind the barn.

4
Dirty Work

MARTHA CRAMER made quite a fuss over Lothers and his burn — moved him into a room at the back of the ranch house till he got well. She and Sadie both treated him better than he deserved. And thanks to Sadie's ointment (so *he* said), Lothers was soon at work again — much his old self, unfortunately.

I saw him from another angle now. I wondered what there was about him to stay a woman's eye. His face had a delicate touch or two. His nose was straight and small. The line down from it cut a deep curl at the end of his mouth. I wouldn't have called him handsome, but he wasn't rough-looking, either — not like me, anyway. He was younger, too, than I. Hell, he must have been younger than Sadie. And growing up seemed the farthest thing from his mind. At work I didn't spare him any; but I kept away from him when I could.

Things never did get back to the way they'd been. For a while I gave up going to town on Saturday. I got myself an extra lamp and tried to do some reading. There wasn't much print at the ranch to hold a man, though — old papers, the Bible, and a doggy volume of Shakespeare.

I got word that Sadie had quit her job — not because of what I'd said, but because Frisco wouldn't budge on the order to mangle Lothers if he came back to the Spinning Wheel. I was glad she'd quit, but the town's other saloons weren't that much better than Frisco's. I half-hoped she might just up and leave. I never thought Paco did her justice.

Then one Saturday night in July I got a jolt from Cramer. The men had all gone off to town. I was in my room at the end of the bunkhouse, sewing the latigo on my saddle where it had almost worn in two. Every one knew how Lothers liked to read: I felt glad Cramer hadn't caught me over a book.

He must have come when he did because he knew nobody would be in the other end of the bunkhouse. I heard him walk around to my door and stop a moment to knock. He didn't always bother. I was in for something whenever he got polite.

"Who's keeping the boys in line?" he grinned as he stepped inside.

"Frisco maybe. I don't get paid for working Saturday night."

I was on my bunk with the saddle beside me. He took the chair at my table.

"Cigar?" he asked, pulling one out of his coat.

"Thanks."

I sniffed it and stuck it away in my shirt. It was better than the kind he usually gave. I didn't want to spoil it on whatever he might tell me. Besides, I knew it burned him to give me one and see me save it.

"Why do you keep on sewing that worthless piece of hide?" he nodded at my saddle. One side of it *did* have patches enough to pass for an Apaloosa.

"It's almost part of my own," I said. "We've been through a lot together."

He bit the end off his cigar and walked to the door to spit. Back to being polite.

"You seem to have the herd — the ranch — pretty well in hand," he said, sitting down again.

"Glad you approve."

He lit his cigar at my lamp and went on as if he hadn't heard:

"So well I doubt you'll find enough to keep the whole crew busy till fall round-up."

"We'll need new horses before then," I said. "And the rest of that fencing you want done will take some time. There's plenty to do."

Cramer shrugged.

"Gilson — Harl — they're as good as I've seen with horses —"

He might have mentioned Lothers, I couldn't help thinking. The boy had a touch with animals.

" — and I'm not in that big a hurry for a fence I've done without this long."

"So what's your thought?" I asked.

He laughed quietly through his smoke.

"I'm thinking back to that talk we had," he chuckled. "You were right: you can have your way."

"Which talk was it?" I asked with a straight face. Even if I'd known, I would have asked.

He quit laughing in a hurry. He didn't like jokes he didn't make.

"The time we talked about Lothers," he snapped. "You can let him go at the end of the month."

"You serious?"

"I sure as hell am."

I put down my needle and shoved the saddle away.

"You could let go one or two of the others ahead of him," I said, "if you want to keep quality hands."

He shook his head.

"As you put it, he's not the same as the others."

"He works hard. What's he done wrong?"

He squinted at the ash on his cigar.

"Well, he doesn't get along with the men — or with you."

"I can take care of myself."

"Maybe," he nodded, "but you play hell taking care of *him*. I heard about that night at the Spinning Wheel."

"So that's reason to fire him?"

"That's part of it."

I had a can on the table for butts and ashes. He flicked his cigar onto the floor.

"What's the rest?" I said.

"He's giving my ranch a hard name. He's unwanted, half the places in town; he owes money, the other half. And everybody comes to me for it. Abe Dalt has a bill against him for more than six months' work could buy. Over at the Silver Pick, they tell me, Lothers started a fight one night and never paid the damages. Frisco showed me three or four notes Lothers signed for gambling debts. And a few less savoury types in town have stopped me about what Lothers owes *them*."

"Less savoury than Frisco?"

Frisco made an effort to get along with the Paco ranchers. It wasn't wasted on Cramer.

"I'm no bookkeeper," he went on, ignoring my remark. "I keep *my* books, but I'll be damned if I keep the town of Paco's."

"You might try telling him so."

"Not worth it," Cramer muttered. "I just don't want him around."

"Things are slack just now," I said. "He'll have a hard time finding work around Paco."

I didn't like defending Lothers, but he *had* done decent work. And if he meant anything to Sadie, a lost job would make it hard on them both.

"He can get the hell out of Paco," Cramer said. "Damned few would smart to see him go."

"I think you're making a mistake."

He shook his head.

"I made one when I hired him."

I took a deep breath — rank of his cigar.

"If you want him to go," I said, "you can tell him yourself."

He grinned around that cigar like it was a word too good to speak.

"I thought *you'd* like to tell him," he said, "since he's kind of sweet on your woman —"

I wondered what he knew, even as I felt myself get mad. Sadie and I had broken off long before Lothers showed. She told me she thought she was falling in love: I knew I wasn't. It was her idea to part, and I respected her for it.

"Leave her out of this," I said in a voice so hoarse he must not have heard.

If I *hadn't* been in love, I'd been almost. But Sadie demanded more than she knew. She wouldn't have allowed me the *thought* of Glenna, could I have allowed her Glenna's place. — She was worth ten thousand of Cramer, though. It got my gut to see him try to use her.

" — and since *she* seems to be sweet on him!" Cramer said with a wink.

"*Shut up!*" I said.

He heard that all right. Maybe his wife and kid in the ranch house heard it. He quit grinning and took the cigar from between his teeth.

"My personal life stays out," I said. "How the hell could I work these men if I let my feelings show?"

He just sat there, beady-eyed.

"You — tell *me* — to shut up?" He looked mad as a snake in a forked stick.

I always slept with my Colt between the mattress and the dog-eared pillow I used. Its handle and trigger guard showed now from under the faded ticking. I glanced down at the gun as Cramer spoke. I wanted to look at something clean. Its blue steel and walnut plates made the most beauty I had in the room.

Cramer jumped so fast he knocked the chair over back of him.

"Sam!" he said quickly, "Sam —!"

I looked back sharp at him when he moved. His face was white as paper. He made no effort to find the cigar he'd dropped. The old fool really thought I was going to draw.

"I wouldn't have said it if you hadn't pushed me," I told him. It was as close as I could come to apologizing.

He breathed easier now and nodded, more to himself than me.

"Lothers'll go" he said, looking down at me as if to be sure I knew my place.

"You tell him," was all I said.

Before I knew it, Cramer had gone. I got up and looked around for the butt of his smoke. Then I lit the one he'd given me and went outside for a walk. When I made it to bed that night, I didn't drift off till almost dawn.

Cramer gave him the word next day: Lothers left at the end of the month. He didn't even say goodbye to me or the men. None of them seemed sorry. If he owed money everywhere else, most of the bunkhouse owed *him*. He wasn't a match for professionals, but he cleaned up at cowhand cards.

He got himself work sooner than I'd thought possible. Pop Maguire, who ran the nearest ranch to ours, signed him on right away. Maguire was never on the best of terms with Cramer. Maybe he hired Lothers just to spite his former boss. We heard nothing but good about him from Maguire, but we figured the news was only meant to grate on Cramer.

Everybody seemed in the dark as to what was really happening. Later we learned it was Lothers' time of probation — no more cards, fights, debts, or drunks. Hard as it was, he must have passed the test. He came off the frying pan, colors flying; and the fire waited with open arms. Six months after he left the Coupled C, he and Sadie drew in on the lifelong gamble. Parson Preble dealt the hands at Paco's little church. Doc Hobbs gave the bride away. I didn't get invited.

Neither party had entered the marriage lightly. Sadie had made him take his life in hand first. She kept the probation short, not wanting to lose her man. And Lothers made the effort, I guess, because it was overdue. Of course, he claimed to love her — but half of Paco claimed as much, even when it was sober.

He quit his job at Maguire's the day of the wedding. He and Sadie spent the night camped out on a piece of land they'd bought six miles the other side of town. It wasn't good land, but Lothers couldn't have paid for anything better. By himself he couldn't have paid for *that*. I heard Sadie put up most of the down payment and signed the mortgage note for the rest. Nate Purvis, who ran the Paco bank, would have squeezed interest out of a body living on borrowed *time*. Even Purvis claimed to feel safe with Sadie's name on the note. Besides, Lothers had made a start at paying off his debts. Money was scarce, but goods were not; and most who saw him paying reopened his line of credit.

Sadie taught him more than minding money. He started shaving twice a week and once in a while put on clean clothes, even if they hurt. He gave up cards and quit telling people what he thought of them. Even Frisco admitted Lothers seemed improved. Sadie managed to patch things up between her beau and her former boss. In fact, Frisco went to the wedding.

By way of a present, he cancelled the ban on Lothers at the Spinning Wheel — even stood the couple to drinks after the ceremony.

The marriage was more than a fortnight old before I saw either him or her. I happened on both together one day when they drove in town to fetch supplies from Ira Caslin. Ira's admiration for Sadie dated from her singing days. He gave her a load of lumber as a wedding present. His was Paco's only timber business. Since the couple needed a house, I guess he knew where they'd have to come for the rest of the wood they used.

I was on my way to the bank that morning with money from a cattle sale. When I caught sight of Sadie and him, they were driving in from the other direction. The street we were on ran the length of Paco. Across it housefronts faced each other like cards in a giant poker game. Sadie and he looked slivery small as they came along between — human chips in a game whose rules we could only guess.

They stopped at Caslin's and went inside. I rode on as far as the bank and went in to mind my business.

When I finished, I made for the Silver Pick on my way back out to the ranch. I horsed up for the ride over and passed their wagon, still in front of Caslin's. Sadie was on the seat by herself, and Ira's boy was loading in the goods. The boy left for a moment as I reined in.

"Hello," she smiled.

I dismounted and tipped my hat. I hadn't seen her since the day we met on the road. She looked even better than I remembered, but I wasn't about to tell her.

"Hope you're well," I said.

"Never better!"

"I want you to know — ," I began, " — know I wish you every kind of happiness."

She smiled again:

"I know, Sam. Thank you."

The boy came back with a sack of flour and heaved it onto the wagon.

"Howdy, Mr. McCallum," he grinned.

"Hi, Pete," I nodded.

I turned again to Sadie when he went back into the shop.

"I would have said it at the time," I told her, "if you had let me know."

"That's why I didn't!" she said. "I would have liked to have you there. But I thought it might be better the way it was. — I hope you understand."

I nodded and glanced away at her horse.

"You've done quite a job on *him*," I mumbled, not knowing what to say.

"You mean my husband?"

I nodded again.

"I had some help," she said.

"From *him?*"

"From him. And you don't have to look at the butt of a horse when you tell me that."

Caslin's boy returned with another sack. I forgot what I was about to say.

"Let me give you a hand," I told him, going to the end of the wagon.

We slung the sack up next to the first, and he went back in for another load. I walked to the front of the wagon and looked up into Sadie's eyes.

"I want to give you a wedding present," I said.

"Why, Sam —!"

She blushed, and I drank it all in straight.

"Sam, I — I didn't expect a present! I mean, don't feel you have to —"

I shook my head.

"I want to — if you'll have it."

"Why, I'd be delighted — only — "

"Only what?"

Pete Caslin came back trundling a keg of nails. I helped him lift it to the wagon bed.

"Only what?" I repeated when he'd gone.

"Only, well, I feel embarassed about not asking you to the wedding, and —"

"And — ?"

"I — I don't feel I deserve it!"

"You haven't seen what I'm going to give you!"

She smiled and blushed again, beautifully.

"Well, what is it?"

I turned to my horse. I always carried my Winchester when I rode with Cramer's money. I pulled it out of its scabbard now and turned again to Sadie. It was all I had worth giving, except my horse and pistol. I knew Lothers didn't own a rifle. Living six miles out alone, they shouldn't have been without one.

"I want you to have it," I said. "It's loaded, so be careful. He'll know how to clean it and oil it. The stock's beat up, but the rifle's good — been with me a long time, tried and true."

"Why, Sam!" she said surprised. "That — that's too much of a present! And you need it!"

"One of these days I'll get another. Till then I can use Cramer's."

"It's very good of you," she said, taking it by the barrel. "And we don't have one."

"Now let me ask *you* a favor," I said, as she laid the rifle under the seat. "That Derringer your uncle gave you — will you give it to me?"

"Sam!" she smiled. "Still looking after my honor? I can't give up that pistol. It's more a keepsake now than anything else. — I'll promise never to use it. Will that do?"

"Will you promise never to wear it? — beginning now, if you have it on?"

She threw back her head and laughed. I'd forgotten how good it sounded.

"I won't tell whether I'm wearing it!" she said. "But I'll promise not to wear it again. Is that enough? Or will you take your present from us?"

"From *you*," I corrected. "No, I don't want it back. But it's a present to *you*."

The sound of boots on Caslin's stoop turned us both that way. Lothers stood there staring at us. Young Pete was with him, holding a parcel in his arms. The boy grinned like a first-quarter moon. Lothers looked as if he'd seen his mother-in-law. He grabbed the parcel out of Pete's hands.

"That'll do," he said, never taking his eyes off me.

Pete disappeared inside his father's shop. I caught a glimpse of his little white face at the edge of Ira's window.

Lothers came down off the stoop and walked to where I stood. He never glanced at Sadie.

"Congratulations," I told him without extending my hand.

His gray eyes seemed to get a shade cooler. He tossed his parcel into the wagon to free both his hands.

"I just wish we were on *my* place," he got out between his teeth, "so I could order you to get the hell off."

"Gifford!" Sadie's voice cut in. "You've given up talking that way."

"Not to him."

His left hand doubled into a fist. His right hung close to the butt of his gun.

"To every one!" Sadie insisted.

"My apologies to *you*, Mrs. Lothers," he smirked. The emphasis on the you and the Mrs. wasn't lost on her or me. I saw tears coming in one of her eyes, so I took my leave.

"Goodbye," I said, tilting my hat brim at her.

I started to wave at Caslin, who'd joined his kid at the window. But I thought it might just make things harder for Sadie. She raised one gloved hand but said no word. I wondered whether she *could* have spoken.

I got on my horse and started again for the Silver Pick. I didn't look back. I heard Lothers climb aboard and lash his horse around for home.

Over a whiskey I wondered what he'd heard of my talk with Sadie. Probably just my last remark: the one I wished he hadn't — for Sadie's sake. I couldn't imagine what he thought, but he wasn't long in letting me know.

5

Elemental Encounter

WINTER LINGERED LATE that year, one or two mild days daring us to think the worst was past. Through it all Lothers worked to finish the house — in between efforts to stock his land on credit. And even during the worst of weather Sadie worked beside him. I wasn't surprised to hear it: once she'd told me she felt she was born to struggle, though born also to win.

I didn't see *her* again for some little while, but I caught a glimpse of her "worser half" at the end of March. It was a glimpse all three of us could have done without.

I'd ridden in with Cramer that day to pick up March's payroll. Cass didn't mind me depositing for him, but he hated to think of the bank paying *out* his money to any one else. Or so he said. Anyway, he and I always rode together on pay day.

As we left the bank, we ran into Lothers on the street. I guess he'd come to borrow some more, or try to. He sported a clean blue shirt and a shave that would have done Sunday proud. A couple of loungers stood nearby, waiting for a bar or some place worse to open. Lothers gave them both a civil hello. Then when he caught sight of Cramer and me, his face went dark enough to need another shave.

I was carrying Cramer's carpetbag with the iron lock on top. We used it when we moved money. Cramer, of course, had to carry the key. Lothers knew that bag and what we were doing. He stopped and gave us his surly best.

"You pretty happy you got one less to pay, huh, Mr. Cramer?"

I hoped Cass would ignore it. But he and Lothers had had hard words at parting. Cramer bristled to the ends of his chalk-gray hair.

"I'm damned happy *you're* the one less," he said.

Lothers grunted.

"And *you* — ," he turned to me, "I guess you're glad you finally got him to fire me?"

I don't know what I would have said. Cramer saved me the trouble.

"You got your*self* fired," he came back, " — your own damned fool self."

"Who're you kidding?" Lothers laughed. "McCallum was out to shed me ever since the day I came. You wised up to who's running your ranch and gave him his God-damned way."

I didn't want things any worse than they were between my boss and me.

"Come on, Cass!" I said. But he rose to the bait like a starving trout.

"You're wrong!" he snapped at Lothers. "I was a while finding out the scum you are. When I did, *I* told you to git."

Lothers laughed again.

"You lie through your wife's false teeth, old man! If you weren't fit *now* to be dead and buried, I'd knock 'em where she wouldn't find 'em for supper."

"Cass, let's go!" I said. Martha was the sorest subject with him: he could talk about her, but he couldn't listen.

"I wouldn't talk about anybody else's *wife!*" he said. It came in his nastiest tone — not that different from his usual one, but telling.

"Huh?" Lothers winced.

Cramer looked at me and shrugged:

"You never get more from a hog than a grunt."

"What about my wife?" Lothers said, his eyes black as tar.

"Cass, for Christ's sake, come on!" I tugged at his arm.

He pulled free and cursed and turned back hard on Lothers.

"Your wife!" he mocked. "My foreman got there before you were born. She's more his 'wife' right now than she'll ever be yours!"

"God damn you, Cramer, come on!"

I almost jerked his arm off. Lothers stood there not knowing whether to spit or wind his watch. The two in the street just nodded and whispered. I swore at what they must have thought.

Cramer swore at me. I turned him loose when I got him away from the others.

"Why the hell'd you say it?" I asked him. "Filthiest, stupidest thing I ever heard!"

"Hell!" he spat back, "I didn't tell that bastard anything half the town don't know."

"That's a lie!" I said. "Just because your wife put that brat of yours to track me once doesn't mean everybody knows what *you* do."

Cramer blinked.

"I don't like being called a liar," he said. "I checked with friends in town. It wasn't any secret you were her man."

"It was till you and your wife got to it."

"I doubt that!" he said, "though Sadie kept it dark about the other one, too."

"'Other one'?"

"He left Paco before you got here. Don't tell me you didn't know."

I knew she wasn't a virgin: she knew I'd been married. But we left each other's past alone. Maybe that's why we'd hit it off. Hearing this from Cramer now burned me as if I'd swallowed fire. I grabbed the front of his shirt.

"You *lie!*" I said hoarsely.

"You've called me a liar twice too often," he muttered.

I let go his shirt. He didn't have the sense not to bring something up, but he knew when he'd said enough. I didn't want to hear about another man. I wanted to wash out Cramer's mouth with a bucket of lye.

He breathed deep and straightened his coat.

"You and me —," he said slowly, " — we got work to do."

He turned and started for where we'd left our horses. I made the effort and followed.

A little knot of people had gathered in front of the bank. Later I learned that Lothers had wanted to go after Cramer on the spot. But Cramer had no gun, and he did have thirty years on the boy. Cooler heads for maybe the last time talked sense into Lothers.

The men were paid — work got done that day. But I felt as if I'd been run down by cavalry. Next day — Saturday — I didn't feel like going back to town. Lothers did, though. I heard about it from the men.

He hadn't spent the night in a bar for more than seven months. In a few wet hours he made up for the long lost time. He drank himself to the ground by midnight — passed out cold in Frisco's gambling room. The real surprise was that Sadie came to fetch him! I don't know who else would have, but it wasn't something a wife in Paco did.

She must have known what was coming when Lothers left her that night. She followed him with the wagon and waited behind the Spinning Wheel. After a while she went in back and asked the girls to keep an eye on Lothers for her. She didn't want to be seen; but when she got word he was out cold, she went in after him. She got there ahead of Frisco's men and hauled him home.

It hurt me to hear all this. The two of them must have had one hell of a row to start that evening off. I feared it was just the beginning. Somewhere short of the end, I felt, Lothers would bring the fight to me. I wanted to humor him early — bury this thing where no damned dog could ever dig it up. If I sought him out at his place, Sadie might get in the way. I had to make him come to me, where nobody else would know.

The year wore into April before I thought of a plan. Touches of green were mocking the near-dead winter; grass poked up like whiskers through the earth's gray face. Birds and rabbits came again —along with things less welcome. A mountain lion from the Granite Hills dropped down to stalk our cattle. Twice I found a gutted heifer not three miles from the ranch. We moved the herd, but I told Cramer I wanted to hunt the killer — alone. He approved; it made no sense to leave a cow-eating cat on the prowl.

Before I left, I took time to down a touch at every bar in town. Along the way I complained about that cat with the taste for veal. I mentioned, too, that I'd be hunting alone — camping at the northeast lineshack close to the end of Cramer's property. Lothers couldn't have missed that trail, even riding drunk.

Next day I borrowed Cramer's gun and rode out leading a pack horse with four days' keep aboard. I didn't sleep in the lineshack. I camped at the end of a little box canyon three hundred yards away. I couldn't be bushwhacked there. Above my camp a circle of boulders topped the fall of a stream that rose high in the Granite Hills. Out the canyon's lower end the stream wound into a pool where cattle drank when spring thaws loosed the water above. To reach me, a man would have to follow that stream bed, fully exposed as soon as he came in rifle range.

I didn't think Lothers would come at night. I felt he would want me to "see the bullet," if he saw himself as my killer. I kept a fire going while I was there, to make sure he didn't miss me; at night I laid a dummy bedroll by it, to make sure he didn't hit me. I slept some thirty feet back from the fire, under a low rock ledge where only a rattler could have found me. I kept Cramer's rifle under my blanket, my own .44 in its holster under my head.

Three dull days stretched into four: I saw no sign of Lothers. And I didn't see hide (though I did see hair) of that cagey mountain lion. At night he would come in close to the bait I laid; but all of himself he deigned to show were tufts of fur rubbed out of his winter coat. During the day I had a go at tracking — through rocks and piney scrub that could have hidden a hundred cats. The occasional rattlesnake I raised didn't make hunting easier. On the fifth day — having drawn neither of my quarries — I figured I'd scrap the hunt.

I returned to camp at noon after a last look 'round for the cat. As I rode up the little stream bed, I saw a print that didn't look like my mare's. It showed in a spot of gravelly ground right at the water's edge. But after four days' coming and going, I couldn't be sure it wasn't hers. I pulled Cramer's Winchester out of its scabbard anyway. I jacked in a round and held the rifle muzzle-up with the butt against my thigh.

As I neared the boulder that hid my camp, I felt sweat coming on me. I paused a moment: all I could hear was the heavy breath of my mare and the purr of the stream at her feet. I hated the thought of being surprised here in my own damned diggings. I looked around me and up at a baffling sky. It was warm and getting warmer. The scabby horseshoe of rock in front of me seemed to shrink beneath the heat. Not a bird, not a breath was stirring.

With my left hand I reached to loosen my .44 in its holster. Then I nudged my horse, and we rounded that last rock.

Sure as death and taxes, Lothers had come. He was hunkered down in a half-squat, his back against the face of the jutting rock I slept under. His horse stood on beyond him with the one I'd left behind. He had no rifle with him. And there wasn't one on his saddle. He stared up at me blankly through the scruff of a few day's growth but made no move.

I kept both eyes on him as I dismounted. Still watching, I put my rifle on safety and shoved it into its scabbard. With a slap on the rump I sent my mare to the other horse.

I stared back at him over the forty-odd feet between us. His left hand held a short stick with a skinned spot near the end. In his right hand he held an open clasp knife. But there weren't many chips in front of him. Either he hadn't been at it long, or the knife was out for something more than whittling.

"Well?" I said, trying to smile.

"Not well!" he shook his head. "You and me got bones to pick."

He wasn't wearing gloves, so I took mine off.

"You speak," I told him.

He looked sadly small, there on his hams and heels, his back to the wall of the canyon. I felt almost sorry for him.

"Have some coffee, if it'll help," I said.

The fire between us was closer to him. It was embers now, but the can of coffee I'd left on it would still be warm.

"I want nothin' of yours," he said. "That's why I carry no rifle."

My eyebrows rose, but I let it pass.

"What *do* you want?" I asked.

"To give you something."

"What?"

"What's yours."

"And that is — ?"

"Maybe I'm not sure yet."

I got impatient.

"You came here to talk riddles?"

"Among other things."

"I'm listening."

"You better."

" — or *what?*"

He grinned in a way I didn't like.

" — or you might not hear!"

I took a deep breath.

"I'm about to break camp," I told him. "If you've got nothing else to say, get the hell home to your wife and tell her she wants you. — And be damned thankful she does."

His grin faded.

"She made me look damned small."

She made him look small whenever the two of them came to mind. Instead of saying so, I just asked,

"When?"

"That night in town she hustled me home like a stiff."

"You ever think how Riper and Grale would have made you look?"

He nodded slowly:

"I ought to kill those bastards."

"You ought to get hold of your*self*. She's the best thing that ever happened to you, and it's time you remembered."

"She may be the worst."

I wanted to call him a fool but I said,

"You're wrong. She's better than both of us put together. And the sooner you start to treat her that way, the better off you'll be. Talk with your life instead of your mouth for once."

He was quiet a moment. Then he looked up quickly at me.

"What's wrong with me — that I can't be like every one else?"

For a moment his face looked wistful.

"You really want to hear?"

"I guess I don't. Not from you."

"I'll tell you," I went on. You've been spoiled — by a God who gave you ability and nothing to control it with. And spoiled by luck that's let you get away with being the child you are."

"You think I'm a child?"

"Worse. You're a man with a child's mind."

He glanced down at the stick he held. Laying his knife across it, he peeled a sliver that curled on the blade like baby's hair.

"What *was* it between my wife and you?"

"What does it matter? Whatever it was, it's dead and ought to be buried."

He glanced up, gesturing with the knife.

"She said in church it was me — that she loved *me!*" he got out slowly. "What *was* it between you two?"

I tried to sound gentle.

"It's a long way finished," I told him. "When you marry, your promise governs the future. The past is best forgotten."

"I don't forget."

"It isn't yours *to* forget. You've got some growing up to do. And while you're at it, you'd better learn to let other people forget, whether *you* can or not."

He stared back, perfectly calm. With almost no expression, he said:

"She lied to me, didn't she?"

I swore and called him a fool.

"You're not good enough to kiss her foot — and you sit there and say to me she lied!"

He nodded deliberately:

"She lied to me."

I shivered in spite of the heat.

"And worse than that," he added, "she's a whore."

I started for him.

"I'll make you eat that filth!" I said.

A month, a day, a moment before, I'd been determined to reason. Now I wanted to tear his tongue out. I watched as I went — him and his sticker. Suddenly it came.

I was fifteen feet from him. It flew up in an underhand curve. I leaped aside and felt the wind from it on my neck.

And I saw why he'd waited till then to throw. I was almost opposite the fire. The only way I could jump was to my right. And under my feet — hidden by a rock from where I'd stood — lay a full grown diamondback, sunning himself like he owned the earth.

I'd drawn my gun as I jumped. But when I landed, I was too surprised even to thumb the hammer back. That snake knew what to do, though. He blurred into a little mountain. The sickening purr I was all too damned familiar with scared me back to life.

I fired the moment he struck. Each of us spoiled the other's aim. I fired again before he recovered. I missed again. But I got off a quick third round that tore his coil in a couple of spots. Tawny circles of snake came apart like a melting steel spring.

I whirled the gun on Lothers. His only move had been to stand up where he was. My breath came hard. Sweat ran off me like blood on a butcher knife. I leaned against the nearest rock. The clammy feel of my clothes made me wince. I don't know now if my pants were wet with sweat or urine.

I took my eye off Lothers to aim a fourth shot into that moving mass of snake. Half its head disappeared in the dirt, along with one of its lidless eyes.

Lothers stayed put, awed (I guess) by what had happened — or by what hadn't. I shuddered as that great hose of a body tried to die at my feet.

The hammer was back on my fifth round. I raised the barrel toward Lothers' gut. The fear in his eyes calmed me.

"You knew it was there!" I said.

My voice was only a whisper. I swallowed, caught breath, tried again.

"You knew it was there!"

He said nothing. His hands reached back for the rock behind him. Sweat showed on him now: his face gleamed like patent leather.

"Did you put it there? Get a snake to do what *you* didn't have the guts for?"

He just stared back like a trapped rabbit.

Suddenly something touched my boot: the snake had reached me. I must have jumped a country mile. Lothers was lucky I hadn't jerked the trigger — but he made the mistake of laughing.

I shifted the gun to my other hand and squatted to grab that snake. I caught it behind what was left of its head. It felt warm and solid.

I stood up, lifting the rattler. A tree limb in a storm would have been easier to hold. The horned tail beat my shin like a drumstick.

"No!" Lothers said as I moved on him. "Don't!"

When I stood three feet in front of him, he suddenly reached for his gun. I cracked my Colt across his wrist. He screamed. His pistol hit the ground, and I kicked it behind me. Then he screamed again, catching his wrist with the other hand.

"That's a good start," I said.

I swung the snake as hard as I could. Body and rattles hit him full in the chest. He fell on the rock behind him. I swung again, aiming for his head.

He rolled away from me to fend the blows. That snake got heavier every time I swung, but I was learning how to use it. One stroke opened his cheek with the rattles. He fell to the ground. I lashed him where he lay.

I must have hit him a dozen times when the snake broke in my hand and skittered away. I threw away the piece I held and walked to where the rest thrashed on the ground. My right hand was slick with blood, but I managed to drop the hammer on my Colt and shove it home at my side.

Lothers got to his hands and knees. He'd screamed like a baby until I knocked his wind out. Now he seemed to be catching breath. I picked up what was left of the snake. I thought Lothers would scream again. He threw up instead.

I stretched that rattler across the length of his spine. The blow flattened him. I stepped to one side and lashed across with my fresh left arm. His shirt and undershirt hung in shreds as bloody as his back. The rattles were curling that tail around him. As he rolled to protect himself, I could see they'd lifted skin off his ribs.

When he turned on his stomach again, I stropped him till my two arms ached. He whimpered like a sick dog. When I couldn't hear him anymore, I stopped.

Sweat and dirt had almost blinded me. I felt sick as a dog myself. I flung the end of that snake away with the last strength I had. My arms trembled. Lothers looked like a side of slaughtered beef and my two hands, almost as bad.

I stepped back, turned, and stumbled toward the stream. I dropped my gunbelt on the way. Next thing I knew, I was on my face in the water, boots and clothes still on.

The little stream was shallow — and cold as a widow's winter. Now it just seemed cool and clean to me, though. I thanked God for it. I wallowed and grovelled and tried to get my head under. Rocks on the bottom stung my cheeks. The pain brought me around. The stream began to seem cold against my legs. I rubbed my hands, wrung them, wiped them on rocks, my pants, my shirt. I wanted a drink, but I couldn't drink from my hands. I bent down and lapped like an animal. I stopped for breath a couple of times, but I drank till I felt all cold inside.

I got up groggy and moved out of the water. I half-hoped I'd see a preacher — *some* one to say I'd been washed clean. Only rocks and the same hard sky looked back. A lone buzzard circling high made me remember Lothers.

I went to him, cleared his mouth, and pulled him around till his head was lower than his feet. The effort it took amazed me.

I removed his gunbelt and took the bullets out of it — unloaded his pistol, too. I put the bullets in an empty can I had. His belt with the gun in its holster I made fast to his saddle. I untied the slicker behind his cantle, rolled up the can of bullets inside, and tied it back again. I picked up my own gun and its belt, reloaded, and buckled up.

I got out the last of the whiskey I'd brought and poured a little over his back. His flesh and shoulders shrank as the alcohol hit. I rolled him over and got my bottle between his teeth. He came around slowly.

I lifted him up and walked him into the stream. When we reached the middle, I let him down with his head to the bank. Then I fetched his hat and began bailing water onto his back.

I stopped afterwhile and sat on a rock to rest. Finally he raised himself and stared through blood and bits of flesh that clung to his hair.

"You gonna make it?" I asked, when his red eyes found me.

He reached up slowly to push the hair aside.

" — kill you!" he breathed out thickly. "I'll kill you for this!"

"Shut up," I said, "or I'll let the buzzards eat you."

Several more had joined the first to circle over us now. He lowered his head and drank as I had.

"You want some food?" I asked, when he got himself to a sitting position.

" — nothin' — nothin' o' yours."

He wiped his face on the rag of a shirt that still hung round his neck. He looked down at his right wrist where I'd struck it. Slowly he flexed the fingers. Then he pulled up his legs and tried to stand. I moved over to grab him.

He shoved my hand away with an effort that put him back in the water. Then he steadied himself against a rock and heaved up on his own.

"What'd you do with my gun?" he said.

"It's on your saddle."

He gritted his teeth and, stumbling along, moved away to his horse. I followed, trying not to look at the mess I'd made of his back.

He flung his arms across the saddle and leaned a moment to rest. The animal snorted but stayed put. If he hadn't, Lothers would have fallen flat.

He held tight some little while and then reached around to where his gun was hanging.

" — bullets!" he mumbled when he saw it was empty, "you stole my bullets!"

"You'll find them when you get home."

I heard him grunt as he felt for the stirrup to mount. He found it and, pulling his leg up with one hand, got his boot in the loop. Then he caught the pommel with both hands and tried to pull up. He didn't make it: the horse shied. I grabbed the bridle and held hard.

"Let go!" Lothers said, keeping his grip on the pommel. "Let go o' my God damn' horse!"

"All right," I said, but I held onto the bridle.

He got his foot up and tried again. The third time he made it. He hung there a moment, bent in two like a snaffle. Sweat was on him again by now, eating into his back. He must have thought he was being boiled alive.

He swung his right leg over at last and straightened up.

"You feel like riding?" I asked.

He acted as though he hadn't heard.

"You never came here to *talk*, did you?" I said finally.

He looked down at me again, grim under heavy brows and hunched back.

"I'll kill you, McCallum," he said. "So help me God, I'll kill you."

He nudged his horse, and I let go the bridle. I walked back to my fire and watched as he moved away. His strawberry back, oozing under the midday sun, almost turned my stomach.

I gathered my gear and closed camp. As I did, I couldn't help wondering about the threat he'd made. I was to wonder about it later. — If he didn't kill me, he came so close it hardly matters.

6
Showdown

AS SOON AS I'D PACKED, I started on his trail. I caught sight of him before he'd gone a mile. I stayed back two hundred yards or so and watched. I don't think he even knew I was there. He by-passed town in a wide swing north, then headed east for his own place. He pushed ahead at a walk and never stopped. I guess he knew he wouldn't be able to get back on if he once got off.

It was almost dark before he arrived. I stopped behind a low rise of ground where I could see him ride in. His house was the only one in sight. Its low chimney and steep roof lay on the sky as if they'd been cut out of paper. It seemed a house that a thief would joy to find — though the only thing in it worth stealing was human.

Against one wall stood a rough lean-to for horses. Blink must have been waiting there. When Lothers got close, the dog ran out, yipping and bounding to meet him. Then the door flung open, light knifed through, and *she* was with him. She ran to his horse, reaching up to catch him. I almost envied him as she got him down. She helped him inside and closed the door: the dark was mine again.

I got back late to the Coupled C. I felt glad no one was up to kid me for missing the mountain lion. Tomorrow would be too soon for that.

In addition to taking guff at the ranch, I found I had plenty to do. I was glad I did. Shingling the barn, laying in stores, pushing men and moving cattle kept me from thinking — part of the time. Nights were harder now than days, and the dreams that came didn't help — visions of a rutted human back, bleeding like a rained-out road.

As days and weeks went by, I wondered why I hadn't killed him out there in the canyon. I could have done it, and no one the wiser — his wife (and him, too, probably) a damned sight better off. But I couldn't kill the thought that he still meant something to *her*. God knows what I would have had to dream if I'd come down on him with all four feet.

The bottle bloomed for me now like a long-forgotten friend. I'm not proud of the way I drank, but I'm thankful something helped. Of course, I paid for it during the day — though sometimes others did. "Bitch-bad" Cramer said I was getting. But I knew the men would take it if I pushed myself as hard as I tried to push them. Then one night after supper Cramer saw fit to remark.

"No need trying to kill the men just 'cause a wildcat give *you* the slip," he said.

I'd never told him what happened that day between Lothers and me. I never told any one. I stayed away from people now. My drinking I did alone.

"You're tight as new wagon springs," Cass went on. "I reckon I don't know all that's eatin' you. — Do *you?*"

I must have been dreaming when he said it. I looked to be sure my hands were clean of snake.

He and I were sitting alone in the kitchen at the time. Remains of supper cluttered the table. The men had gone; Martha and the boy were out at the pump; I'd been trying to light my pipe. Cramer even worked in a word about me and

John Barleycorn. It tickled me, hearing it from him: he could have taught a fish to drink.

"Whatever's on your mind," he said, "you can drown it deader in women than in whiskey."

He must have thought he was about to lose his foreman to a case of the shakes. He glanced around to make sure Martha was still in the yard.

"Let's hit town this Saturday," he said, turning back to me. "Drink alone never did a man good. I'll stand you to a night you won't forget."

I turned him down, but Saturday next I took off to Paco on my own. The winter-stiff mud had turned to May. I figured the ruts in *me* might loosen under some different rain. I wasn't that set on drinking. I wanted to see new faces and hear about troubles that weren't my own. I heard plenty from bar to bar.

Lothers, I gathered, was alive, well, and full of himself as ever. Weeks had passed since the rattlesnake damned near killed us both. Lothers seemed to have put it farther behind than I. He was back in town with a scar on his cheek and more than a chip on his shoulder.

He had to face worse than creditors now. Cramer's droppings that day in the street afforded the town a handle for all of its old ill will. And Lothers' exit from the Spinning Wheel under the wing of his wife added fuel the fire could have done without. As Doc Hobbs put it, "What's sauce for the goose is another man's sass."

The scar on his cheek, where the rattler's tail had cut him, got things off to a roaring start. Joe Grale at the Spinning Wheel had asked if it meant Lothers couldn't hold down his wife. Lothers knocked him into the nearest spittoon, I'm glad to say. And when Carl Riper repeated the question, Lothers went after *him*. The crowd at Frisco's hollered for a fair fight —

parted them long enough to lay some bets. Frisco took advantage of the pause to move the fight to the street. It all brought out the best in Lothers. He bent Carl over a hitching rail and beat a few knots on his head. The crowd had to pull them apart.

After that, people got careful. They held off heckling until Lothers drank the fight out of himself. I figured on being careful, too. Riper and Grale might just have been drunk — as they claimed, and as they often were. But I made my mind up not to let Lothers catch me drunk.

I was with Doc Hobbs at the Silver Pick that night when Lothers showed. The scar below his right cheekbone glowed liver-red. I was glad I couldn't see the rest of him: Hobbs (I learned) had never been out to treat him. Sadie had nursed him back alone.

He didn't see me at first. Hobbs and I were standing at the inside end of the bar. Lothers stayed at the street end, close to the door. He'd had a few drinks already: his hand shook as he reached for the nearest bottle. He threw down a drink and poured another before his throat got cool. He looked around as he worked on the second. With a hand on the butt of my Colt, I watched. Our eyes met: the glass he was holding stopped just under his lip.

He never took his eyes off me. Hate came through them, over the whiskey. He nodded slowly as if to tell me, all in God's good time — or the devil's. Then he downed his drink and left.

I'd downed my own and started to go when Hobbs spoke up.

"You better leave him alone."

"He better leave me alone," I said.

I cleared the swinging doors and stepped aside, out of the light. Flat against the front of the building I waited till my eyes got used to the dark. Lothers wasn't hiding. In a moment I saw his solid back, moving away from me down the street.

The doors opened again, and Hobbs was with me on the verandah.

"Just thought I'd tag along," he said.

"You think somebody'll need a doctor?"

"Somebody's going to need a friend." He squinted at me and tapped his hat down tight on his head.

"Who the hell's friend are *you?*" I asked.

"Who the hell ever needs me."

I smiled, and we stepped off into the street. The night was warm, well-seasoned with stars. A near-full moon rolled through it all, a gold mote in its own white dust. — I wondered afterwards whether the things of that black night could ever have happened outside, under such a sky.

Lothers headed for Frisco's place. Why I followed, I couldn't exactly say. What I'd heard (and seen) of him bothered me, though. I didn't fancy his sobering up while my back was turned.

When he reached the Spinning Wheel, he pushed through the doors like he was king. By the time Hobbs and I got there, he was seated with a bottle at one of the front-room tables. Two of the town's best soaks sat opposite him. I learned that the others at the table had moved as soon as Lothers sat down. The ones remaining were too far gone to get up.

I walked back to my spot at the bar and asked Jukes for the usual. Hobbs got his, and this time both of us drank slow.

Many had noticed Lothers' presence. Nudges and whispers made the rounds. A fellow named Frenchy — Paco's grayest, grimiest miner — seemed to have most to say. He was dirty enough to use like charcoal to write your name on the wall. He'd just left the table where Lothers sat down. From the bar he heckled the two who couldn't move.

"Who you drinkin' with, Moon?" he called over his shoulder.

Jim Moon was older than Frenchy — whiter of head, if not of heart. He'd spent his life chasing "fool's gold and sinner's silver," and lately a gut full of whiskey. He surprised us all by being able to answer:

"Polson — drinkin' wi' Polson."

Moon's partner claimed his name was Leopoldson. Paco knew him as plain Lee Polson. He was the third (and farthest gone) at Lothers' table. He and Moon — and Frenchy, too — had put their money on Riper the night Lothers took him apart.

Polson said nothing. Moon rapped him on the chest with the back of his hand:

"Here, you — Polson, yo' son of a bitch! You drinkin' wi' me or not?"

Polson belched.

"I tol' you!" Moon grinned.

Some at the bar laughed. The banjo boys cut further comment with "The Yellow Rose of Texas." It was almost on key. At the end of it Frenchy made his way to the banjo stand.

"Things been like this long?" I asked Hobbs.

"Long enough. Worse here than some other spots in town."

Frenchy returned to the bar. He leaned there, scratching with whichever hand wasn't full of a glass. The banjo player he'd spoken to hollered for quiet and announced:

"By special request for Jim Moon's table — 'The Girl I Left Behind Me'!"

Frenchy led a round of applause. Some who knew the song, and more who didn't, joined in on the chorus. Moon grinned like he couldn't shut his mouth. Polson just sat there, giving his glass the dead man's eye. Lothers never moved, except to down some whiskey.

When the song ended, a couple of Frisco's "girls" came out and did what I guess was a dance. When they left for the roulette room, Frenchy started entertaining again.

"Moon!" he hollered. "You keep sittin' there drinkin', your *wife*'ll come clean you up!"

Lothers put down his glass. He stared around at the bar like he couldn't be sure who said it. The place quieted. Moon's voice came over the rattle of glasses.

"She'd have to come from Kansas City. — Ain't a broomstick made'll bring that witch this far!"

Laughter and cheers from the bar.

"Maybe *your* broomstick will, Moon!" some one remarked.

Another hoot from the bar. Moon was the local Methuselah. He poured himself an unsteady drink.

"Ain't nothin' wrong with me," he said, "that whiskey and women won't fix!"

The place erupted in a shout of laughter. Even in that huge room it sounded like an avalanche.

Lothers slumped in his chair. The house got back to its drinking.

"Why the hell does he come here?" I shook my head at Hobbs.

"Why do *you*?" he said.

But I couldn't answer. My eyes fixed on the doorway to Frisco's gambling room. I wondered whether my sight was going. Sadie stood there, pale and still, her figure outlined darkly in a dress of blue homespun. Any one else would have looked small under the beam of that double doorway.

Hobbs and most of the bar saw what I was staring at. They all turned to watch. It came out later she'd followed Lothers and waited for him out back, thinking he meant to drink himself dead again. The sound of that shout a moment before made her think he'd done it.

Lothers saw her as soon as he looked up out of the glass he held. The crowd hushed as if it feared the two of *them* might whisper. I guess Sadie didn't know *what* to do, now she'd shown herself. She just stood fast and tried to stare him down.

"Get out!" Lothers said thickly. "Go home. Get out!"

"You come *with* me," she answered.

"Get out!" he said. "Don't make me tell you again."

Somewhere somebody dropped a glass; there wasn't another sound. Every eye in the house was on them. Sadie held both arms at her sides, fists so tight her shoulders trembled.

"Come home with me, Clifford," she said quietly.

Lothers swallowed. His head twitched at the faces 'round him. He groped for some straw to break the back of her pride.

"I'll not go home with a whore," he said.

I felt my body stiffen. The whole crowd seemed to feel its starch. Sadie lifted her chin. Her eyes grew wider — her lips parted in two tight lines across her teeth.

"What did you call me?"

Her voice came cold and distant, as if from another country. Lothers reached for his drink and tossed it off.

"You heard," he answered. "The word's not new to you."

I thanked God he didn't repeat it. Sadie took one deep breath and then another. Her hands clutched her legs in a spasm of self-control. Suddenly she turned and made her way out through the back-room crowd.

Unbelieving silence gave way to the hum of voices. I felt too ashamed for Sadie even to look Doc Hobbs in the eye.

Jukes claimed he'd never heard a woman called such a thing to her face since he'd been tending bar. Somebody said a woman like Sadie was "too damned rare to get called a whore, no matter what she was." Some one else said, if a man called his wife a *Chinaman*, he hurt nobody but himself. Ugly as it was, it *did* seem a matter now between Sadie and him. I wondered what good it would do if I or any one beat those words back down his throat.

Several in the house would have liked to try. Frisco knew it better than I. He strode in from the back room and signalled the piano player. The fellow jumped into a tune head first: the banjos picked it up. Noise seemed to calm the place. Frisco made his way to the bar and ordered a round on the house. He wanted no more trouble: it kept our minds off spending money.

Hobbs took off to see where Sadie had gone. I figured I'd wait where I was till Lothers sobered, or until he left the place.

Jim Moon quit drinking as soon as Sadie left. When Polson roused and reached for a drink, Moon slapped his hand. Polson blinked like a kid at the cookie jar. Moon nodded toward the door. After a moment Polson managed to get to his feet. Moon stood up, and the two of them lurched to the swinging doors and went. Frenchy followed them out.

Nobody missed any one of them. Saturday night just rotted on. The longer I watched, the more unreal it seemed. Lamps and candles flickered in a hollow effort to fill the dark. The gilded mirror behind the bar mocked their tiny flames. People looked at *me* as often as they looked at Lothers. He kept on drinking and so did I, reckless of whether I got ahead of him.

Hobbs came back to tell me Sadie and the wagon had disappeared. He'd checked a couple of houses where he thought she might have gone. No one had seen her. We figured she'd headed home.

Hobbs had a drink or two himself — a drink or two more than usual.

"Why don't you go and leave Lothers to me?" he asked, as the night drew out. "I'll see he gets home — and tell you about it."

"I'm not finished here," I told him.

"I'd hate to see you do anything you might regret," he said.

"Maybe I already have."

He shook his head and glanced at Lothers.

"Maybe I'll wind up getting *you* home and telling *him* about it."

"Maybe."

A fiddler joined the band now: it wasn't a happy marriage. I began to feel tired, bored with it all. But I didn't know what was going on. None of us did.

I was almost ready to leave when we all found out. More than an hour had passed since Sadie came and went. The crowd had thinned. Lothers still sat alone with his liquor. Jukes moved up and down the bar, serving the few who hadn't worn out their pay. Frisco was back in the gambling room, and the band played like noise was God.

The fiddler must have been first to see. He tapped the piano player with his bow. The banjo boys had noticed by then. They stopped and followed the fiddler's stare. So did every eye that still could see.

She'd entered this time through the swinging doors. Her face was even paler now, her hair and dark dress salted light with dust. Otherwise, Sadie looked the same — except for the Winchester in her hands.

The scraping of chairs and shouts from the card room faded. Heads and shoulders crammed the back-room doorway. The whole place hushed. She stared at Lothers like he was the only thing she could see.

Some one at the other end of the bar must have moved toward her.

"Don't come near me!" she said, raising the rifle.

Whoever it was stopped. Boots began to tickle the floor. People inched back against the walls. Those behind Lothers moved fastest.

He must have seen her as soon as she entered. He never showed it, though. He was half-facing her where he sat, but he just stared down at the table top. Even when she came and stood in front of him, he never raised his eyes.

"What do you want?" he asked finally, still not lifting his head.

She eyed him hard, the rifle pointing up at the ceiling. I must have moved to go to her. Hobbs pulled me back and started for her himself.

"Keep off!" she said and lowered the gun at Hobbs.

She never took her eyes off Lothers. With the rifle pointing at Hobbs, she levered a round up into the chamber. Hobbs stopped where he was.

"What do you want?" Lothers repeated.

She took a breath and tightened her whole body.

"Say you were drunk!" she told him: "say you were drunk and take it back."

"I'm *not* drunk!" he snapped.

He got to his feet with an effort. The chair crashed over behind him. He steadied himself with both hands on the table. His clothes were all that held him together — like the paper ring on a cheap cigar.

"I can smell it on you from here," she said, lifting her nose at him. "You reek of whiskey."

"So — Jonah didn't smell like fish when he got where the hell ever *he* was goin'?"

We were all too tense to laugh.

"Then *apologize!*" Sadie said, and levelled the rifle at him.

Lothers straightened and took a step backward.

"'Apologize'?"

It carried all the contempt he could muster.

"I apologize to *nobody!*" he got out. "Till God Almighty apologizes for how he made me, I don't apologize to a soul. — Whore you were and whore you *may* be. Whore! whore! whore! — and be damned!"

Silence fell like a funeral pall. It lasted only a moment.

"You're not worthy to father my children," she said deliberately.

The roar of the rifle made me jump.

Its bullet caught Lothers high in the chest and flipped him backward. He fell on a table, smashing it under his weight. He kicked and rolled on his stomach, clawing the floor.

Sadie walked to one side of the table between them. She levered a bullet as she went. The rifle sounded again. The cold white of her face was melting now in tears. But she worked the lever — aimed that Winchester one more time.

When the third bullet struck, Lothers quit kicking.

7

Persuasion

LOTHERS WAS DEAD when Hobbs reached him. Sadie turned away from the body, her own wrenched with sobs. She must have forgotten she still had the gun. Suddenly she remembered. Raising it over her head, she flung it across the bar. It smashed into Frisco's gilded mirror and hit the floor.

"God help me!" she cried into her hands. "I give myself up!"

We all held back in a kind of awe. I felt as if I'd been shot myself.

The room came to after a moment. Somebody went for Marshal Gage; some of the rest got Lothers onto the nearest table. Hobbs thought to shed his coat and lay it over Lothers' face. Jukes began cleaning up the mess behind the bar. Little by little the talk began, but only in whispers.

Meanwhile Sadie stood straight and alone, right in the middle of the room. She stopped crying and just stared down at the floor. No one ventured near her. She stood that way till Marshal Gage arrived.

Gage was not the assertive type. Maybe that's why he was still marshal. One way or another, the brash kind didn't last long in the job. He approached Sadie like a preacher opening his Bible.

"Understand you done in your man, Mrs. Lothers," he said as he tipped his hat. His black handlebar moustache danced a jig as he talked.

"I killed him," Sadie replied in a whisper.

Gage blinked at the body.

"I guess that's him yonder," he muttered, almost to himself. "All you people see it?"

He glanced about at the nods that came.

"I'll have to lock you up," he said, turning back to Sadie. "Will you come with me?"

"Let me look at him — before I go," she said.

"Certainly — certainly," Gage nodded.

She walked over to the body. The house got quiet enough to make a heathen pray. Slowly she folded back the coat that covered Lothers. Then she closed his eyes with her fingers. She studied his face some several minutes, her own impassive and stained with tears.

"He was a handsome man — my husband," she said.

She put the coat back carefully and turned to the marshal. "I'm ready now."

Gage nodded and gestured toward the door. With her head high, she walked before him to the street. If Paco had just crowned her its queen, she couldn't have moved more beautifully.

As soon as they were gone, the talk began.

"By God, she did it!"

"Dead as a outhouse mouse!"

"Died too quick, the son of a bitch."

Some one asked what to do with the body. I think it must have been Frisco.

"Got a dog I ain't fed . . ."

"Burn it!"

"Take it to McCabe's."

The last suggestion carried. Carpentry was one of the trades of which McCabe was local jack. He barbered for a living, but the back of his shop also served as Paco's lying-in-state room. All whose heirs could afford it rested there till McCabe put what he called the "last roof over their heads."

The bunch that left with the body came back shortly to say McCabe refused to take it. He figured no fee was coming from Sadie and wouldn't open his shop till he knew who was going to pay for the box. Frisco finally said *he* would, just to get shed of the body.

I left when Lothers did. But my sleep wasn't half as sound as his. In fact, I wonder whether I slept at all. It was more like being in a black daze. Dawn put a welcome end to it. I was up before the ranch had stirred, heading for town on a cold-coffee breakfast.

That Sunday was the only time in my life I beat the preacher to church. A low white fence enclosed the building and its burying ground. I was waiting at the gate when Parson Preble crossed the street from the yellow house he owned. There wasn't another soul in sight.

"Morning, Mr. Preble," I said as he approached.

"Good morning, Mr. McCallum!" He eyed me hard from head to foot. "You're hardly in Sunday attire. I trust you're coming to church, however?"

If looks made preachers, Preble would have been a Jeremiah. His coat fitted without a wrinkle, and his white stock gleamed like the waters of holy Jordan he loved to talk about. He made fair comment on how I looked. I hadn't changed since the night before. I'd even passed up a Sunday shave to make sure I reached him in time.

"I was planning to come," I nodded.

"It's all too rare a pleasure," he nodded back.

He started past me into the church. I called after him.

"Mr. Preble! May I have a word?"

"I've a lot on my mind, Mr. McCallum," he said, as if he were preaching. "I'll be glad to see you any time you care to call. At the moment I must prepare for service."

"That's what I came about," I told him. "Have you heard what happened last night?"

He took a deep breath and let it out quick, as if trying to blow a fly off his lip.

"I heard Sadie Lothers shot her husband, if that's what you mean," he said.

I nodded. Preble had a way of finding out most of what went on. Not that it was hard — but we were all impressed at how quick about it he was.

"Did you plan to mention it in church?" I asked.

"I did — and do," he replied.

"It might go easier on her," I told him, "if you held off speaking about it."

"Mr. McCallum," he said, taking a step back toward me, "I'm not concerned with how easy or hard 'it may go' in this world for that unfortunate woman. I *am* concerned with the morals — if they can be called that — of this bedeviled community. If I think the general good can be served by referring to something that touches us all, I shall indeed speak about it — and that right early. — Now if you'll excuse me, I'll see you at service."

With that he moved off into the church. I started to say he would see me somewhere else a damned sight sooner. Instead, I walked uptown and got some food and a shave.

When the service was due to be over, I strolled back out to the church. The congregation was just beginning to leave. I felt sure Hobbs would be there — along with Mayor Garvey and some others I wanted to see. They were all there. I stopped Hobbs first.

"You weren't inside?" he asked, nodding at the church.

I shook my head.

"Probably good you weren't," he said. "It would just have made you mad."

It seems Preble waxed unusually glib. He called it shameful that a killing could happen under the very nose of the town. He made the shooting an excuse for denouncing liquor and cards — again. He mentioned the Spinning Wheel by name — called it (and every bar on earth) a sink of sin and the devil's temple.

I looked at Hobbs and swore. Instead of going home, the congregation broke into little groups to talk outside the church.

"We've got to get her away from here," I said.

"What do you mean?" Hobbs scratched his head.

"Get a committee to run her out — tell her not to come back."

He bored into me with his eyes.

"You think that's fair?" he asked.

"'Fair'? Fair to whom?"

"Well, to her, for one thing. — You were there last night."

I tried giving *him* the stare:

"You think Judge Perkins'll be any fairer?"

Perkins was the territory's circuit judge. Twice a year he came to hear any suits there were. Some thanked God he didn't come oftener. He'd fought in the Union army till he got himself captured at Spotsylvania Courthouse. For the rest of the war he cooled his ardor *and* his heels in prison at Andersonville. His right arm rotted from some disease he caught there. After the war he lawyered in Kansas till Grant made him a federal judge. They said he'd been weaned on a bullet, but the years had made him harder than ever his mother had.

"Well?" I prodded, as Hobbs stood there thinking.

He swallowed hard. Perkins was due in a couple of weeks for what was called "spring term."

"What do you think the judge'll give her?"

"Ten — fifteen years," I shrugged. "What the hell choice does he have?"

Hobbs glanced around at the people talking in front of the church.

"Let's speak to Mayor Garvey," he said.

Garvey was talking with Henry Beeman, who published the *Paco Gazette*. I started toward them and felt Hobbs grab my arm.

"Let's take them one at a time," he smiled. "Old Garvey has a stomach complaint. He'll feel better with lunch inside. Come on: I'll buy you a drink — unless you've taken the pledge."

After a drink and some lunch of our own, we paid a call on the Mayor.

Garvey had been one of Paco's earliest settlers. He'd done a number of things, I gathered — homesteading, farming, store-keeping, and (lately) running the assay office. He looked like a man who'd worked hard all his life without a lot to show for it. But he seemed solid in spite of his years. His handle of "Mayor" was honorary — the only thing honorary in town, as far as I could tell. He'd held the title since long before I came. No one dreamed of taking it from him by anything so mundane as a vote.

We sat on the porch in front of his matchbox house. His wife left us alone there.

"What you suggest," he told us, after I'd said my piece, "is quite beyond the law. You may be surprised to hear I've wondered about it myself. But we — we've never done anything like it in Paco before."

I glanced at Hobbs, who was sitting on Garvey's other side.

"The town has run people out," I said, "even since I've been here. It's done a sight worse to a couple of rustlers I could name."

"*Suspected* rustlers, you mean," the old man said, shaking his white head slowly. "It pains me to think of those things. They cost this town, and every one in it, more than a thousand stolen cattle."

He paused and looked out over the dazzling sand beyond his porch.

"And nobody's been run out for killing," he went on after a while. "Card sharping, maybe — claim jumping, stealing — things like that. Or for just showing up with a bad reputation. I'd like to see us so strong we didn't *have* to run any one out. You don't settle something by turning your back on the wrongdoer. And some in town we tolerate only because they've been here a while."

He stopped and stared out over the rail again. His eyes seemed fixed on something close that, even as he watched it, was melting fast away. He stared so long I began to wonder. I coughed and twirled my hat.

"I know you're there," he said, never shifting his gaze. "I'm just thinking — I've thought about little else all morning."

He raised one hand to the back of his head and smoothed his already smooth white hair.

"Though what she did, this woman who killed her husband, was something just between him and her, they were both a part of *us*, in a way. You can't take life from one without affecting the lives of all. Are we — you and I, this town, and what this town will *be* — justified in freeing a person who did the worst she could to another human being? — who did it in the sight of all, not caring for the law's most basic restraint?"

I couldn't think how to answer him. A feeling almost of
shame came on me. — I tried my last, long chance.

"She has friends," I said: "friends who won't want to see
Judge Perkins punish her."

"I know! I know!" the old man nodded. "That's what
scares me! Not that I fear her friends: I fear what they'll make
of the law. If she's held and tried and *they* refuse to abide the
issue, will I have done a greater wrong than they? — to insist
she stay and be made the cause of their rebellion?"

I had sense enough to keep my mouth shut now.

"If she wasn't already in jail!" Garvey sighed. "If we just
didn't have her in custody!"

Hobbs kept quiet, too. We both waited on the Mayor.
Finally he looked around sharp at each of us in turn.

"I told Henry Beeman I'd talk to him later about this thing,"
he said. "Why don't you two come with me?"

We rose together and walked uptown to the newspaper
office.

Beeman and the boy he called his "devil" were setting a
one-page extra on the shooting. Beeman was small and spindly
— thin as one of his papers, with a face like a page of its print.
His cheeks and forehead were white as chalk; they made the
line of his brows seem all the darker. A thin moustache ran
along his lip, and a wispy fringe of jet black hair traced the
edge of his jaw.

He'd set up only the banner and head, but the price showed
twice what the weekly cost.

"Work on Sunday comes high," he winked at us. "Sunday
is a day of rest!"

Garvey came to the point and asked what Beeman thought
of escorting Sadie out of town.

Beeman whistled.

"Novel approach to law enforcement!" he said. "When word of *that* got around, you'd play hell trying to punish any one else who killed her spouse."

"Circumstances here are special," Garvey said. "I'm sure I needn't elaborate to *you.*"

"But the next time," Beeman went on, "the next time a woman shoots her drunken husband — she gets run out of town, too? Why it might even be *my* wife!"

"It might at that," old Garvey nodded.

Only he could have gotten away with it. I kept a straight face, and so did Hobbs; but the type-setting boy guffawed till Beeman slapped him.

"It might be more humane," Beeman mused aloud. "Fine figure of a woman, Sadie Magrath. — It beats salting her down in prison."

He fingered the spidery fringe at his chin.

"I don't know *what* to think," he said at last. "But it would make a hell of a story!"

Beeman eyed his press. It stood at the back of the shop like a tiny guillotine, its uprights looming over the bed where ink instead of blood was spilled.

"Be that as it may," said Garvey: "you could help by explaining it all. *Some* one'll have to. Lothers wasn't the town's most popular citizen. His wife may well have been. I tend to agree with Mr. McCallum: her friends won't like to see her punished. If you could make this town understand why shipping her out was the only way — well, it just might make them see why such a thing must never happen again."

Beeman pulled a rag from his pocket and dabbed at his mangy beard as if he thought it might drop off.

"Yes," he said, still staring at his press, "it would make one hell of a story!"

He turned to the boy, now setting type as though his life depended on it.

"You, Jethro!" he snapped. "Go find Mr. Purvis. Tell him he's wanted in the newspaper office — right away. Mr. Caslin, too. — *Move*, 'less you want your backside stropped!"

Jethro moved. When the boy had gone, Beeman smiled benignly at Hobbs, the Mayor, and me.

"We better convince the 'vigilance committee' first," he said. "Should we summon any one else?"

I knew Ira Caslin was Sadie's friend. About Nate Purvis, I couldn't tell. He'd never been to the Spinning Wheel — said it didn't look right for a banker to enter a gambling den. He was new in Paco, but he'd wormed his way into most things except the town's affections.

"What about Preble?" Garvey asked.

Beeman agreed:

"If he's not with us, we'll hear about it from hell to breakfast."

"Maybe even if he *is*," I said.

"He should be here," Garvey nodded. "Will you fetch him, Mr. McCallum?"

I looked at Hobbs.

"Doc, *you're* on better terms with the man."

Hobbs laughed, but he went for Preble at once.

I began to think the morning's sermon might have done Sadie more good than harm. By noon the whole town must have heard her story. And feeling ran high that something unusual had to be done.

While the group gathered, Beeman asked if the Mayor cared to read his piece on the shooting. He said he'd written it after church — hadn't even stopped for lunch. The Mayor took Beeman's copy and looked it over. Without his specs I knew old Garvey couldn't have read a bull's butt; he never put them on, though — and Beeman never noticed. Maybe the Mayor meant it as a lesson to me in patience.

Jethro got back ahead of Purvis and Caslin. When they arrived, Beeman ordered the boy out till the talk was done.

Caslin looked as green as last week's lumber. He agreed at once to the exile plan. Purvis had more trouble with it.

"I lent them money to buy their spread," he complained. We all knew they couldn't have borrowed it anywhere else.

"Since *he's* dead," Purvis went on, "I hate to see *her* skip town not paying a nickel."

His face got pinched as a prune when he talked about money, which he did most of the time.

"What do you think you'll get if she goes to jail for fifteen years?" I asked.

Purvis shook his head and swore and said the whole thing was damned depressing. He liked to talk big, but he wasn't the kind to buck a crowd. He finally said he'd go along, but griped at having to foreclose "another miserable mortgage."

I was glad he agreed before the preacher came.

I'd hoped Doc Hobbs might somehow soften Preble. No such luck. As the two of them entered, Hobbs looked my way and shook his head.

The Parson thought he was still in the pulpit. Sadie was a "taken transgressor," and Preble stood ready with the first stone. He thought the town should hold her and make her some kind of example.

"Running her out isn't making her example enough?" Garvey asked.

Preble wouldn't budge:

"It's not making an example of the thing that's wrong with the *town!*"

Beeman smiled:

"You can't turn men off drink by keeping a woman in jail!"

"No more'n you can close up one saloon by opening a hundred Bibles," Caslin remarked.

The rest of us laughed. Preble just got sore: he had as much humor as a blunderbuss.

"I'd like to close more than *one* saloon in Paco," he went on. "This shooting mightn't have happened if half the crowd who saw it hadn't been beastly drunk."

For a preacher, Preble knew little about his customers. Cow hands six days out of seven looked forward to nothing but salt pork and sundown. For them, a saloon on Saturday night meant a damned sight more than church on Sunday.

"I didn't see it," Garvey shook his head. "I don't know that I could dispute you if I had. But *now* we're faced with something that seems to threaten what little respect for law this town can boast."

A murmur of approval swept the group.

"We think," Garvey continued, "that escorting this woman out of Paco may have a good effect. At least it'll keep the town from trying to set aside such penalty as the law might have to impose. She's well known and well liked. If we send her off, we may avoid something even worse than a bar-room shooting."

The Mayor paused to wipe his face on a large, white pocket handkerchief. The closeness of Beeman's little shop had raised sweat on all of us. I was wetter than most: Preble had directed his drinking remarks at me.

"Putting aside this thing of saloons," the Mayor went on, "how do you feel about sending the woman away?"

Preble blinked above cheeks that were growing redder.

"Isn't it against the law?" he said. "What'll our Marshal do?"

"Gage'll do as he's told," said Purvis.

It wasn't the most reassuring thought, in terms of Paco's future. But we all knew it was true.

"What do you think about running her out?" Beeman pressed the Parson.

"It would be too easy on the *town*," Preble said quietly. "It would let us all forget — and forget too soon. It would be like sweeping this business under the first convenient rug. That such a thing could happen here! — that respect for life and another's soul could be so frail! The wrong already done can never be made good. This we should not be hastening to forget. We all must suffer when we allow killing to happen. By keeping her with us, however short a time, we can't fail to remember — and perhaps even repent."

I don't think Preble ever knew how deep his words then went. I felt them chew my very heart, though I longed to get Sadie away. The sweat on my back went cold: I sensed agreement with Preble rising in the room.

Suddenly Garvey spoke. He raised both arms shoulder-high in a gesture stronger men than Preble would have found hard to resist. His words came like a chant:

"With you as our conscience, Parson, this town before God will never forget!"

It was a master stroke. The whisper that had begun for Preble rose to a murmur for Garvey. Beeman reached to shake Preble's hand. Then he turned and shook with the Mayor, as though it was all decided.

Preble looked surprised, but happy, too. A compliment on his preaching was the shortest way to his vote. Anything less than letting him pronounce on *all* our acts would have raised his wrath forever. Before he quite knew what he had done, Preble agreed with us all.

8

Late Learning

WE DECIDED TO SEE HER as far as the hills just north of town. She could take her husband's horse and the wagon, which Gage had brought to the jail. We planned to ride out with her to the house and give her time to prepare. Then we would all swing north together and see her away by dusk. We broke up to get our horses and meet at the jail in half an hour.

I didn't want to get to the jail before the rest. I already had my horse, so I went with Hobbs for his. When he was ready, we mounted and left for the jail at a walk. I wish we could have galloped. Word of what was afoot had spread: little knots of people stood about, watching as the party of horse converged. What we were doing sickened me to the soul. I wished it was all over and long lived-down.

When Hobbs and I tied up at the jail, we found our group had grown. Of those who'd been at Beeman's all but Garvey and Preble were there. So was Cass Cramer. He'd ridden in that morning and heard the news over noon whiskey. Frisco and one or two others had come to the jail with him.

Marshal Gage walked out on the stoop to ask us what was up. We thought we should wait for the Mayor, so no one ventured to say.

Garvey didn't keep us long. But he brought word that Preble wasn't coming — felt he couldn't participate, being a man of the cloth. He sent his blessing by Garvey, though — for whatever that was worth.

Garvey welcomed the new to our group and explained it all to Gage. The Marshal scratched his stomach.

"You want me to swear you people in?" he asked.

"*Hell*, no!" the Mayor told him. "This ain't any *posse*. — And *you* better not ride with us. Stay here — keep and eye on the town."

Garvey led us past him into the jail. The building had formerly served as a general store. In front, where a counter or two had stood, were Gage's desk and gunracks. The wall that once marked off the back room had been replaced with a row of bars. It divided the jail almost in half. Perpendicular to it another iron grill partitioned off two cells. The ironwork had changed only the face of things. The place still smelled like a store, odors of bacon and camphor coming out over the gun oil.

Sadie occupied the right-hand cell. She was standing now behind the bars that walled her off from Gage's office. She watched us as we entered, searching every face that came. She looked pale and tense under her dark brown hair. She still had on the same blue dress, which looked as tired as she. It shouldn't have, but it surprised me not to see her fresh and clean.

I couldn't meet her eyes. I let my own wander 'round the office. They came to rest on the rifle. It stood in the corner by Gage's desk, a white tag tied to the trigger. I couldn't look long at the rifle either.

The group filed in and waited. Some of us greeted her. Most kept quiet. When we were all in, the Mayor began, knowing nobody else would.

"Mrs. Lothers," he said, his tone no harder than it had to be, "We're all aware of what went on last night. Some of us even saw it. The whole community is shocked and deeply disturbed. — Feeling the way we do, we've come to escort you out of town."

"To — to what?" she asked. Her pallor heightened the worry in her face.

"To escort you out of town," the Mayor repeated. "We'll ride with you to where you were living and let you gather your things. Then we'll take you north to the Granite Hills. Where you go from there is up to you."

"Up to me!" she murmured.

"The only condition," the Mayor went on, "is that you never return. You must leave this town and its environs forever."

She grasped the bars of her cell to steady herself.

"I can't !" she said in a hoarse whisper.

"You can't accept the condition?" Garvey asked.

She stared at the floor and shook her head.

"Our action may surprise you," said the Mayor, "but I'm sure you don't realize the position you're in. Granting you this opportunity is the town's most generous concession."

"*Too* generous!" she said, her voice almost breaking. "I cannot leave."

The Mayor glanced at the rest of us.

"You *what?*" he said.

"I cannot leave," she answered, more firmly, "I've given myself up."

Whispers started around me.

"I don't understand," Garvey said.

"I've thrown myself on the law's protection," she came back quietly.

"The law can hardly protect some one in your position!" he told her.

Again she shook her head.

"It's not myself — my person — that I worry about!"

She looked quickly into the Mayor's eyes:

"I've never run away from anything in my life. — I've run into danger, but never from it. I've done foolish things, things I regret — but never a thing I'm ashamed of."

"You killed your husband!" Garvey said.

"There are things no woman can bear," she told him, " — and shouldn't be expected to."

The Mayor gasped:

"Do you know what you're saying?"

She tossed her head to shake that dark hair back. Her nose didn't look so big any more. Her face, though ashen, took on a strength I'd never seen.

"I'm not ashamed of what I've done," she said. "If I could have killed him with a single bullet, I would have. I knew what I was doing. If I must suffer, I will abide the punishment."

The Mayor's face went white as his hair. Marshal Gage was scratching himself, but none of the rest of us moved.

"You refuse to leave?" the old man asked.

"I *cannot* leave!" she said simply.

She still had hold of the bars. I saw her knuckles go white.

"You — you cannot!" Garvey repeated.

We all stood as if struck dumb. I could almost hear the afternoon sun beat down on the roof above. Not a boot or a board creaked. And then the faintest trace of a smile licked at Sadie's lips.

"Have you come to force me, Mr. Garvey?" she asked. "Is it a lynching mob you're leading?"

The Mayor's head bowed almost imperceptibly. His eyes grew wide and fell to the floor at her feet.

"None of us here will touch you!" he said in a voice gone husky.

The place got graveyard-quiet. Finally the Mayor squared his shoulders back.

"I — I believe I have no business here," he said to no one in particular.

Shaking his head, he turned and made for the door. We moved to let him through. Then we followed him one by one to the street. It was like coming out of a church. We looked at each other and shrugged and gathered around the Mayor.

"That woman has taught me a lesson!" he said, as if in a daze. Without more ado he untied his horse and headed away to his house.

I didn't know what to make of it. But I didn't stay to talk. I got on my horse and rode out into the wilds. My mare didn't understand it any more than I. She was young and full of spirit and kept pulling 'round for home. But I rode her off till the white sweat on her flanks reminded me of my own. The heat of the day was merciless, even through my shirt. It made me feel some aching kin to the scorched hills that formed this uncouth country. The dust, the glare, the dryness singed my very lungs. I cursed it all for its ugliness — wondered what kept me there.

I got back late and slept that night, exhausted. Next day I put the men to work and told Cramer I was off to town. He said nothing — just nodded. I was grateful to him for it.

Noon was on me before I reached the place. I drank lunch at the Silver Pick and headed out to the jail.

Marshal Gage was half-asleep. (He always sat a chair better than he did a horse.) His booted feet covered the top of his desk and looked tired even from pounding that, their usual beat. Gabby Macrae, the "sexton" of Paco's jail, was sweeping the floor with a worn-out broom. Their prisoner sat on the cot in her cell, some sewing on her knees. She got up as I came in.

I told Gage I wanted some time alone with Sadie. He shifted feet to the floor and spat through the front window. I knew he liked my tobacco. I sat on the desk where his boots had been and offered a brand new plug. He took eight good teeth's worth.

"Keep it," I said, when he handed the plug back. "I talk better without it."

He nodded and stuck the plug in his vest. He glanced down at the Colt I wore.

"I know you value your gun," he said. "I reckon you wouldn't be giving it way, even in a cause like this."

"I give away bullets now and then," I told him: "never the gun."

Gage nodded and rolled that chunk of tobacco under his big moustache.

"I reckon there ain't any harm," he said, getting up, "so long as I keep the key."

Gabby Macrae was leaning now with chin and hands on his broom.

"Knock off, Gabby, 'fore you give yourself hernia," Gage drawled.

Gabby threw the broom in a corner and left licking his lips.

"I'll be back in fifteen minutes," Gage told me from the door. "Think that'll do?"

"Sure," I nodded.

He followed Gabby. I turned to Sadie Magrath.

We talked first about silly things — how she liked jail and whether she had what she needed. There wasn't much privacy, she admitted; and she liked her own cooking better than what was brought from the nearest bar. Aside from that, she said she couldn't complain. Two of the girls from the Spinning

Wheel had been to her house to fetch some clothes and sewing for her. Parson Preble had sent her a Bible. She had on a clean dress now and was making herself a new blouse. It lay on the foot of her cot.

The girls who'd gone for her things hadn't found Blink, she told me. The dog seemed to have disappeared.

"He'll turn up," I tried to smile. "You know — the 'bad penny' and all that."

"He wasn't so bad," she said. "I feel sorry for him now — a waif again. Like me!"

I flapped my hat against the leg of my pants.

"I came to talk about something else," I told her. "It's not too late to do what Mayor Garvey wanted. I think right now I could get them to give you another chance."

She tilted her head and let those dark eyes fix me.

"I don't want it."

"Sadie, do you know what you're up against? Judge Perkins gives ten years for *stealing*. You can't expect mercy from him."

"What greater mercy *is* there — than to give me something that'll make good what I've done?"

I felt like swearing at her.

"Sadie, you've got to get *out* of here!"

She looked straight back at me, simple as a child.

"Where would I go, Sam? What would I do? — Do you think killing my husband is something I'll ever forget? Do you think I can just shuck it off — like a rattlesnake shedding skin?"

"Don't talk to me about rattlesnakes," I muttered.

"Do you think it won't be with me always?" she went on, " — in my sleep, in my work, in *me*? — I'll stand up before Judge Perkins — and any other judge there is. I didn't kill him lightly, my husband. And it wasn't just him I killed."

I blinked at her:

"What do you mean?"

"It was much, much more," she said. "It was all my dreams — all I'd ever hoped life might some day hold for me."

"What are you talking about?"

She took a deep breath — pushed back her hair with one white hand.

"I wanted a home," she continued, "a home of my own — something I'd never had, even as a child. My old uncle did what he could, but he wasn't my father and mother. — I wanted a man I could love, and who loved me. I wanted a family — my own family — to love and share and give my life to. I wanted so much — and yet so little. Isn't all I've said what every one wants? And isn't it what most women get — whether they want it or not? — whether they deserve it or not? But I can't believe you don't know all these things!"

She turned abruptly and took a step back from the bars.

"I know!" I managed to say.

"I thought you did," she said, still with her back to me. "I wanted a man I could look up to — a man I could respect — who'd make me ashamed to be untrue to him — who would touch whatever is best and deepest in even the worst woman's soul."

She raised one hand to her face. I think she was wiping away a tear.

"I thought I would have a chance out here," she said.

She took the few steps to the end of her cell and looked out the tiny window there.

"I'm not beautiful," she went on, "but I'm healthy and I'm strong enough."

"You have more beauty than you know," I told her.

She laughed:

"That's the old Sam!"

She turned and walked back up to the bars and me.

"You *did* tell me once I had a beautiful body!" she said.

I swallowed hard:

"That's not what I'm talking about."

"Well, what does it matter? My uncle once told me, 'Looks are nothing, though they sometimes get you what you want!'"

"Sadie, Sadie — !" I shook my head.

"Oh, don't look at me that way!" she laughed again. "You had your chance and didn't take it! — I had mine and did. It's always a gamble. I just lost."

"Sadie, you haven't *lost!*"

"Ah, but I have, Sam. Though I don't regret the gamble. For a while I had everything I wanted. It was all so glorious I think I never knew till then exactly what I *did* want! — He gave me things I would never have had. He was weak and small in some ways, but he made me feel like a God. He thought I was nothing but noble and pure. He did whatever I told him, as if I held his soul in my hands. — For a time I was able to mold that man. I made him all I prized on earth — all I think he, in his own little way had ever dreamed of making himself."

"And then — !" I was half-afraid to hear.

"And then," she said slowly, "they told him something here in town — probably the truth about me."

She glanced down and grasped the bars in front of her.

"He went back to being an animal," she said: "drinking — fighting — the way he always had. I went through hell with him then. Once he got drunk and told me I could go back to being the way *I'd* been. — He couldn't understand there was *no* going back for me — that I couldn't have if I'd wanted to. I told him my life and love were his 'till death us do part.'"

She shivered in spite of herself.

"I don't believe he ran with other women," she went on. "It wasn't his way — whatever faults he had. But he tried to make me admit — that I was degraded. And I *wouldn't* admit it. I told him I didn't care about his past and refused to talk about mine. — I almost wish I *could* have said what he wanted. It drove him mad that I wouldn't confess."

She breathed deep, turned, and walked back to her window.

"I suppose the reason I didn't," she said, "was that I believed it might make things even worse between us. It would have given him justification for the way he only *thought* he had the right to be."

"You — you needn't tell me," I got out.

She went on as though she hadn't heard:

"And then one day six weeks ago somebody beat him. Beat him with a whip like I've never *heard* of any one beating another. Flayed the skin off his back and ribs as if with a knife."

"Sadie, don't —!"

My mouth was so dry I couldn't speak. I grabbed the bars of her cell as if I thought I could rip them out.

"He never told me who it was," she said, still at the window. "I think it must have been Carl Riper over at the Spinning Wheel. Carl always liked me, brute that he was. And he hated Giff. I guess Carl caught him alone — unarmed — and just plain cut him apart. He's good with a bullwhip, Carl is."

I must have groaned or knocked my head against the bars. She turned and walked back toward me.

"What's the matter?" she asked lightly, and touched my hands where they grasped the bars. "Are you in jail or am I?"

I let go the bars as if they were hot and scooped my hat off the floor. She gave a nervous little laugh and stepped again to her window.

"I nursed him back after the beating," she said. "He just lay flat on his stomach a couple of weeks. Until he got strength again, it was almost the way it had been in the very beginning. He was so weak he could hardly talk. He just looked at me, and kissed my hands when I fed him. — For the second time, I felt almost that I'd created Giff."

She sighed and walked back to where I stood.

"When he got back all his strength," she said, "it was even worse than before. He started drinking — came back to town — had that fight with Riper, and Joe Grale, too. (Maybe Joe had helped Carl with the whipping.) When Giff came home from beating those two, his hands looked almost as bad as his back had looked before. — He began to frighten me. After that fight he started to talk about killing people."

She came up close — showed me the deeps of her eyes.

"He told me he was going to kill *you*, Sam. He knew all about you and me by then."

"The damned fool!" I muttered.

"One thing about my killing him," she whispered: "I'd like to think that, by doing it, I may have saved your life."

I shook my head:

"You mean you saved me from killing *him*."

"Maybe it's the same thing."

I felt sweat break beneath my hair.

"Sadie, Sadie, you've got to get *out* of here!"

"I'll never leave. — I thought my telling you all this would make you understand."

She glanced down at the floor again.

"After the whipping," she said, "he started to use that word to me. He even beat me once. We had some awful nights."

She put her hands up to her face. Then she dropped them and looked straight at me.

"He said you made me your whore, Sam. — One night he got drunk and threatened to denounce me before the town. I said I would kill him if he did."

I stared back. Thoughts I couldn't stop tore through me — through the bars, through her past and mine.

"If you and I had been together," I said, "what would you have done — if *I'd* called you that name?"

She almost laughed, then shook her head.

"You wouldn't have called me that!" she said.

"I might have called you something worse!"

"*Is* there something worse?"

I closed my eyes and opened them again slowly:

"What would you have done?"

She studied my face a moment and smiled:

"I would have kissed the word from your mouth."

"With a rifle butt?"

"With my own two lips!"

I wondered whether her eyes or mine would be the first to overflow.

"Sadie, Sadie, it's too *late* for you and me to be talking like this!"

Before she could answer, we both heard boots on the stoop outside.

"Much too late," she nodded.

The door opened and Marshal Gage waked me back to life.

"Are you through?" he asked, shedding hat and gun.

"I'm through," I said, not looking at him.

I turned and walked out into the street.

9
Trial and Error

SEVERAL TIMES AFTER THAT she and I talked alone. Whenever I found an excuse for the trip, I rode in and stopped by the jail. Gage got enough plug-cut in the process to make a grown goat sick.

Even before I saw her, she was with me all those times. She haunted my mind like some one new, a woman I'd never known. Maybe I hadn't seen what was there — or maybe she'd changed from the inside out.

I still had hopes of getting her gone. Judge Perkins was almost on us; and though I didn't urge her, I tried to make her *want* to leave. I pray that I wasn't cruel. Once I asked her, didn't she really feel she could make a go of it somewhere else?

"What do you mean?" she came back sharp.

"I mean, give yourself another chance."

"I didn't give him one."

"You gave him too damned many."

She squared up as if her shoulders bore a weight I couldn't see.

"Sometimes," she said, "you get just one chance to mind your own business. Sometimes you get just one chance to do what you must to keep your self-respect. My time — my chance — came. I took it."

"Don't you feel sorry?" I asked, " — sorry you took his life?"

She never batted an eye.

"What he did was filthy," she said. "Yet it wasn't in hate that I killed him. Maybe from too much love of me, but not for hate of him. — It's just that he would have taken from me even the little that I had. What he said was like hitting a woman in the breast. I can't feel sorry for what I did."

"Well, aren't you sorry for your*self?*"

She didn't flinch.

"I've never in my life felt sorry for myself," she said. "Not for long, anyway — though God knows I've been tempted. I've had as many good things as I have been denied. No, I've never felt sorry for myself. And I can't afford to now."

I almost wish she'd slapped me. But I guess she knew she didn't have to. It was one of our last little talks before the Judge arrived.

Perkins was late that year. Most of us hoped he might be even later. He was old, and every one thought the next judge couldn't be any worse. He came with his clerk on the stage that touched at Paco. A couple of lawyers came, too. They followed him 'round his circuit, arguing cases along the way. We had no lawyer in Paco then. There wasn't business enough to keep one man at the bar, much less the two it takes to sue and line each other's purse.

We had no courthouse, either. Perkins judged in the post office, though it was smaller and dingier than most saloons in town. Assay work and claims registration both went on in the post office then. It was our only "government" building. Each spring and fall, tables and counters got shoved back to let in the territorial court.

The building had a single ground-floor room. Perkins sat at a big oak desk against the room's rear wall. He always brought a Union flag along — tacked it up on that back wall where all but him had to look at it. Left of the desk stood a testifying chair; the jury had the opposite side; and two small tables faced the judge where lawyers, clerk, and parties sat. Onlookers got the rest of the room: the clerk would line up rows of chairs behind the two front tables. Any overflow from the chairs watched things standing up.

Most of the time seats went begging. Things were different now, though. Sadie Magrath was up, and Paco felt the trial would be her star performance. Even standing room was scarce: at fifteen minutes to trial time the "courtroom" looked (and smelled) like a sardine can.

The day was hot as any in June, but the heat discouraged none. People sat or stood on the counters shoved against the walls. Some were milling around the door, watching from the street. When one of the counters broke under all the bodies on it, pieces got passed out the door and a few more people pushed inside.

Judge Perkins didn't much care for the look of that crowd. He'd never seen its like in Paco. He scowled about as if he wanted to try the whole damned town.

When he judged, he always wore a coat and a string bow tie. That morning he was almost the only one to brave the weight of a coat. Sweat ran down his face like basting on a Christmas pig. He had a water glass, some books, and a gavel on top of his desk. He used what remained of his bad right arm to weigh down a pile of papers. In his left fist he held a palmetto fan. He waved it under his chin and now and then used it to tick sweat off the end of his nose.

Sadie was at the far side of the table to Perkins' left. Marshal Gage sat between her and Perkins' whey-faced clerk. Sadie looked pale, but apart from that, cooler than most of us there. Her hair was up off her long, white neck; and her dress, of some dark gray material, opened at the throat and folded across her chest.

Two civil cases were on the docket. Perkins heard them ahead of hers. He must have been hoping to thin the crowd. I almost hoped he would myself. I'd come too late to get a seat and stood wedged in behind the chairs at the back. Not a soul got bored, though; at least, nobody left.

The first case dealt with water rights in one of our scanty streams. The other involved a title to land. I couldn't pay them much attention. As words and deeds flew to and fro, my own mind wandered back to the war — the biggest title case I'd ever see. Perkins' flag made me remember — the flag I'd fought not long before. The people of Paco I'd come to accept — even the ones I didn't like. But the Judge and his bunch and that blue burlap were salt to an inside sore. Many in the room were from the South; I'd begun to wonder how *they* were feeling when a gravelly voice spoke up:

"No more civil actions. A criminal case remains before the court."

It was Perkins' clerk. The tight little room came alive. Voices rose in the street.

Perkins mopped his face as the talk grew louder. Then he reached for his gavel.

"Order. Order," he said calmly, rapping the top of his desk.

He waited till all were quiet.

"Criminal case to be heard at two o' clock," he announced. "Court will adjourn for lunch."

The bang of his gavel made a few of us swear. It was lacking half an hour of noon. The crowd felt cheated, especially those with seats. Even the clerk, lean and hungry as Cassius, looked surprised to hear about lunch. Perkins must have hoped the curious wouldn't stick around. He just sat still, waiting for the room to clear. I swore at the man myself, him and his Yankee flag. If it would sweat the Judge, I thought, I'd like to beat hedge and highway to make the mob come in.

I had my lunch standing up at the Silver Pick. I tried not to hear the talk. Sadie's case and more than a drop of whiskey lived on every tongue. Speculation as to what she'd get — and laying bets accordingly — occupied even the kid who emptied cuspidors. Ten years seemed the odds-on favorite — though some were betting she'd go scott free, since no twelve men would ever find her guilty.

By twenty of two the court was overflowing. Perkins had gotten his clerk to bring in extra chairs. Seated spectators took more room than standing ones, and more seats meant fewer folk. Some of the chairs got broken, though, in a fight over who would use them. The broken chairs (and a couple of good ones) flew out the door in the fight. Mayor Garvey arrived when I did and got the last surviving seat. The crowd outside, meanwhile, got thicker: it would have been a great day to loot the town.

By the time the Judge and Sadie showed, there was hardly any room left. Perkins inched his way at the head of the little procession. In his wake the clerk, lawyers, Sadie, and Marshal Gage threaded a path to the front of the room. The crowd closed behind them like the Red Sea on Moses.

I stood wedged in again at the back, and the place felt hot as green brandy. The street door opened behind us: those outside were straining to get a little closer in. Faces crammed each of the building's windows, even those that caught the sun.

The oak desk had been pushed closer against that Union flag. Perkins barely had enough room to get in his chair. The clerk and the others couldn't sit down at first.

"Move back! Move back!" Perkins hollered.

Mutters and shoves materialized a little more space up front. In the back we stood packed solid. If some one behind me had hollered "Fire," I couldn't have turned around to spit.

When all up front got seated, the Judge relaxed a bit. He stared about and fanned himself and waited for the crowd to quiet. Under his stringy gray hair his face looked tired already. His eyes were pouched and heavy-lidded, and his jowls hung down like wattles on a turkey. When the place had simmered some, he nodded to his clerk.

"Hear ye! Hear ye!" the clerk called the court to order. He looked around nervously and announced:

"The People of the United States versus Mrs. Gifford Lothers."

Some around me grinned at each other.

"'People'?" I heard them whisper. "'*Yoo*-nited *States*'?"

Perkins tried not to look annoyed. He dropped his fan and rapped for order. One of the lawyers, who acted as prosecutor, started to read the charge. I forget the creeping *whereas's*, but it did accuse Sadie of shooting her man in a bar called the Spinning Wheel.

"The prisoner will stand and face the court," said Perkins, when the lawyer finished.

Sadie rose and looked at the Judge.

"How do you plead to the charge?" he asked.

"Guilty," she said in a husky whisper.

A groan of dismay ran 'round the room. The Judge dropped his fan and banged for silence. He looked at Sadie, as unbelieving as any of us.

"The court will allow you to reconsider," he said. "Do you wish to avail yourself of counsel?"

"No," Sadie answered in a firmer voice.

Another murmur got several blows from the gavel. Perkins blinked his puffy lids.

"Do you wish to change your plea?" he asked.

"No," she replied.

The room's whisper rose to a shout in the street. Perkins shifted in his chair. When he dropped the fan this time, he never bothered to pick it up. He grabbed the gavel and beat a tattoo on the desk.

When order returned, he leaned forward and opened both eyes wide at Sadie.

"Are you aware," he asked, "of the seriousness of the charge? It says you shot your husband 'with deliberate intent to kill.' Do you know the meaning of those words?"

"I meant to kill him," Sadie said quietly.

"Then you still don't wish to change your plea?"

She was silent a moment.

"I meant to kill him and that's what I did," she said.

Another groan from the crowd died under Perkins' hammer.

"Had you deliberated on this act?" the Judge pursued. "I mean, had you reflected on what you were going to do — and then determined to do it?"

"I knew what I was doing," she said.

Perkins leaned back in his chair.

"You are, of course, entitled to a jury trial," he said, "on the matter of whether you're guilty. But if you so plead, you forfeit that right. In fact, you throw yourself on the mercy of the court for sentencing. Do you understand all this?"

"I understand."

Somebody swore in the street. Perkins lowered his eyes to the battered desktop and shook his head. You might have thought the wind had stirred his jowls, if there had been any wind about. I smiled to think what a beautiful box Sadie had put him in. Perkins couldn't have found *one* man — much less twelve — to call her guilty. Since no jury would be involved, she was *his* responsibility. I'd heard of Judges "clearing the court" for less than what had already happened. Yet Perkins, armed with only a gavel, knew *this* court might take a notion to clear itself of him.

He raised his head slowly. His string tie had long since wilted. Sweat was coming through the front of his shirt.

"Would you tell the court just why you killed your husband?" he asked.

Sadie lifted her chin.

"He — he destroyed all I had in life, or ever hoped to have."

"What exactly did he do?"

"He called me 'whore,'" she said softly.

Perkins blinked.

"That was *all* he did?"

"It was all he had to do."

"I mean, he didn't raise his hand to you — strike you — threaten you in any way?"

"He threatened me in a way you wouldn't understand."

Perkins raised his brows.

"But he didn't offer you physical harm?"

"No."

"Just called you a name?"

"That's right."

The Judge coughed and glanced at his own copy of the charge.

"You were both in this saloon — the Spinning Wheel — at the time?" he said.

"We were. He'd been in the place some time already. I came to him there."

"You came to him? For what purpose?"

"To take him home."

"He was incapable of taking himself home?"

"I thought he might be."

Murmured assent came from all around.

"Had you done him such service before?"

A snicker crackled the room like fire.

"Once before. I got some one at the Spinning Wheel to help me get him out of the place."

"And on the night you shot him, you went to him simply to take him home?"

"Yes."

"Why were you so anxious to take him home?"

Sadie took a deep breath and shrugged:

"I feared what might happen if he drank himself insensible. — There were many who hated him."

Cries of "*Hell*, yes!" and "Still do!" filtered in from the street. Perkins banged for silence.

"And you," he said, when quiet came, "you were not among those who hated him?"

Sadie stared back grimly.

"He was my husband. I loved him."

Another seething whisper had to be gavelled down.

"On the night you shot your husband, what happened when you came to him?"

"He refused to go."

"He was capable, then, of getting home on his own?"

"*He* thought so."

And then she added, after a pause:

"He was capable anyway of calling me that name."

Perkins studied his papers a moment.

"Had he called you such a name before?"

Sadie glanced away, as if unwilling to answer.

"Once," she said in a whisper.

"Once before, you say, he called you the name?"

"Yes."

"Privately?"

"Privately. He threatened to do it in public. — I told him I would kill him if he did."

The crowd gave a raucous cheer. Perkins banged like a blacksmith.

"This court will come to order!" he shouted, when relative calm returned. "Such outbursts make more difficult a duty hard enough already."

The clerk trembled in his chair like an old mule passing the soap works. The two lawyers looked as though they were ready to run for the hills. Perkins just looked angry.

"Let us continue," he said to Sadie. "How long prior to the night of the shooting did you have this private conversation?"

"Oh — several days."

"And at that time did you form the intention to kill him?"

"No. I never believed he would do what he said."

The Judge eyed her steadily.

"You had no specific intent to kill him till the night he called you the name in public?"

"That's right. I couldn't have stayed with him if — if I'd thought he would ever do it."

Her voice almost broke. She took a deep breath, tossed her head, and was ready when the next question came.

"The charge says you shot your husband with a rifle. You were not carrying a rifle, were you, when you came to take him home?"

"No," she shook her head. "No, I wasn't."

"Where did you get the rifle?"

I winced at the question.

"It was ours — mine and my husband's."

"Where was it that night?"

"It was at home — where we lived."

"Where were you living, Mrs. Lothers?"

Sadie swallowed hard.

"A little house we built — outside of town."

"How far outside?"

"About six miles."

Perkins opened his eyes wide.

"After he called you the name, you left this place, the Spinning Wheel, and went home to get the rifle?"

"Yes."

"How did you get there?"

"I'd come to town in the wagon. I drove it back."

"You drove out, got the rifle, and then returned to town?"

"Yes."

"How long did it take?"

"I don't know — maybe an hour and a half — maybe two."

"You returned straight to the Spinning Wheel?"

"Yes."

"Your husband was still there?"

"Yes."

"What happened when you saw him?"

"I told him to take back what he said. And when he didn't, I shot him."

"You shot him not once, but three times, according to the charge."

"Yes!"

Her answer was only a sigh. Another murmur swept the crowd. Perkins waited till this one, too, subsided. Gavel and fan both lay abandoned on his desk.

"Have you anything further to say," he asked, "before receiving sentence?"

"Nothing!" Sadie shook her head.

The room got quiet as a church. Those at the windows shushed the noisier ones outside.

"The court is aware," the Judge began, "that the defendant surrendered after the shooting and made no attempt to escape. Also, the defendant has saved us the time and trouble of a trial by pleading guilty. And the court is much impressed with the defendant's frankness in responding to questions."

He paused to mop his face.

"This is no ordinary defendant," he went on. "Nor is the crime, of which she admits her guilt, an ordinary crime. But circumstances hardly disguise the nature of the act. The act was murder and must be so regarded in a community governed by law."

It was the first time Perkins had used the word "murder." Some of us shuffled our feet.

"Now, there are various kinds of murder," he continued. "The law makes due allowance for acts done in the heat of passion. Taking life on the spur of the moment under over-powering provocation is different from taking life where time permits reflection on the deed. This latter act — killing on previously formed intent — is the most serious personal crime our law forbids."

He glanced about at the stony faces watching. He was talking now to the crowd, not just to Sadie. Whether they understood or not, they listened.

"In the present case," the Judge went on, "the crime appears to have been committed in violent anger. The deceased called his wife a name, and the act provoked her to take his life. Now, the law is clear that words alone, however vile, can constitute no legal excuse for physically harming another – much less for taking that other's life. Where neither word nor circumstance implies a threat of injury, neither the one nor the other can be a defense to the charge of murder. Indeed, the defendant here seeks to assert no such defense. It is greatly to her credit that she does not."

He coughed and took some water from the glass that had been provided.

"In view of her attitude and answers," he went on, "the court is willing to accept as true the statement that, notwithstanding the earlier threat, she had no intention of shooting her husband until the night he called her the forbidden name. In trying to fix an appropriate penalty, the court finds a single question determinative. That question is whether the defendant, after her provocation, had time to form the intent necessary to render her act *premeditated* murder.

"The defendant's own account of her behavior decides this question for us. Had she killed her husband as soon as he spoke — had she acted, say, with a weapon she was carrying, or had she used a weapon that came immediately to hand — the case would have been decidedly different. Having no weapon with her, however, she left to procure a rifle from her home six miles away."

His words stabbed my very soul.

"The total journey of twelve miles," he said, "took her at least an hour and a half. In the eyes of the law such a space of time is more than enough to let hot passions cool. Her armed return to shoot the deceased was an act of reasoned vengeance. The law and the Lord are the only powers who may exercise this dread prerogative. Out of a mistaken sense of honor — out of a reverence for her own integrity exceeding that which she was willing to accord the state — she arrogated unto herself the role of executioner. She is guilty of planned and premeditated murder, and must pay the penalty for it.

"The statutes under which we are governed leave me no discretion. Death is the punishment fixed for any person who willfully causes the death of another. I accordingly order that this defendant, Mrs. Gifford Lothers, be confined till the seventh day following this present, and that on such day at eight o'clock in the morning here in the town of Paco she be taken from her place of confinement and hanged by the neck until dead."

We were all of us stunned. The Judge was even able to bang that gavel a final lick. Then a roar like a stampede sounded. Every voice in the place must have shouted "NO!" together. The roar died — I made out individual cries:

" — hang *you*, y' son of a bitch!"

"Heat up the tar!"

"Go get a rope!"

The room seethed like a kettle of snakes. Perkins jumped to his feet and stood with his back flat to the Union flag. Clerk and lawyers leaped their table to get beside him.

A rock came through one of the windows. People started to duck and shove. I felt myself pushed forward, almost off the floor. Some at the back were fighting their way to the Judge. Pop Maguire, who'd lost the water-rights case that morning, seemed to be pushing hardest.

Chairs were thrown aside and smashed. People got knocked to the floor. Somebody came up swinging, and a free-for-all began.

A window — panes, frame, and all — crashed across the two front tables. Three men tumbled after it, pushed by others trying to climb inside. Something hit the back of my head — a rock or a piece of chair. I was twisting around to swing when the roar of a pistol stopped me. It filled that reeling room like an earthquake going off.

Another shot followed. Plaster and bits of ceiling rained down like buckshot. The smoke thinned: every one stopped and turned front to see what was going on.

Marshal Gage had fired both shots. He was standing on Perkins' desk, holding the dragoon revolver he always used. Sadie, I learned later, had gotten him to fire.

We in the back had lost all sight of Sadie. Gage now gave her his free hand and steadied her onto the top of the desk. Her hair streamed down loose. One sleeve of her dress had been torn off at the shoulder. And her eyes flowed fire enough to scorch the Sierra snows.

"Stop it! — Stop it!" she screamed.

She stared at us like some maimed and angry god. One or two picked themselves off the floor. The room milled to a surly silence. Then she spoke in what was more her normal voice:

"Stop this madness before you hurt your*selves*! — The sentence is just. I hold no hate for him who gave it. May each of *you* have no more to complain of when *your* judgment comes. — Behave like men — not like the children you *want* to be!"

Hers was the room and the mind of every man who saw her. She just stood looking down at us — chin high, eyes alive with all she didn't *have* to say. In the dead hush that came she pinned each wriggling one of us to the farthest wall of his being.

She turned to Gage, who gave her his hand and helped her back to the floor. He put up his gun and followed her down. Then she walked with confident step in front of him, never looking behind. The crowd drew back, afraid to touch so much as the hem of her ragged dress.

I got to the street myself in time for a last glimpse of her back. She and Gage were walking side by side — he loose as a bag of bones, she like a Roman statue. I wasn't even aware of the grumbling mob around me.

10
People's Posse

TO HIS CREDIT, Judge Perkins reached the street with a little more dignity than speed. He didn't stop for his flag, though — just brought the papers off his desk. The crowd watched, sullen and muttery. Clerk and lawyers followed on the Judge's heels — stayed there, too, till the four of them cleared town together. They decided not to wait for the stage. They all went off in a rented buggy before the darkness came. It took some guts, what Perkins did. But nobody cried to see him go.

I rode back out to the ranch that evening not sure what to think. A death sentence hadn't occurred to me: it was like throwing good life after bad. It must have occurred to Sadie, though. I wondered what I could say to her now, or she to me. For the first time since I'd known her, she just plain scared me dumb.

I went through two of my blackest days. All that kept me sane was work. I thanked God then for every chore I had. Things I used to swear at made me smile — broken thongs, leaky roofs, cattle and men that summer sun just made a little lazier. — I planned to see her, but I wanted time to get myself in hand.

At the ranch they talked of nothing but Sadie. Yet out of some primitive courtesy, the men never mentioned her in front of me. They clammed up like so many mutes whenever I was around. Even Cramer and his wife got careful of what they said. Meal-time talk became so scarce as to make us all at the table sweat. It didn't much bother me: my appetite had grayed and gone. But a decent meal was one of the things the men always looked forward to.

In Paco, talk of Sadie must have been even worse. I got the gist (or thought I did) from Cramer, who went to town both days on business. Rumor had it that Perkins was sending an army of marshals to make the "final arrangements." In fact, the Judge sent only three; but something happened before they came that made me wonder if three would be enough.

It happened the third night after the trial. We were finishing supper at the Coupled C — all three Cramers, the men, and I. I'd hung my gun belt on the back of my chair, as I always did. Every one else had gotten to the apple pie. I still had pork and gravy on my plate when I heard the horses.

"Company!" Cramer muttered, shoving back from the table. He got up, walked around my chair, and went out through the parlor.

Few people ever came in that way. The kitchen door was the one we always used. And my chair wasn't in the shortest line from Cramer's place to the parlor. None of it registered with me then. I just stared down at the tabletop, chewing a crust of bread.

I didn't look up even when the first man entered the kitchen. Then I heard the click of a rifle bolt, and the smell of gun oil hit me.

I turned and looked up into Frisco's string moustache. Riper and Grale were right behind their boss. All three had on sidearms. Frisco and Riper carried a Winchester apiece. Light from the table lamps daubed the gun barrels gold.

Next came Frisco's bartender, Jukes, hauling a double-barreled shotgun. Pop Maguire followed, along with some of his men. Jim Moon and Polson tagged behind with several more from town. On Moon the smell of liquor overrode the gun oil. Last came Mayor Garvey — the only one not sporting a weapon or two. It gave me a jolt to see him with those others.

When the group came in, Martha Cramer grabbed her son by the arm. The two of them went into her room and stayed there. I glanced around the table and caught a couple of the boys nodding at each other.

The table stretched from the kitchen hearth to the parlor. All of us seated there stayed put. The newcomers spread around us. Frisco headed for the hearth. Cramer followed. Garvey stayed by the parlor door.

Helloes went back and forth. Nobody said any more. I became aware that all were looking at me.

"What's going on?" I said.

"Something you should know — you and your men."

Frisco spoke from down at the hearth. What was left of the fire gave his grin a rusty glow. With his snake moustache and that red grin he could have passed for Satan.

"Like what?" I said.

"Tomorrow marshals come," he said. "Tonight we move. Sadie Magrath will not hang."

Whispered approval filled the room.

"All Paco feel like we do," he said. "Others wait at the jail until we come."

He stopped, and the silence almost ate me alive.

"You're taking a long way 'round to the jail," I said.

"We think *you* want to come with us," Frisco nodded.

"You came here for *me?*"

"For you and whoever else want to ride along."

"What'll you do with her once she's free?" I asked.

Frisco shrugged:

"We bring her a horse. Where she go — *her* business."

"What do you need me for?" I said. "You've got every gun in town."

Pop Maguire spoke up:

"We thought Miss Sadie might show more interest if *you* were with us."

He said it straight, but I didn't like the snickers I heard from some of the rest.

"You try to get her away before the trial," Frisco said. "We think you want more *now* to get her away."

"She wouldn't leave," I reminded him.

He nodded:

"We think she leave now."

"What if she won't?"

Frisco smiled as if he felt sorry for me.

"She'll go!" Maguire answered. "Before I see her hang, I'll carry her out of that jail myself."

Gleaming gun barrels scored his point better than any words.

I felt sick at head and heart. I thought of the house and the life that Sadie had tried to build. I thought of the life in her splendid body. But the guns, the cover of night, these sullen faces — they rubbed me raw somehow.

"Mr. Garvey," I turned to the Mayor, "have you come here to urge this thing?"

He stood with bowed head, his hands clasped behind him. He looked like a hanged man himself.

"No," he answered simply.

I wasn't surprised. But the others started to whisper. Frisco spoke for them all.

"Before trial you go send her away," he said. "You come send her away tonight!"

Garvey shook his head:

"I was wrong. I had no right to do what I did. That poor woman made me see it."

"Then why you come?" Frisco asked savagely.

Garvey glanced around at the others.

"To talk you out of it," he said.

Frisco swore and thumped the butt of his rifle on the hearth.

"Is too *late* for talk!"

He must have been hoping the rest would shout the Mayor down. But Garvey was a mean talker. When he spoke, people listened — even if they didn't agree.

"What you're planning," Garvey began, "may look like an act of mercy. But it's the worst thing you could do for the town of Paco. — When I first came to this place, there wasn't such a thing as a court of law within three hundred miles. When the court finally came to us, I thanked God we had the chance to become something more than a bunch of men who lived and died by their guns.

"Even so, some cases never made it to our court: cattle-thieving cases, mainly. Some of us still took life and law in two rope-ready hands. The thought of it makes me tremble — not just for the ones who died, but for the living — and for those who'll come when you and I are gone. They're the ones who'll have to bear with what we've done, and what we've failed to do."

Some in the room had helped dispense the "midnight justice" he referred to. One had handled the rope. Garvey's voice came husky: he couldn't hide the hurt his words caused him. Maybe that's why the room was listening.

"The sight of a person buried in mid-air does teach a lesson of sorts," the Mayor went on: "a different lesson, though, to every one who sees it. I know I've stared at the body of a lynching victim till his blood became my tears. — But what'll be the lesson of the thing you plan tonight? You would free a person who was legally sentenced. With one hand you snuff out a life that the law has never condemned; with the other you grant a life the law holds forfeit. Can there be one justice for suspected thieves and another for a known murderer?"

His question took its toll of me. I must have been the only one.

"Them rustlers all was strangers," Jukes piped up. "It don't seem right, hangin' somebody we know."

" 'S not murder to kill some son of a bitch like Lothers," Grale put in.

"No!" and "*Hell*, no!" others agreed.

"We hang cattle thieves to end rustling," Cramer said. "What are we hanging Sadie for? She did us all a favor."

"Such favors are a curse," the Mayor replied. "Nobody asked any one of us what kind of *man* he was going to be, before he was given life. And the law forbids any one of us to take that gift away. Only the whole community, through its court, can do such a thing."

"Well, by God," said Riper, "if we ain't the community, who the hell is?"

"You haven't got the *authority*!" Garvey countered.

"We got it till the marshals come!" Riper said, lifting his gun.

"And we're *saving* her life," said Cramer, "not taking it."

"Save her life and you kill the law," Garvey answered.

"Then we kill the law!"

Frisco said it. The group concurred noisily. Unflinching, the Mayor waited for quiet.

"If you wanted to free this woman," he said, "in order that there might never be another hanging — why, I'd lay down my worthless life to help you. As it is, I just pray God to help us all!"

He left, and white-haired wisdom with him. For a moment the room and the night were perfectly still. Then, as the sound of the Mayor's horse died away outside, Maguire turned back to me.

"Well?" he said.

"Count me out," I told him.

"We already count you in," Frisco said.

"Count again."

I tilted back in my chair. And then I knew what this whole thing was about. As the chair swung on its hind legs, I could tell my gun was gone. No one stood behind me. Cramer must have taken it on his way to let in the mob.

I looked at him now. He pulled back the front of the jacket he wore to supper. The butt of my Colt was hanging over the top of his pants.

"For your sake as well as hers," he said, staring at me blankly. "When she leaves town, you'll know we did what's best for you both."

I dropped my chair onto all fours and glanced down at the tabletop. My plate was still there — cold remains of a meal I never wanted. All this really had happened.

I could fight, but they were more than too many for me. That bunch had come to get me: they would have me when they left.

"You gonna come quiet?" Maguire asked.

"Better to bite the bullet than the dust," I shrugged.

"Smart!" Frisco grinned. "I never figure you got so much sense!"

"I'll have to fetch my horse," I muttered, giving Frisco the eye.

"Somebody fetch horse *for* you," he said.

Charlie Currus looked across the table at me. I nodded.

"Carl go, too," Frisco said with a glance at Riper. "Make sure he just bring horse — no guns."

He turned back to me with another grin:

"We got plenty guns already!"

Charlie and Riper left together. I looked hard at the faces 'round me. They grinned back like a cage of apes.

"Where do you think Marshal Gage will be, when this bunch hits the jail?" I asked Maguire.

He scratched himself below the belt.

"Home, cuttin' his wife's toenails," he said.

The others thought it was funny. I said no more till Charlie brought my mare. On word from Frisco, Charlie led her around to the front of the house. All of us inside moved out through the parlor. Maguire and his men surrounded me.

The cool night air came like balm to my hot insides. My wet shirt clung, and the breaths I sucked down made me dizzy at first. But under the moon I felt a lot bigger than I had in Cramer's kitchen.

Charlie Currus stood behind me as I prepared to mount.

"Me and three of our crew," he whispered, "are with you, if you cut."

"No use," I said. "but thanks."

"Mount up, McCallum!"

Riper gave the order. He was up already, pointing his rifle at me.

As we got under way, I marvelled at how this whole night's work had been thought out. Seven riders hemmed me in — three out front, two behind, and one on either side. I guess I should have felt flattered.

The ride to town seemed longer than the "preacher's hour" it always took. The other men and the rocky scrub we passed seemed all unreal. Horses hooves drummed my brain like waves from a sea of dust. I was glad when Paco came: it meant the end of *my* trip, if it meant the start of another's.

A small crowd was biding its quiet time at the jail. Between them they must have had more guns than the whole Mexican army. The Marshal had been coaxed off to some saloon. Gabby Macrae remained in charge of Sadie.

We dismounted and tied our horses out front. Pop Maguire told one of his men to keep an eye on the street. The rest of us moved inside.

Frisco went first. I was directed to follow. Riper, Grale, and Maguire came right behind me. Gabby sat in the corner farthest from the gunrack. He was playing checkers with the kid who cleaned cuspidors at the Silver Pick. One of Maguire's men lounged against the wall, watching. He was armed, but Gabby wore no gun. Sadie was on her cot, sewing by the light of a kerosene lamp. She dropped her work and stood up as soon as she saw the mob. Gabby just stayed put and stared.

"We come for your prisoner," Frisco told him. "You will not make trouble?"

By now most of the mob had gotten inside.

"Don't seem like trouble's worth makin'," Gabby said.

Frisco turned to Sadie. I'd avoided meeting her eyes, but I watched them now as she looked at the others. Her face seemed thinner and drawn tight; otherwise she was all herself.

"Good evening!" Frisco removed his hat and made a cramped little bow. "We come set you free."

"Free?" she murmured. Her eyes opened wide, but I think she hardly saw him.

"We come take you away," Frisco said, trying to sound official.

"Why? What's the matter?" she asked.

Frisco stared:

"You stay here, they hang you!"

"I know."

She stood straight with her hands clasped in front of her. No one moved.

"All of you came to take me away?" she asked.

Her eyes lit on mine. Muttered "yeses" rose around me. I said nothing — just looked back as calmly as I could.

"All those guns!" she said, when the place got quiet.

"We mean no harm to you," Frisco told her. "Guns are for any who try to stop us."

"Including me?" she asked with a tired smile.

"No harm to you," he repeated. "We start you out tonight. Marshals come tomorrow. Too late after that."

Sadie stood straight as a flag in the wind. Slowly she raised her chin and looked at Frisco down the length of her nose.

"You torture me by coming!" she said. "What you're doing is not right —"

Frisco cut her off:

"We not here to talk right and wrong! We here to take you away!"

Her eyes fell full on me:

"And are you here, Sam, to take me away?"

"He's with the rest of us," put in Maguire. "We've all come to get you out."

"I want to hear it from him," she said.

I felt what I knew was a gun muzzle grinding into my spine. I don't know now who held it. I stiffened, though I knew I wouldn't get hurt unless I started something. As it was, I could hardly move. Maguire and Frisco had me wedged between them.

Sadie must have known there was something wrong. She could see I wasn't wearing my gun: she knew I never went without it.

"I didn't *want* to come," I told her.

"Shut up!" Frisco said in my ear.

"Let him speak!" she cried and grasped the bars in front of her: "I won't go till I've heard him!"

Frisco looked across at Maguire, who nodded slightly. They both relaxed.

"Who the hell ever has a gun in my back better take it out while he has the chance," I said, looking straight ahead.

This time Frisco gave the nod. The gun removed itself. I looked deep into Sadie's eyes.

"It's not so much what you get in this world," I said, "as who it is gives it to you. I've had to take plenty myself — some from men I could respect — some from men I hated. From them I couldn't respect, I never took — except when I had no choice."

I stopped and threw a quick glance to left and right.

"From *this* bunch," I went on, "I'd as soon take death as life. But before God — or whatever else is ordering this whole business — I want to see you *live!*"

She swallowed hard. Perspiration gleamed in the dark hair at her forehead.

"Thanks, Sam," she said, "for being honest!"

The room seethed like a spat-on stove. I heard cries of "Give it to him!" and worse. I just looked hard at Sadie, and she at me with the ghost of a smile in her eyes.

"We waste time!" Frisco shouted, turning to wave at the mob. "We not here to beat up surly cowpunch'. We here to get Sadie out — pronto!"

But Sadie spoke up:

"I won't go!"

She stepped back in her cell, arms rigid at her sides.

"You *must* go!" Frisco said and flung around to face her.

"Why 'must' I? What further right has any one to say what I must do?"

Now Frisco started to sweat.

"Is no question of 'right'!" he said thickly. "I no want to see you hang. Nobody in *town* want to see you hang!"

"Then mine will be in part *your* punishment, too," she said.

Frisco blinked. A line of perspiration dropped to the end of his thin moustache.

"Keys! The keys!" he said, turning on Gabby Macrae. "Unlock!"

Gabby stayed where he was.

"Unlock it yourself," he said.

Somebody grabbed a ring of keys off the peg by the gunrack. The ring jingled from hand to hand till Frisco seized it and flung himself at the lock. Sadie watched with a wild glaze in her eye.

Three or four keys were on the ring. The second one worked the lock. Frisco threw back the heavy door with a clang that jarred us all. The mob hushed as he entered her cell. He was stepping toward her when it came. Sadie moved to meet him and swung with all her strength.

It was a wild, roundhouse swing that any one expecting it could have ducked. But Frisco wasn't expecting it. The blow caught him behind the moustache.

He reeled backward over the cell's one chair. On the way his head struck the open edge of the door. He rolled away from it on his stomach, both hands clutching his face. He lay there dazed, blood trickling between his fingers.

Sadie's eyes went wide with horror. She pressed both hands to her cheeks as Frisco moaned deep in his throat like a wounded bull.

Maguire got to him first. Joe Grale came around me and stooped at his other side. With an effort they got him up. His head hung forward, blood and wet hair dripping over his face.

"God damn!" he said, breathing hard. "God *damn!*"

Grale held his arm above the elbow. Frisco pushed him off and took an uncertain step away from the cell.

"What about Sadie?" Maguire asked. He still had Frisco's other arm.

Frisco shook free. His eyes started almost out of their sockets. Before he could speak, Sadie screamed:

"You wouldn't let me live in peace! At least you can let me die!"

She burst into tears and threw herself on her cot.

"Hell!" Frisco said, rubbing his eyes, "let her hang!"

Slowly, feeling the way with his feet, he started for the door. The men made room as he went. Grale and Riper followed. Several others went with the three of them into the street. The door slammed: the only sound inside was a muffled sob from Sadie's cot.

I didn't look at Maguire. I turned to the others, seeking a face I thought I could move. I caught Cass Cramer's eye. I stared back and said:

"Let's go. We've done enough."

I didn't know what would happen. Finally, though, he turned and left. I held my breath as I heard him ride away.

Then, one and two at a time, the others followed without a word. Maguire and his men were the last to go.

Left alone, I glanced at Gabby Macrae. He still sat next to his checkerboard, staring back as if he blamed me for interrupting the game.

Sadie's body heaved a last long sob or two. Her hair spread out across her pillow like rays from a blackened sun.

I took what I guess was the coward's way. I left like the rest without a word.

11
Marshal and Strangler

I GOT MY COLT from Cramer as soon as I made it back to the ranch. He was in his usual parlor chair, reading a paper — or pretending to. The gun lay on the table by him. I just walked over and scooped it up. Neither one of us spoke. I guess he knew *my* feelings; I didn't give a damn for his.

I found my belt still on the kitchen chair. I shoved the gun home and strapped up again like day was just beginning. I had it on when I flung out, boots and all, across my bunk. I lay there, stared into the dark, and cursed the day, the night, myself. Sleep came down at last — hauled me back from the end of my tether.

I'll go to the grave remembering that night's rest. Sufficient unto itself it was, like the evil of the coming day. For that day brought the U. S. marshals to us — a hateful one to live again, even in the telling.

I woke up just past daybreak, shaved, had coffee, and headed for town. I figured Cramer owed me a damned day off.

Gage let me talk to her, gun and all — though after what happened the night before, he stayed on the stoop out front while I was there.

Sadie wore a loose-fitting, long, blue dress that morning — the one I'd seen her working on before. It had a high, white collar that made her face look a bit less pale. I asked how she felt. She said "fine," but she wasn't the kind to complain.

"I'm sorry about last night," I said: "sorry in many more ways than one."

"It was awful, wasn't it?" she admitted.

"Worse!"

She watched me in silence a moment. Then without taking her eyes away, she slowly shook her head.

"You know what I most regret?" she asked through a faint, white smile that made me think of daisies. I shook *my* head.

"I don't believe you understand — what all this means to me. I would have wanted you to. You of all people."

I ground my teeth together:

"I understand."

"No. No, you don't!" she said gently. "But then, why should you?"

I swallowed — tried to look confident.

"Well, maybe I will some day," I told her.

"Yes, maybe you will!"

I wondered what I could say that wouldn't hurt her. Everything that had been in my mind left like a ghost at dawn.

"Well, what good to talk about it?" she shrugged, and tossed her rich, dark hair back out of the way.

"What good?" I nodded.

"So many other things to talk about!"

I nodded again. But I couldn't talk about them.

"If Blink turns up, I hope you'll find him a home," she said.

"I'll take care of him," I answered hoarsely.

She looked up at me with a smile I couldn't return.

"Will you do something else for me, Sam?" she asked.

"Anything!" I managed to say.

Some of her old laughter curled like a flame around her eyes.

"Go have yourself a drink somewhere," she said.

I couldn't help smiling.

"Good!" she nodded. "I knew you could still laugh!"

I almost told her I could still cry.

"I'll be back!" I promised as I left.

The federal men arrived while I was at the Silver Pick. I wasn't able to see much else, but I sure as hell saw them. Somebody ran in to say they were coming, and every one who could move went to the big front window to watch. In addition to sidearms, each of the three had a rifle and a double-barrelled shotgun slung to his saddle. I heard them called some ugly names behind that window. I couldn't think of one ugly enough. I just let them pass.

Afternoon wore into evening. I was holding onto the bar with both hands when Doc Hobbs sauntered in.

"They told me you were here," he said, as he put down an elbow next to me.

I offered him the bottle. He shook his head.

"You better get hold of yourself," he said. "You can't drink like you used to."

It took a while to sink in.

"How the *hell* do you know how I used to?"

"*You* told me!" he grinned.

I grinned back:

"Have a drink!"

"Well — a short one," he nodded.

Long — short — I didn't know the difference. I spilled half of it, pouring him one; but most got into his glass. It didn't get inside *him*, though. I had to finish it off myself.

I don't remember what we said, or whether we even talked. But he stayed with me all the way. By the time I'd had enough, it was night and black as a bear outside. Hobbs offered me a bed. I laughed at him. I *did* have trouble getting on my horse; but once I was up, I stayed. I even made it to the edge of town before I got sick.

I wasn't much good next day. Hobbs was right: I'd put on years since the last time I'd spent nine hours in a bar. I stayed out cold till noon. I hadn't done such a thing in all my time at the Coupled C. Martha Cramer said it was a hell of a pass when the help got drunk in the middle of the week. Cass had sense enough not to remark.

I couldn't shake loose again till only two more days were left: today, tomorrow — then "hanging day," as everybody was calling it.

When I made it into town that evening, I found the federal men had taken over the jail. They walked around armed to the teeth — looked at us like we were all a bunch of chicken thieves. One of them sat on the stoop with Gage, where I was made to check my Colt. Another sat inside and watched while the third one rested.

The inside man was the surliest of the lot. The only word he spoke was "no." He sat at Gage's desk and kept his pistol cocked beside him all the time I stayed. I'd been able to say damned little to Sadie before. I could say even less now. I'd never liked being under a gun. With the gun a stranger's — *and* a U.S. marshal's — I felt almost at war again.

Sadie looked well, though her color came and went. Once she squeezed her hands together as if she was in some kind of pain.

"These fellows making you comfortable?" I asked.

"They're most considerate," she replied.

I glanced around at the one who was skinning my back with his eyes. His right hand lay a hair and a half from the butt of that cocked gun. I may not have known what to tell Sadie: I knew what I wanted to tell *him*.

Sadie spoke to cool me — probably good she did. We talked for a while of simple things — weather, the town, people we knew. Afterwards, we both got quiet. My heart fell as I wondered how to end our talk. She took the matter off my hands.

"Sam, I think we should say goodbye," she told me all of a sudden.

I passed in a moment from shock to anger to shame. I tried to say, "If you want it so!" But I couldn't speak.

"Tomorrow we might not be so calm," she said. "The day after that, I'm afraid will be too late for anything personal."

I stared back stupidly. She gave a tiny shake of her head and tried to smile.

"I had to ask you once before — remember?" she said gently. I nodded.

"You did what I asked you then," she murmured. "Will you now? — I won't ask again . . . ."

We weren't two feet apart — the cold steel of her cell, the frailest token of all that lay between us.

"Can't go — without telling you — ," I began, half-afraid to utter the words.

Each of her two white hands held one of the bars where death had already started. She reached out to touch my mouth with trembling fingers.

"Don't!" she whispered, her calm belying the warmth I felt against my lips. The hand was gone before I thought to kiss it.

"I know the way you feel," she said. "It would just be harder for both of us — to hear you say the words."

I blinked at the wet that made it hard to see her.

"I know, Sam!" she went on quietly: " – all you've done for me – all you *would* have done! – I'll have that with me to the end. It's more than I deserve. – Go, and don't feel harshly toward yourself."

I nodded, unable to speak. I took a deep breath – unlocked my teeth:

"Goodbye, then – Sadie Magrath!"

She smiled beautifully.

"Goodbye, Sam!"

I watched her cheeks warm to a blush.

"I'll remember you," I told her. "I'll remember you strong and smiling."

"I'd like that!" she said.

Then again, looking deep into me, she repeated:

"Goodbye, Sam!"

"Goodbye," I said.

I turned to the door in a daze. When I cleared the stoop, Gage had to holler after me did I want my gun. I took it without looking at him and climbed back onto my horse. I didn't even feel like drinking. I rode back out to the ranch and went to bed – though not to sleep.

Next morning the hangman came – a fat little man who looked more like a cook than a killer. Nobody had a good word for him. "Strangler" was the one that stuck, though he seemed to know his trade. He saw to building the scaffold himself – swung on the rope to test it. Then he went for a look at "the Condemned," as he referred to Sadie.

I went to the jail myself that evening, against her better judgment. There seemed so much we hadn't said, or maybe even thought. When I hit the front stoop, Gage informed me Parson Preble was with her. I felt I should wait until he left.

While I waited, Gage told me of "the Strangler's" meeting with Sadie. As soon as the hangman entered the jail, she seemed to know who he was and why he'd come. She stood up and greeted him from her cell as if not a thing was wrong.

"I'm five feet ten," she said, without being asked. "When I came here, I weighed a hundred and thirty. They've fed me well, and there hasn't been much to do. I'm afraid I've put on a pound or two, but not more than five."

The hangman (who claimed he'd never been asked to do up a woman before) seemed more shaken by it than Sadie.

"And he *should* have been!" Gage concluded. "She was as calm as if she'd been talking to *you!*"

He tapped my chest with his finger:

"In fact, a damn sight calmer!"

I swore at him and walked away.

The crowd had already started to gather. The federals weren't letting any one enter the jail. They let in the preacher, of course. I counted on Gage to get me admitted, too. But Preble showed no sign of leaving.

I left the jail a couple of times and walked to calm myself. I passed the scaffold, its beam and uprights dark against the black of night. I walked past all the bars, too, where the town was winding up for what would happen at dawn. In spite of the crowd it all seemed like a bad dream I didn't have to have.

One hour, two hours, three dragged by; still the preacher made no move. He was sitting in front of her cell: through the jail's window I could just get a glimpse of his back. Sadie must have been on her cot while she and Preble talked. I couldn't see her. Two of the federal men were watching inside with them. The third sat on the stoop with Gage.

I didn't want to, but I struck up talk again with Gage. The federal man on the stoop never said a word. He just fingered the shotgun he held across his lap. Gage started in on the hangman again. I gritted my teeth and listened.

It seems that after his bit with Sadie he headed over to the Spinning Wheel. It was afternoon, and the place was fairly quiet. It got a lot quieter when "the Strangler" showed. Those at the bar moved away like he was a thing unclean. He'd downed a stiff one and ordered another when Frisco appeared from the back room. Jukes looked to his boss before putting up that second drink.

"Coffee!" Frisco told him.

The hangman faced around at Frisco:

"I ordered whiskey!"

"Coffee," Frisco repeated.

Every soak in the place laid down his glass to watch. Grale and Riper came in and stood behind their boss.

"If I can't get it here, I'll go where I can," the hangman said.

He licked his lips as if to get the last of what he'd paid for. Frisco walked over and stood directly in front of him.

"You drink coffee," he said.

He nodded at Jukes, who took off for the kitchen. Grale posted himself by the door. Riper moved around beside his boss. The hangman started to fidget.

"What's the meaning of this?" he asked, looking from Frisco to Riper and back.

Frisco spoke with a calm he wasn't known for:

"It mean Sadie Magrath die quick and clean."

The hangman licked his lips again:

"You mean — you mean Mrs. Lothers, the Condemned?"

"You know who I mean. She don't die right, you next one through God damn' trap."

By this time Jukes was back with a mug of the blackest. He set it on the bar, where it smoked like a bucket of pitch. Frisco watched the steam curl up.

"Her blood and body," he said with a slow nod: "they better pass quick."

"But I — I don't like coffee!"

Frisco didn't budge:

"You drink."

The hangman's face began to look like a mess of maggots. He wasn't wearing a gun, and nobody pulled one on him.

"It'll make me sick!" he pleaded.

"You drink."

Steadying himself with a hand on the bar, he raised the mug to his lips. He swallowed a little and put the mug down.

" 'S too hot! Too *hot!*" he cried.

"We wait," Frisco nodded.

They waited. According to Gage, not a soul in the Spinning Wheel moved till the hangman drained that mug and left with one hand over his mouth. Where he was passing the night nobody seemed to know.

The federal man sitting with Gage chuckled and spat in the dust beyond the stoop. Gage laughed, too. I couldn't begin to try.

"The preacher," I asked finally, "how long has he been here?"

"Since supper," Gage said. "She sent me for him as soon as she finished eating."

"*She* sent for him?" I asked. As far as I knew, Sadie hadn't spoken to Preble since her wedding.

Gage nodded:

"Told me it was the last thing she'd ever ask."

It baffled me. I'd meant to ask Gage to make the preacher leave so I could see her. But the fact that Sadie had sent for him made me reconsider.

I don't remember saying another thing, or hearing one. I got on my horse in a stupor. She brought me home almost without my knowing it.

12
Last Dance

THAT NIGHT HELD ME numb between the nothing of yesterday and tomorrow. If I slept, it must have been for lack of something worse to dream. The last time I came awake, my hair felt as if the dews of dawn had drenched me.

Dawn! The sky already had started to sicken with day. Would I be in time? I hardly dared to think what for. I threw on clothes and buckled my gunbelt, trembling.

It was almost seven o'clock before I started. Every one else had long gone. And they'd been damned quiet about it — thinking, I guess, to let me miss the hour of eight.

Martha Cramer was the only one at the ranch. Even her boy had gone. She offered breakfast when I went to fetch my horse. I couldn't eat. As I left, she stood and watched from the kitchen door — as alone in her own way as Sadie Magrath.

I pushed my mare. The miles crept by. I may have been hoping I *would* get there too late.

It was almost eight when I arrived. Paco's one street bulged with wagons, buggies, horses, dogs. For fifty feet around the scaffold there wasn't room for a rifle barrel. A tame Indian or so watched from the edge of the crowd. Women and children stood in wagons farther back.

I tied my horse where I found a spot on the rail at the Silver Pick. Then I headed for the scaffold — tried to shoulder through the crowd. Some were eating breakfast — or maybe it was lunch, if they'd travelled half the night. Some laughed and joked together. A few were drunk and smelled like it.

I pushed on in. All the noise, all the swearing at me beat my ears like rain on an iron roof. And it was a God's own glorious day — cloudless, bright — impossible day for breaking a woman's neck.

When I couldn't get closer, I stopped. I could hardly move in the press. My heart tried to tear me in half. I felt dizzy and sick. Thank God I had no breakfast in me to lose.

At a little past eight the jail door opened. The whole street was watching for it. Every one hushed at once. The little procession began. The crowd was so thick they had to come single file. One of the federals led. Then came Sadie, pale with her hair tied back in a tight little bun. I almost choked at the sight. I remembered the walks we'd taken together, her hair billowing out behind like a black flame.

And was it? — it was — Parson Preble, walking behind her! I wondered whether he'd stayed the night. Gage and the other two federals followed. The hangman waited at the foot of the scaffold.

They moved forward, compact and quiet. With an awed murmur the crowd shuffled aside. The scaffold was only a hundred feet from the jail. The little group stopped in front of the steps.

Preble shook her hand and said a few words in her ear. I marvelled at him — having anything left to say. She smiled and thanked him. Then she turned and climbed the steps without even touching the rail. Only the hangman went up with her.

The rope was already fast to the beam. She stopped and stood with her back to the noose. Her eyes, as if they couldn't see, fixed on something above the crowd. I could hardly breathe as I watched the hangman tie her hands and feet with straps.

Something filthy about it — this shameless watching the life wrung out of another! I'd never thought so till that moment.

"Have you anything to say — before sentence is carried out?"

The hangman spoke in a high, nervous voice after he'd done the binding. It sounded like he was talking to the crowd and not to her. My mouth went dry as sand.

Sadie straightened her shoulders. Her whole chest heaved under the dark blue dress I'd seen her make in jail. She lifted her chin. With eyes still fixed on something nobody else could see, she spoke out strong:

"I give back more than the life I took. No one can do more. I die content."

A whisper like a gentle breeze stirred the crowd. I half-expected God to save her — hoped for some late miracle. I even prayed that *we* might die and she go on to live.

The hangman stepped up close. He fumbled for something black beneath his coat. I could look no more. I turned and started shoving now to get back out, away. People cursed me under their breath. My chest came up against arms and elbows.

"The black hood — he's puttin' it on her!" I heard somebody say.

"Didn't know they used them things out here."

"Knows what he's doin', the Strangler."

"He better."

I felt I was drowning in a sea of heads and shoulders. I pushed harder to get free.

And then came a crash like thunder in that bright, sun-filled day. The trap banged down. The crowd groaned. I stopped and stood there stunned. People around me shifted and relaxed.

"Look at 'er spin!"

"Dead soon as it caught."

"Ol' Sadie, doin' her last dance!"

I wanted to hit somebody. But all my strength had gone. It went as my own heart beat the echo of that incredible crash.

The crowd loosened. I pushed on. It felt as if the mud of a hundred winters caked my boots.

Whiskey had helped before. When I came to the Silver Pick, I went in, caught up a bottle, and slouched back to the farthest table.

I sat facing the wall and made myself take down a swallow or two. The raw brown taste of it almost made me retch. Others drifted in and set up the usual fuss. It melted to a misty sound, like a train or a waterfall.

After a while — maybe and hour — I sensed some one behind me. I didn't bother to turn around.

"Sam?" he said in a low voice.

It was Willy, the bartender.

"I don't want any more," I said.

"That ain't it," Willy came back.

"Well, what is?"

"The preacher — he's out front. Sent word he wants to see you."

I looked around at him.

"Preble?" I said. "Must be some mistake."

Willy shook his head:

"Asked for you by name."

I had another pull at my drink. It tasted better now. I got up, wiped my mouth, and left. People stopped their talk of the hanging to eye me as I passed. Parson Preble never got this close to a bar. I guess everybody (including me) was wondering what had brought him.

When I came out, he was there in the street, fanning himself with his hat. He looked like a one-winged chicken. I walked to the edge of the verandah and waited for him to speak.

"Mr. McCallum," he began, "I'd like to tell you something — though this hardly seems the place."

No one else was on the verandah. Except for the odd horse there wasn't a living thing close enough to hear us.

"What's wrong with it?" I asked. I wasn't for going anywhere with any one, especially him.

"If you insist," he said and put his hat back on. "Sadie — Mrs. Lothers — sent for me last night."

"*I* know that," I snapped.

"If you *please!*" he snapped back. He took a deep breath and hunched his wet coat collar off his neck.

"When I came," he said, "she asked me to stay there with her in the jail."

He cleared his throat like he was about to pray.

"I told her I would do whatever I could," he went on, "though she wasn't a religious person — as I'm sure you know."

He eyed me sharp. I didn't blink.

"But she *was* remarkable," he admitted. "From all I'd heard, she *must* have been. — I learned last night for myself. A remarkable, even a humbling person — albeit misguided."

I opened both eyes wide. I wouldn't have thought the person lived who could humble Parson Preble.

"I asked her why she'd called me," he continued. "She said she would tell me this morning, if I stayed the night."

He glanced down almost shyly at his boots. Then he looked up at me straight:

"She did it for your sake, Mr. McCallum. She feared you might try to see her again. She didn't want you to torture yourself. She thought, if you found *me* with her, you wouldn't try to come in."

I felt as though he'd stabbed me. I walked the few steps down to the street.

"And you stayed with her!" I said, when I stood before him. With one punch I could have sent him to hell — or wherever he was going.

"I did," he said, unflinching. "This morning Marshal Gage told me you had come by the jail. Last night neither she nor I ever knew you were there."

His face broke into a tired smile:

"Perhaps the right or wrong of her thought — her request of me — is something you can judge better than I."

My tongue went dead. The Silver Pick loomed loud behind us. Dregs of the hanging crowd milled at the end of the street. We could both hear carpenters, tearing the gallows down. But neither one of us saw anything except the other — and maybe a shadow of her in the unforgiving sunlight.

"Thanks," I managed to say, "for whatever you did for her."

I stuck out my gun hand. He took it in his that lived with Bibles.

"I wish I could have done more," he said, " — for you both."

His grip was strong for a preacher's.

"Now, if you'll excuse me," he finished, "I must go home — and rest."

I watched till he was out of sight. He walked like an old man, I thought — older than his years made him. I moved over to the verandah and slumped down on the steps. I felt old myself.

I must have sat there some little time. People came and went, going about their business. Once in a while I told myself I ought to be about mine . . . .

A man on horseback stopped in front of me. I looked up at Mayor Garvey.

"I was just riding out to the Lothers place," he said, "to take up anything there worth saving. I wondered whether you would show me the way."

I stared at him.

"I know where it is," I said.

I didn't feel much like going. But I thanked God Garvey was making the trip, not Gage or the federal men. I got the feeling that, yes, I wanted to go. Town seemed stale as my own black-bordered mind. And I guess I was hoping to find a remembrance of *her* — something to keep her more alive in the days to come.

"I'll go," I told him.

My horse was standing handy. I got up, stretched the stiffness away, and freed her reins.

We headed out at a walk. We were almost past the last house when I heard a holler behind us. I turned as Doc Hobbs trotted up on his roan. He'd figured where we were going and asked to ride along.

Garvey had no objection. I never wondered why Hobbs wanted to come. Enough was on my mind already and what was left of my heart.

We touched up the horses and started to cover ground. It was level and easy most of the way. Nobody talked. The sound of horse hooves came cleaner than any words. Dust and stunted scrub went by like carpet jerked from under us. We had little over a mile to go when I saw something that made me swear.

"What is it?" I heard Hobbs call.

My mare slowed to a walk and stopped. The others pulled up by me.

"There!" I said, squinting against the glare. I pointed off to where the gray earth soldered itself to a chamois sky.

Three hundred yards away stood a yellow tepee — a jagged blot thrust up like a knife to gut the sky. An old mule grazed near it: no other sign of life was showing. I hadn't seen Momma Skyfoot these twelve months or more. I wasn't seeing her now — though a gray rope of smoke rose up on the far side of her tent.

"That old Indian woman!" Garvey muttered. "Probably came to sell her trash to the hanging crowd. — I thought she'd long since left us."

Would to God she had!

"*You have in your hand . . . ,*" I heard her say.

And I shivered — like Saint Peter, I guess, when he heard the damned cock crow.

"*. . . to wipe white blood away, but you will not.*"

I cursed that wretched woman. I wanted to ride over and clear her out of my sight and soul forever. The presence of the others checked me. Get her on the way back in, I thought — lag behind, have it out with her then. But when I returned, she and her mule had made like time and tide. I never saw her again.

"We better push on," Garvey said.

I spurred my mare and didn't look back.

We held our way as before to the tiny house on the flats. I'd seen it only once — that twilight time when I followed Lothers home. It had seemed lonely and fragile then: it seemed lonelier now. Tufts of sage and powdery dust had blown all over the low front porch. The door swung out like the mouth of a corpse nobody'd bothered to close.

We dismounted and tied our horses. Next thing I knew, a streak of yellow hide was on me, licking my boots and slapping me with his tail.

"Blink!" I laughed in spite of myself, "where the hell you been?"

I guess he wandered off that night when Sadie drove back for the gun. Those who'd fetched her clothes and sewing probably left the door ajar. Once he found a way in, the dog must have decided to stay.

"Looks like he knows you!" Garvey grinned.

"He should!" I said as I patted Blink. "He followed me home from the range one day. I couldn't keep him, so I gave him to Sadie."

I stooped and scratched his ears as the others entered the house. When I followed them, Blink ran ahead and beat me through the door.

There was little to see inside — a few books (which I guess had belonged to Lothers), oil lamps, cooking gear, homemade chairs and a table. The house had only two rooms. The one we were in had served for cooking and living. A small bedroom adjoined it. Garvey lingered over the books. Hobbs walked back to the bedroom with Blink and me behind him.

The dog had made this room his den. He'd torn apart the double bed it held. The straw mattress with its cover sagged halfway onto the floor. As we surveyed the damage, Blink just sat and wagged his tail.

"Seems proud of what he's done," Hobbs said and eyed the dog.

"Must've liked that side of the mattress," I nodded at the part on the floor. "*Her* side, I guess."

I felt my face get red as I said it. Hobbs looked away and walked over to the downhill side of the bed. Blink scurried ahead of him, growling.

"Here's something else he likes," Hobbs said and stopped. "Seems to be a blanket."

Garvey entered behind me. I walked over by Hobbs. What looked like a yellow ball of wool lay under the corner of the mattress resting on the floor.

"He doesn't want me to touch it," Hobbs said.

Blink was crouching next to the mattress now, his back to the yellow ball.

"Maybe you could pick it up," Hobbs turned to me. "I'd like to see it."

I grunted:

"Just a yellow blanket. Sadie must have made it for him."

I walked around to where Blink sat. He stuck up his muzzle at me.

"Blink!" I said. "That your blanket?"

I reached out to stroke his head and stooped by the mattress corner.

"Sadie let you sleep in here by her?" I said and scratched his ears.

With my left hand I reached for the ball of wool. It had been stuffed between the mattress and the bed frame. I had a hard time pulling it free. Blink whimpered and winked that trick eye of his, but he let me have the blanket.

I stood up and unfolded it. The dog had shredded it here and there. Bits of its yellow fluff floated to the floor.

"Too good for a dog!" Hobbs mumbled.

I think I whistled at the softness of it — finest carded wool, knit by hand. One of its corners bore a small embroidered "L."

A tiny bluebird sheltered in the angle of the letter. The whole blanket couldn't have been any more than three feet square.

"Too small for *this* dog, too," Hobbs added under his breath.

I turned on him. Eye to eye we were, his face yellow as what I held. God knows what mine looked like.

"Something fell when you picked it up," he said.

"*What?*" I asked thickly.

He swallowed hard and nodded:

"On the mattress — at your feet."

I glanced down at a yellow blur against the striped gray ticking. I stooped and quickly grabbed it up. Blink brushed my leg as I did. Something soft — the same fine wool: my arm shook as I squeezed it.

I stared at Hobbs till I felt raw soul oozing out of my eyes. Garvey walked over and stood behind us. They watched me in a funny way.

I opened my hand at last. I saw my fingers trembling before I knew what they held. A pair of yellow booties it was, each with a ribbon drawstring. I gazed at them, dumb as the dog at my feet.

"When they cut her down — asked me to look — thought she was quick with another life."

Hobbs whispered, but I heard him.

"You mean we hung a babe unborn!"

Garvey spoke with the horror of the damned in hell.

"Must've hidden it," Hobbs murmured, "even from her husband."

She would have, I thought — until she felt he was ready to know. And my eyes sweat the passion I'd held in check till then. I wiped them on the blanket. Still squeezing it, I blundered past the others to the open air.

Outside, the sun fell like a blow on my head: I knew I'd lost my hat. It didn't matter.

Then I felt something against my leg. It almost threw me. I stopped and glanced down at the mud-colored muzzle nipping my boot. Blink yapped when I looked at him. Then he jumped and tried to bite the little blanket. He was only playing. He stopped when he had my notice.

I shifted blanket and booties into my left hand. With the other I rubbed my eyes until they cleared. When they did, the dog was sitting a few feet off to my left, panting, watching the way to town.

I don't think he even saw me draw. He was looking for something else. When I cocked the gun, his ears perked up; but he never looked away from the road. I aimed carefully. He never knew what hit him.

The shot brought Hobbs and Garvey running.

"What the hell — ?" Hobbs called.

"You seen a snake?" Garvey asked, puffing along behind.

They stopped short when they saw the dog. Blink lay out quiet now. One foreleg had buckled under him. I straightened it with my boot. Except for the blood on the back of his neck, he might have been taking a nap.

"The dog!" Hobbs said. "Why'd you kill the dog?"

Their stares burned me till I wished they would look at each other. I couldn't take my own eyes off the dog.

"He never had *any* one — any home — but her," I said.

They looked at each other then. The Mayor came a step closer — laid a hand on my arm.

"Sometimes the world makes an ugly face," he told me. "Don't *you* make it uglier."

He couldn't have known what was in my mind. I stood there feeling ill, while a scorching sun ate into my neck. I almost wished some one could have shot me then in the back of the head.

I thought of her fingers — sensitive, strong — as flies settled on the animal's wound. It was a heavy thought — like a dream of what could never be.

I buried the dog in the yellow blanket out behind the house. The booties I buried in a rusty ironbound trunk I have that I'm still afraid to open.

The Death of
Granite Hendley

To the memory of my father,

EDWIN PARKER CONQUEST

19 October 1894 – 10 May 1966

"There be three things which are too wonderful for me, yea, four which I know not:

The way of an eagle in the air; the way of a serpent upon a rock; the way of a ship in the midst of the sea; and the way of a man with a maid."

Proverbs 30, 18 and 19

1
Angry Meeting

ONCE IN A WHILE you meet a man who goes through your life like a war through the pages of history. And when he's gone, you feel that something in you has gone — part of your soul, a lot of your hope, a bit of what little charity you might have had. And perhaps because all of that has gone, you feel somehow at peace. You know that life is through with you, that it won't have time or take the trouble to make such demands again.

Granite Hendley was such a man.

Nobody ever knew where he came from. (Though lots of people had an idea of where he was going — or so they said.) And I understand every one in Paco County today has a different notion of how he got the name "Granite." Some think it was because of his hair, which turned a tombstone gray before his time. Some say it was because he had a stone face that scared the bullets away. And some remember what happened between him and the Grayson brothers up in the Granite Hills north of Paco Courthouse.

But nobody really knew why he *deserved* the name, let alone how he got it. Nobody, that is, but Millyanna and me. And we didn't know till he died. Even then I suppose we shouldn't have been surprised, and maybe Millyanna wasn't. But she was a woman — Indian woman at that, and you never know what they're thinking.

I knew "Old Granite" when he wasn't old or granite either. I knew him when he was plain Tom Hendley -- a smoky stalk of a man, gristle and grime under frowzy hair the color of a black boot with Paco dust all over it. In those days his cheeks had a touch of red, too — enough to make a woman envious and a man laugh, if they'd been somebody's cheeks but his. Fact is, he was handsome in his day. But the time came when his own mother couldn't have called him handsome.

I think it must have been his eyes. In all the years we knew each other, they were the one thing about him that never changed. Set deep back under his forehead, they were — two black caves cut in the rock face of a cliff, with a tiny gray fire burning away in each of them. They were that way up to the night he died. And when he went, his eyes didn't shut or roll or stare the way some people's do. They just seemed to go out like a bright flame in the dark.

The first time I ever saw Hendley, he didn't even have a gun. He was so broke that all he owned was a horse and saddle. I remember it well because it was quite a day for me. And it was quite a day for the whole town of Paco. — That's all Paco was in those days: a scrubby little waterhole in the sun-baked, rattle-snaked Southwest, trying to keep its head above the sand. It had a couple of stores, two or three saloons, post office, jail, bank, and the rest. It didn't get to be Paco Courthouse and give its name to a whole county till a long while after.

That first time was a Saturday evening in June of 1873. Ranch hands, farmers, and a few miners from up in the hills had drifted into town to make up for the rest of the week. Bottle and bath were on most of our minds — in that order.

One of the best fellows Paco ever saw for making Saturday night count was a Georgia boy named Barney Gilpin. A farm just south of town used to keep him occupied six days out of seven — that and a wife, a few head of cattle, and a baby daughter. But regular as clockwork he rode into town of a Saturday to get wound up for the next week's work. Or to unwind from the last — nobody was ever sure which. And if he ever missed a Saturday, you could bet he'd be that much worse the one following. I guess he must have missed two or three in a row before *this* one. Anyway, he was in Paco, drunk and shooting before sundown.

Barney liked to shoot when he got oiled. And he was a good shot, too. But not so good that we didn't mind. It usually meant risking a notch in your ear to be around when the hooch was on him. So before long Barney found himself without drinking friends. When it got so nobody would serve him in saloons, he used to get drunk around in Thompson's livery stable where he'd worked before he was able to borrow enough to buy his farm. Then, often as not, he would lurch into one of the saloons and clean house with a little target practice.

Everybody liked Barney, because six days a week he was as decent a man as you'd hope to meet. Our Marshal, Jeff Gage, never seemed to find it in him to lock Barney up. The Marshal wouldn't go near Barney drunk. (Nor would anybody else, I should say, to Marshal Gage's credit.) And "Who'd want to lock Barney up sober?" Gage always asked. So in spite of all Mayor Garvey said to try to make Gage assert himself, Barney kept it up week after week.

Like I said, this particular Saturday was worse than most. Barney got twitching drunk at Thompson's and then managed to make it to the Silver Pick. He had a "standing engagement" there, as he used to say. Jukes, the Silver Pick's bartender, had been the first one in town to refuse him whiskey, and Barney got a kick out of heckling him. He would stagger in and glare at Jukes like a horned owl. But he was usually satisfied to cuss a little, shoot some bottles off the bar, and then pass out to sleep it off. This time, though — either because Jukes hadn't moved fast enough or Barney had moved too fast — he shot Jukes twice and splintered his left shoulder.

This was pretty serious, since Doc Hobbs was out of town delivering a baby and nobody knew when he'd be back. The saloon had emptied in a matter of seconds, and everybody was standing outside at what seemed a safe-not-sorry distance. I'd been at a bar across the street when the shooting began. I came out and joined the crowd when I heard all the noise. By then Barney was thrashing around in the Silver Pick like a madman, singing and cussing and shooting glasses off the tables. Soon the whole town was out in the street. And a few of us started laughing and egging him on — till we found out about Jukes.

Things hushed up pretty quick then. And all you could hear was old man Garvey out in front of the crowd haranguing Marshal Gage against the background of noise from the Silver Pick. Gage was making his same excuses, and Garvey just got madder and madder. All of a sudden the old man turned on the crowd, his white moustache trembling like the mane of a wild stallion.

"Ain't anybody here man enough — " he roared at us. — "Ain't anybody man enough to go in there and stop that drunken fool?"

Nobody in Paco would have harmed a hair of Barney's head, just as Barney wouldn't have hurt us if he'd been sober. So we all hemmed and hawed and looked sheepish while Mayor Garvey fumed. Barney always passed out if you let him alone, and we figured the only thing to do was wait till he did and get on with our own Saturday night. Then, too, we'd all been a little shook up after taking a look at Jukes's shoulder. Nobody would have set foot in the Silver Pick, even for a dozen drinks on the house. That's why we were all surprised when we heard a voice say:

"I'll go if somebody'll give me a gun."

We all shut up like we'd been slapped. The crowd parted and every one turned to see who had spoken up. Sure enough it was nobody from town — nobody we'd ever seen before. It was Tom Hendley. He had on a beat-up black hat and a long gray coat that looked as though he had lived in it all his, and its, natural life. He was standing at the back of the crowd with his hands tucked into the top of his breeches and his face as calm as if he'd just ordered breakfast. He was young — hardly more than a boy, I thought then. But he had a thick, dark moustache that made him seem older. He stood a little shorter than average, and he had a tired look about him that came from the way his moustache drooped down around the corners of his mouth.

"What's that, son? You got no gun of your own?"

Mayor Garvey was on him in a minute, but he stopped and looked skeptical when he saw how young the fellow seemed. Hendley just stood there, not making a move except to shake his head.

"You're a stranger in town, huh?" Garvey asked, looping a thumb in the front of his vest.

Hendley spat some tobacco juice off to one side.

"I reckon."

Garvey blinked.

"Then you don't know Barney Gilpin, I suppose?"

Hendley shook his head.

"Well," Garvey went on slowly, "I — er — I mean — well, it doesn't seem exactly fittin' to ask a stranger to settle something that's pretty much a family matter."

I was surprised (and half the town with me) that, after all, old Garvey had a soft spot for Barney like the rest of us.

"You want somebody to get him, or don't you?"

The stranger spoke with almost a sneer. It didn't set well with the crowd. Old Garvey was still hesitating. But he looked now as though he couldn't decide whether the stranger was trying to make fun of him. Finally somebody piped up:

"Give the kid a chance. Barney'll cut the ears off him!"

We all laughed except the stranger. He shifted his wad of tobacco and spat sideways with a motion like a snake trying to scratch its back on a fence rail.

"It's your town," he muttered. "Have it full of trash if you want. But make up your mind. I'm just goin'."

We were all a little put off by that. And Mayor Garvey seemed to take it as a personal reflection on the way he was running things — or trying to. He looked at the stranger a minute in silence, and then his face split into a laugh.

"All right, young feller," he chuckled. "But don't come cryin' to me if you lose your *moustache* in there."

We all laughed again. Even the stranger gave a wry little smile as he settled his hat down tight on his head and asked who'd give him a gun.

"How about you, Sam?" the Mayor grunted, turning to me. "You got the best gun in town. Will you lend it to the kid here for a few minutes? If he's able to talk when he comes out, I don't want him to have an excuse."

Much laughter from me and the rest.

"You think you can handle it?" I asked him. My Colt was easily the best pistol in Paco, and I was proud of it. I'd won it in a card game off a Navy lieutenant in New Orleans just before I came west, and I never saw but one revolver in my life that was better. But more about that in its place.

"I think I can," the stranger replied.

I watched his face as I drew the gun out of my holster and held it out to him. He weighed it in his hand a moment, tossed it up lightly and caught it again, grasped the handle, spun it on his finger, felt the balance, and then suddenly looked up at me. He stared into my eyes, moving the gun up and down lightly with his wrist. It was hard to tell whether he knew how good the pistol was or whether he was just getting a little nervous.

"She shoot straight?" he asked.

"Just a bit high and to the right. It won't make any difference in there."

I nodded toward the Silver Pick. Somebody in the crowd laughed, but the stranger seemed not to hear.

"I could fix that!" he muttered.

He kept on looking at me, feeling the weight and balance of the gun while every one waited. Finally I nodded again toward the saloon:

"He's over there, in case you forgot."

Barney was cussing and kicking over tables now, noisy as a bull in a burning barn. All the fellows laughed again.

The stranger nodded slowly, never taking his eyes off me.

"I got a good memory," he said. And tucking my pistol into his pants, he turned and started toward the saloon.

Just then Barney cut loose with a rebel yell that made me jump. He followed it with a shot apiece through two of the panes in the Silver Pick's big front window.

The stranger stopped and looked around at us with a little smile:

"I reckon that means he's drawn."

Nobody laughed. He looked up at the two shattered panes, pulled my pistol out of his pants, and started once more for the saloon. He stopped at the verandah steps and hollered out:

"I'm comin' to get you in there!"

"Come ahead on, you black son of a bitch!"

Like I said, Barney was from Georgia. When he got drunk, everybody in earshot was a black son of a bitch.

Hendley "went ahead on." He walked gingerly up the three front steps as if they were too hot for him. Then suddenly he leaped for the big swinging doors like a wild animal smelling a kill. He pushed them open and sprang in to one side all in the same motion.

Barney fired twice, and then I heard my Navy Colt sound off — just once. Somebody fell and a table and glasses went down with him. There wasn't a sound in the street. We waited for what seemed several minutes, almost without breathing. And then the doors of the Silver Pick swung open and out walked the cocky little stranger, my gun tucked into the top of his pants. Neither he nor it had suffered a scratch.

He'd gotten Barney, all right. Gotten him square in the stomach. All of us looked at the body afterwards. I couldn't have placed the shot better myself if I'd had all day and Barney standing still in front of me. Not that Barney's stomach was such a small target. But indoors with a bad light and a strange gun, though a good one — well, we all agreed it was nothing short of miraculous.

Almost everybody ran in to see Barney, but I waited for my gun. The Mayor waited with me, and so did one or two others.

"Son," the Mayor said, as the stranger came up, "if you want it, the post of marshal in this town is yours!"

I took my pistol back, broke it, replaced the empty, and shoved it home at my side. The stranger never took his eyes off the gun.

"I'm just goin'," he answered without looking at the Mayor. He spat and walked over to the rail where his horse was tied.

"Room and board and forty dollars a month!" Garvey said, following him.

"I'm just goin', Mister."

He swung up lightly into the saddle; and with a flick of his hat brim that was almost a sneer, he loped down the street and out of town.

He had hardly disappeared when some one came running out of the saloon to tell us Barney Gilpin was dead. Everybody in town was sorry. At least, they said so — especially the ones Barney owed money to. And that was damned near everybody.

It didn't take long for people to go from feeling sorry to feeling angry — at Mayor Garvey. Most of them blamed him for Barney's death. And the ones that didn't, blamed me for lending my gun to the killer. Telling them the stranger meant to do us a favor was like throwing kerosene on a fire.

Things got hotter and hotter till the crowd shut up for a few minutes to let Nate Purvis speak. Purvis owned the town bank and believed money was the best policy. He allowed that he wasn't one to condone killing but he hadn't liked the looks of the stranger any more than the binges Barney used to pitch. He said he felt damned glad to be rid of them both. And losing the town drunk, according to him, was little enough to pay for getting shed of a gunslick like the stranger. Purvis was a young man, and he'd struck me before as being jealous of Garvey's influence in the town. Sure enough, he didn't miss this chance to let fly at the Mayor.

"And why the hell *you* —," he turned on the old man, " — why *you* went and offered that fellow the job of marshal is beyond me. We're damned lucky he didn't accept. No need for a hoodlum gunner like that around here."

Purvis had been in Paco only a short while. I guess the past deeds of some of his fellow townsmen hadn't come to his attention yet. There were quite a few who winced – or winked – when they heard this. And Mayor Garvey got hopping mad. Since there wasn't much else he *could* do, he took it on himself to stick up for the stranger:

"I don't think he was any hoodlum gunner, Mr. Purvis! But even if he was, he went after Barney with the approval of all of us here. – And Barney might not have behaved like he did if he'd known there was somebody in town who wasn't afraid of him."

Garvey paused and looked around him like a cornered lion.

"The atmosphere in this town don't encourage sober living!" he ground out between his teeth. "If we had a competent marshal, this place would be a lot healthier!"

At which point Jeff Gage spoke up to say that he took that remark as an insult. He accordingly tendered his resignation, along with the tin star he was wearing.

"Accepted!" snapped the Mayor without batting an eye.

There was a little snicker from most of the crowd. Everybody knew that no one wanted Gage's job. It never occurred to any of us, least of all to Gage, that the Mayor wouldn't try to coax him into taking back the badge. It was a standing joke around town that Garvey had been trying to find a new marshal for more than a year. Almost anybody who came to town and wasn't an Indian could count on getting asked.

But the snickering died when Garvey turned his back on Gage and glared out at the crowd. Nobody wanted to miss a word of what he might say. Old Garvey could really talk when the fit was on him. He ran the government assay office in town, and he had a reputation for honesty that went a sight farther than most of the gold he weighed. He was walking up and down on the edge of the crowd now, looking at us like a fire about to break out.

"If I can't get a respectable marshal from amongst you people," he hollered, "I'll be marshal myself before I'll live any longer in a place that's got no notion of common decency!"

He was a white-haired old man, Mayor Garvey. He couldn't have beaten his wife, we used to say behind his back. But he could make even the roughest of us shut up when he spoke. Whether he had once been elected Mayor or people just called him that, I don't know. But ever since I had come to Paco, Garvey had been the Mayor. And nobody ever called an election as long as Garvey was alive.

"Well, how about it?" he went on. "Have I got any volunteers? Or are you *all* willing to live in a sty the rest of your lives?"

I didn't think it was possible, but we got even quieter.

"I'm as sorry as any of you about what happened this evening," he continued. "And I aim to take collection for Barney's widow and child before any of you leave this street. Because — you — we — we're all of us responsible. All of us. Things have gone too far in Paco. The law's been too light-handed, and it's a disgrace that makes a man almost ashamed to be alive. — I wouldn't have stood it as a young man. I wouldn't have lived in such a town. And I don't plan to start now. I'm too old to change and I'm damned *well* too old to move. It's got to be the town that does the changing. — Like I said, I'm sorry about Barney. Ain't anybody here any sorrier. But if something like this has got to be done in the future and nobody else will do it — well, by God, I'll do it myself or else die tryin'. And at this stage, I'm not particular which."

Not a sound from the mob. I guess we all knew there was something to what he said. There were goings-on around town that Jeff Gage wouldn't have touched any sooner than he would Barney Gilpin. Most of us knew something ought to be done.

But nobody seemed willing to take on the job. We all just stood there while Garvey walked back and forth in front of us like a man cursing a dog he was too disgusted to beat. Every step he took, every ugly look he gave us, was the worst kind of insult.

When he'd spoken his piece, Garvey began calling names. And the worst of it was he started with me.

"How about you, Mr. McCallum?" he said, walking over to where I was standing. I must have flinched inside when I heard my name, but I tried not to show it.

"You've lived in Paco a few years now. You haven't got a wife and youngsters yet. But maybe some day you will. There's hope for everybody, they say."

I heard a laugh somewhere behind me, and I spun around, mad enough to swing. Whoever had laughed cut it short when I turned. And old Garvey went on as though he hadn't noticed:

"Maybe you'll want to pass 'em on a decent place to live in — give 'em all the things you never had yourself. — How about it, Mr. McCallum? You've got the gun. Have you the guts?"

I don't rightly know what it was, but something made me speak up:

"Give me the badge and we'll both find out."

Nobody was more surprised to hear it than me. Of all the jobs in this world, being marshal seemed the farthest from anything I'd ever thought of doing. Boots began to shuffle and people started whispering and I felt old Garvey grab my hand and damned near wring it off at the shoulder.

I'm a little foggy about what happened next. Some of the crowd seemed glad I'd accepted, some skulked away and shook their heads, and most didn't know exactly what to do. I reckon I was in that last category myself.

But I knew what to do when Jason Bigelow came up and slapped me on the back. Jason was a thick-set, heavy-handed fellow I never had much liking for anyway. He ran a place just down the street called the Blue Chip, where I used to do my drinking.

He laughed like hell as he pounded me between the shoulders, and said this was the best joke he'd heard all week. I smelled the liquor on him, but that wasn't any excuse to me then. I spun around and hung the best punch I'd thrown in the past three years on what should have been the point of Jason's fat chin. I laid him flat on the ground — came damned near busting my hand doing it — but it sure as hell was worth it.

I felt a lot better then. And after I helped Mayor Garvey take up collection for Barney's family, he and I walked over to the jail and he swore me in.

2

Return Match

ABOUT A WEEK before Barney Gilpin got shot, I had quit a damned good job as foreman at Cass Cramer's ranch. Cass had called on the hands to ride with him one night and "reclaim" a few lost head. The next ranch to Cass's was run by a chippy little Irishman named Pop Maguire — who was handling it for Jason Bigelow, I might add. And Cass, who *had* lost a few head recently, figured Pop Maguire wasn't being too careful about whose beef he branded. The two of them had already called each other every name they knew. Now things had gotten to the shooting stage. I'd been through a cattle war back in Texas, and I wanted no part of that again — especially not for foreman's pay. So I told Cass I hadn't signed on to do somebody else's gunning. And when I quit, four of the boys who saw it my way did the same. — Well, after Garvey's harangue on the street that Saturday night, I found myself stuck with a whole town's gunning, and for not much more than what Cass had paid me! I guess I figured anything was better than wearing out pants and savings in some two-bit saloon.

But gunning wasn't the worst of it. The next morning Mayor Garvey and I — and every one who could muster clean clothes — rode out with the body to inform Mrs. Gilpin. It wasn't the first time some of us had brought Barney home stiff in a buckboard, but that didn't make this trip any easier.

We did our best to comfort Mrs. Gilpin, but she was too upset by it all to make much sense of things. Like most people in town, she held the Mayor and me responsible. I'll never forget the sight of her when the two of us left. She stood in the doorway of her house hollering "Murderer!" at Garvey and me while the little girl clutched at her mother's skirts like a tiny animal looking for a place to hide. I felt sick as we rode away.

Mrs. Gilpin didn't notice, but we'd had to return Barney without his gun. Nobody could find it in the Silver Pick, and we figured the stranger must have walked off with it. Neither Garvey nor I remembered seeing the gun on him, but he could easily have hidden it under his coat. It was too dark to go after him that same evening. And by morning he would have enough of a start to beat the devil. Anyway, it didn't make sense to go to all that trouble over a gun. But it did give people something else to talk about when God knows they had enough already.

It was more than three months before I saw Hendley again. I was sitting in my office trying to do some of the paper work that went with marshalling. That was the most laborious part of it all for me. The big roll-top desk that stood in the corner by the gunrack used to scare me whenever I looked at it, so I did my work at a table across the room where I could look out the door when I got bored.

I was slouched down in my chair behind the table, both hands in my lap, when Hendley walked in. Barney's pistol was the first thing I noticed. He was wearing it in a well-oiled holster on his right hip. The gun was a late model Union Army revolver, and I'd seen it often enough to know it like an old friend — or enemy. I didn't move when he spoke.

"Howdy," he smiled at me.

"Howdy."

"So you're the law around here now?"

"That's what they tell me."

"I hear you been telling a few people yourself." He jerked his head over his shoulder toward the Blue Chip.

"I wouldn't put too much stock in what passes around Bigelow's bar," I said. I'd given Bigelow (and Cass Cramer, too) warnings about keeping the peace — at least, as long as they stayed in town.

He shook his head:

"You're gonna have trouble there, friend."

"So?"

The way he looked when he said it made me a little uneasy. But I didn't feel like talking about it till I found out why he'd come back. He didn't waste any time letting me know.

"So maybe I've come at a bad time. But I'd like to buy that gun off you, if you still have it."

"You mean you came back here just for that?"

I would have thought it laughable if anybody but me had been the owner — and anybody but him had wanted to buy.

"Just for that!" he grinned.

"It's not for sale!" I grinned back.

His face clouded. I guess he was used to having his way.

"I'll pay three months' good wages — *good* wages, I mean. You'd have to work five years around this dust trap to make money like I got."

He pulled a leather bag out of his pocket and chunked it onto the table in front of me. It had the rich, happy clink of real gold. I would have given a lot just to feel it. But I grabbed tight hold of my legs under the table and didn't say a thing.

"You could damn' near buy the best horse in the territory for that," he went on.

"Not for sale!" I got out finally.

Neither of us made a move. He stood there glaring at me and I just looked at that little leather bag. For some minutes he said nothing, and then suddenly he reached into another pocket and pulled out a second bag the same size as the first. He tossed it down beside the other and grunted.

"All right. There's the same amount again. I borrowed it just before I came here. You can have it all for the gun."

My eyeballs must have looked ready to hop on the table beside that gold. I could have gone to Denver or San Francisco and parlayed a stake like that into a *gentleman's* living. But I dug fingers into my knees and told him the gun was not for sale.

For a moment he stared at me dumbfounded, his moustache seeming to droop a little more than usual. Then he scooped up the two bags full and rammed them into his pocket.

"What do you want for your gun, McCallum?"

His jaw clamped to on the sentence like a jail door swinging shut.

"Name your price!" he went on, when I said nothing. "Every man's got one. Name yours and give me a time limit. I'll get the money and bring it to you."

"Every man, maybe. Not every gun," I told him. "This one stays with me till I die. And I don't plan on doing that any time soon."

"Don't be too sure, McCallum. Don't be too sure."

With a little snicker he looked over his shoulder toward the Blue Chip and spun on his heel to leave.

"Just a minute!" I said before he reached the door. He stopped and turned around slowly. "Now that we're straight about my gun, let's talk about yours. You took it off the fellow you shot in the Silver Pick, didn't you?"

"So?" he cocked his head and gave a sour little grin.

"So you can leave it with me right now. It's the rightful property of the man's widow. I'll see she gets it, no questions asked."

"You want me to tell you what *you* can do?"

"Don't waste my time," I said. "Like I told you, I don't plan on dying yet. I've seen you operate, Mister, and I'm not taking any chances. I got you cold from under the table — and you know what this gun'll do."

I was lying like a scared kid. I had hold of my knees, squeezing hard with both hands, and I could feel the sweat from my fingers making my pants legs damp. He took a lunging step towards me.

"Why, you —"

"Hold it!" I said without moving. "You're not facing a drunk this time."

He stopped, and I could see that moustache twitching as he ground his teeth. He walked slowly back to the table and very deliberately started his right hand toward the butt of Barney's gun.

"With your left hand," I corrected.

He cracked his mouth as though to say something. Instead, he just took a deep breath. And reaching across with his left hand, he drew the gun from its holster and dropped it awkwardly on the table in front of me.

"Is that all? Or do you want my underwear?"

I brought my left hand above the table and picked up the gun.

"If you feel that way about it, I'll give you back the bullets," I muttered, opening the cylinder.

"There ain't any!" he snapped. "If there had been, I would have used 'em!"

He was right about there being no bullets. The chambers were clean as glass. I glanced up at him quickly. He looked so mad I knew he must be putting it on. A real gunner never lets himself get that way, especially when he's close to doing business.

"Well, now, who's kidding who?" I said and reached up with my right hand to scratch the back of my head.

He jumped like a rabbit and his eyes got as big as mine must have been when he threw that gold in front of me. He grabbed the edge of the table with both hands and jerked it off my lap till he saw my pistol still in its holster. He eyed first me and then my gun as though he would have liked to chew us both up. Then all of a sudden he burst out laughing — a long, hard laugh. I felt so relieved to hear it that I had to join in myself.

He told me later he'd intended to return Barney's gun when he first came in. That was why he'd removed the bullets and cleaned it. But after I'd made him mad by not selling mine, he'd determined not to give back Barney's.

We were still laughing when Jim Potts, the stableboy at Thompson's, came running in the door. I boarded my horse at Thompson's now, and the boy, who I saw almost every day, had taken a liking to me for some reason. He always came to tell me whatever he overheard. He was a cheeky kid, ragged and barefoot and not very bright. But I'd taken a liking to him, too. My only complaint was that he talked too much. But now he took one look at Hendley and shut up as if he'd been kicked.

"This is a friend, Jim," I told him quietly. "Maybe he'll be as interested as I in whatever you have to say."

Jim had been outside the Silver Pick that night when Barney Gilpin was shot. And now he just bulged his eyes at Hendley like a stuck frog.

"You *did* come here to tell me something?" I prodded, as the boy continued to gape.

Jim swallowed without taking his eyes off Hendley.

"They comin' to get you to arrest Mr. Bigelow!" the boy managed, finally.

"Who's 'they,' Jim?" I asked.

"Everybody!"

I smiled at Hendley, who was returning the boy's stare with an expressionless look. I figured I wouldn't get much more out of Jim under the circumstances, so I said:

"Well, don't you think you'd better get back to your horses and let me get set for that mob?"

"Yessir!" Jim said, still eyeing Hendley. "Yessir!"

And as if glad of an excuse to leave, he bolted out of the office.

When he'd gone, Hendley and I looked at each other and laughed again. Then he stuck out his hand to me.

"My name's Hendley, Mr. McCallum," he said. "Tom Hendley. They told me yours over at Bigelow's."

"Glad to know you," I said. "Call me Sam."

And we shook.

I felt a shiver go through me as I touched his hand. It was like squeezing a piece of raw beef — muscle without a bone in it, and delicate as a woman's hand. He told me later he never did anything with his gun hand that he could have done with his left and that he always wore gloves for heavy work.

"Glad to know you," I said again, trying to cover up the funny feeling his hand had given me.

"Well, I'll be goin'," he said, tugging at his hat brim. "If anything happens — if you change your mind about that gun — will you get word to me?"

He mentioned a hotel in Denver and said they'd know how to get hold of him there. It made me feel damned strange — like I was about to die and making a will — but I told him I would. Then he said a good-natured farewell and started for the door. He turned before he got there.

"I was just thinkin'," he muttered, feeling his moustache and not looking directly at me. "Bigelow the tall, fat one over there — in a blue suit?"

"That's right."

Hendley looked down at the floor and shook his head.

"You got trouble, McCallum."

"Why? Bigelow's not that good at taking care of himself."

"That's just it. He's the kind who gets somebody else to haul his dirt for him. And Ben Craigle was over there this morning . . . ."

The name meant nothing to me. I told him I didn't understand. Hendley just laughed.

"I *could* sit back and let 'em cut you up!" He licked at one corner of his moustache. "But then somebody else might get that gun. — Besides, you deserve a little better than to go down in front of a bunch like that. Not much, but a *little* better . . . !"

He laughed again. I cleared my throat and was about to say something I would have regretted, when suddenly he asked me,

"Would you have a spot on your staff for a spare deputy?"

I couldn't have been more surprised if he'd asked me to dance.

"You serious?" I said.

"Sure as hell!"

And he gave me the same level look I remembered on his face the night he went after Barney Gilpin — like it was all for fun and putting a bullet in a man's gut was not much more than butchering cattle. I remembered a lot in that little moment. I remembered the remarks people had made after he'd gotten Barney — "hoodlum," "gundog," "killer." I knew he couldn't have learned about guns just from riding the range. But, hell, nobody ever asked what *I'd* done before I got to Paco. Maybe that's why I settled for the place . . . .

Just then, out the window and over his shoulder, I caught a glimpse of Mayor Garvey and some angry-looking people coming down the street. After what Jim Potts had said, I figured they were coming for me. And I had the feeling I might need a friend, or at least another gun, on my side.

Hendley hadn't flinched under the long look I gave him. And as I looked, I thought of *my* pillar-to-post existence, before I found myself middle-aged with this sand-sieve town to try to call home.

All of a sudden I couldn't help grinning.

"I believe I do, Tom Hendley. You're on."

This time I stuck out my hand.

"There's just one thing — " he cocked his head at me. "I get to use your gun."

"As long as we're together — and on the same side," I nodded.

He caught my hand in a good, strong shake that felt a little better than the last one.

We'd just finished shaking, when Garvey walked in. Behind him came the group I'd seen, among them Cass Cramer and some of his men. Garvey had a rolled-up paper clenched in one fist, but he almost dropped it when he caught sight of Hendley. In fact, the lot of them stared at Hendley as though they'd thought he was three months dead.

"The gunslick's back!" . . . "Fellow who shot Barney Gilpin!" . . . "Stole his gun, too!" . . . "Widow and baby daughter —"

They began muttering, and Hendley must have heard their remarks. Garvey was so surprised he couldn't say anything, so I coughed to cut off the comments.

"Mr. Garvey," I said, "I'd like you to meet my deputy, Tom Hendley. He — er — he came back to return Barney Gilpin's gun and to take you up on that offer you made him."

For a minute I didn't know what was going to happen. I hoped Garvey would find a way to take it in what looked like his stride — and get the others to follow suit. Everybody in the room shut up. Some turned to look at each other, but the Mayor just kept staring at Hendley. Finally Garvey seemed to come to. He walked across the room to where we two were standing and stretched out his hand.

"Well, Mr. Hendley," he said in a hoarse voice, "I hope this visit will be more pleasant than the last — for *all* concerned."

"I hope so," Hendley nodded as they shook.

With that the gang across the room began all over again. Somebody remarked they didn't need *that* kind of deputy, and others asked who brought him back and what about Barney and a lot of other things I can't remember.

This time Garvey cut them off. By now he'd found his voice, and he asked the others whether they'd forgotten what they came for. They quieted down for a moment and Garvey turned to me:

"There's been trouble, Sam. Bigelow's stuck his neck out damn' near far enough for the rope."

With that the locusts descended. Every man in the crowd had a different version of the details, but as near as I could make out, this is what happened.

Some strangers had been seen the night before trying to drive off cattle from the little draw down at the south end of Cramer's property. A couple of Cass's men were riding home late that way and just stumbled on them. Cass's men had hollered at the others (apparently rustlers) and fired a few shots — as Cass had it — "over their heads" to run them off. Instead of running, the rustlers had fired back and shot both men out of the saddle. One died almost immediately, but the other made it back to the ranch house. Cass and his boys didn't waste any time going after the "bad uns." When they caught them up, there'd been a running gunfight for a mile or so till the rustlers split up and got lost in the Granite Hills north of town.

But not before Cass's new foreman had winged one of the rustlers! They got him back to the ranch-house, and somebody identified him as a puncher who had ridden for Pop Maguire and one or two other cattlemen. He was in rough shape when they brought him back, and he died before morning. But Cass got out of him before he went that Maguire had been leading the rustlers under orders from Jason Bigelow. Doc Hobbs certified the death and confession. Cass had been pretty cagey about the questioning. He'd kept the puncher alive with hot blankets and whiskey and hadn't started asking questions till the Doc got there.

The upshot of it was a general holler for Bigelow's hide, Cramer leading the chorus. Mayor Garvey, on his own authority had drawn up a warrant for the arrest of Bigelow *and* Maguire. He was carrying it rolled up in his fist, and every once in a while he would wave it around like a stick of dynamite. Maguire was out at Bigelow's ranch (if he was still around). But the group with Garvey wanted me to arrest Bigelow, who was holding court at the Blue Chip as if nothing had happened.

I'd never seen a warrant before. I studied it out with some interest. All the time I couldn't help thinking there was nobody I would rather bring in than Jason Bigelow.

"I'll go get him," I told them, when I'd finished.

I was just starting for the door when Charlie Currus, who had come in with the others, stopped me. He and I had worked together for Cramer, and Charlie quit when I did.

"Bigelow allowed he wasn't goin' to be taken," he told me.

Charlie's straight blond hair, coupled with a fresh, new-scrubbed look, made him seem a mere boy. But he had the solid soul of a man and I knew I could trust him.

"Thanks, Charlie," I said, giving him a hand on the shoulder as I went by.

"He means it," Charlie said, as though he thought I hadn't taken him seriously.

"I'll watch him," I said, trying to look grim.

Tom hadn't said a word during my confab with Garvey and the others. In fact, I'd almost forgotten him. When he spoke up now, I suddenly felt glad to hear his voice.

"Lend me a gun, Sam?" he grinned.

I grinned back and passed him my Navy revolver. He turned it over in his hands and nodded slowly without looking up.

"Hasn't changed much, has she?" he muttered more to himself than to anybody else.

"If you want a full belt, take one off the wall," I told him. I always kept several spare belts hanging over the roll-top desk.

He broke open my gun and saw that it carried a full six.

"This'll do," he said, still eyeing the gun.

"Well, let's go!"

I picked up the spare pistol I used to keep in my top desk drawer and started out the door.

3
Dead Reckoning

THE CROWD that had come with Garvey parted for us without a word. And for the first time I began to wonder what I'd gotten myself in for. Those dusty faces might be parting for somebody else tomorrow! The door of my office slammed like thunder and jarred me back to today. Everything I heard sounded louder than it ever had before. My boots beat down like drumsticks on the boards we had for sidewalk. I stepped off the boards after a bit and Tom came right beside me.

As we walked, I realized why all the little noises sounded so loud. Word of what was afoot had made the rounds, and the place was quiet as a ghost city. People were leading horses away, clearing the street as the two of us moved down it.

The day wasn't that hot, but I felt the sweat coming out on my back. I glanced at Hendley out the corner of my eye. He didn't say a word, but he looked like he might have been walking to school. I felt damned thankful he was there. — And I wondered for a moment who would have come with me if *he* hadn't.

It was only a short step from my office to the Blue Chip, and it seemed shorter than ever that day. Past the barber shop, Dalt's store, post office, Purvis's bank, then across the street and we were damned near there. I stopped in front of the saloon and looked at Hendley. I don't know what I was about to say or do, but he saved me the trouble. He grinned and pulled a piece of tobacco out of his pocket. After biting some off, he held out the plug to me. (He told me later he liked to feel something between his teeth when things got tight.)

I shook my head. I couldn't return the grin, and it put me off a little to see him looking happy just then. I turned away impatiently and started up the verandah steps without a word. He was with me all the way, and we walked through the swinging doors side by side.

A bar ran the length of the room on the right and a few tables stood along the opposite wall, where some of the usual crowd were drinking and playing cards. Several men were standing around one of the far tables watching what looked like a fair-sized game. Bigelow wasn't around. I nodded to a few people I had bent elbows with in the past and walked over to the bar. Some of the card players noticed Hendley, and I saw heads turn and fingers begin to point.

"Where's Bigelow?" I asked Pim, who called himself the bartender. I had about as much use for Pim as I did for his boss. He stole Bigelow's whiskey and the customer's money — when he could. How he missed getting killed by one or the other I never could understand.

"In the back room," Pim grunted without looking up from polishing the bar.

"Get him."

"What for?" Pim looked up with a surly stare. "He don't like to be bothered."

"Get him."

Tom stepped over to the bar and leaned back on it casually with his elbows. Pim eyed us both suspiciously and then threw his rag down and started for the other end of the bar. I kept my eye on him as he disappeared through the door at the back.

Jason must have been expecting us — or at least me. Almost immediately he shoved himself into the doorway and stood there, trying not to sneer. He looked as slippery as ever; but he wasn't wearing a gun, that I could see. Behind him I caught a glimpse of Pim's little head bobbing up and down, craning to get a look over Jason's fat shoulder.

"Well! If it isn't our new marshal!" Bigelow said, as he moved a few steps into the room. "Haven't seen *you* in so long I thought maybe you'd died. — What's up?"

"Your number, Bigelow. You're under arrest for causing the murder of Tim Blalock."

"Tim Blalock?" He cocked his head and looked at the ceiling. "Don't believe I knew the man."

By this time the place had quieted down. The bar flies declared a truce on their bottles and turned to look at Bigelow and me. Pim moved over to the end of the bar, but all the rest stayed put.

"He used to ride herd at the Coupled C for Cass Cramer," I said. "Got shot last night by a gang trying to drive off some of Cass's cattle. Cass's men got one of *them*. And before he died, he said you'd put him up to it."

"First I've heard of it," Jason shrugged. "Cass is always slingin' mud my way."

"Mud maybe. Murder charge, hardly ever."

"Anyway," Bigelow said, "I've noticed some people believe Cass quicker 'n others. — Take you, for instance. You used to work for him, didn't you?"

"Watch yourself, Bigelow." That kind of remark made me sore as hell. "I've got Doc Hobbs's sworn statement. He witnessed the dead man's confession — Hobbs and four other people out at the Coupled C. You're keepin' me waitin'."

"I'll keep you waitin' a damned sight longer!" Bigelow got out between his teeth. "I was home in bed last night, and I'll be damned if I go to jail over any trumped-up charge like that!"

I took a deep breath.

"I'm the law around here, Bigelow, in case you forgot. You goin' to make me ride you out o' here on the end of my pistol?"

Jason gave an uncomfortable little laugh and arched his neck to peer around me at Hendley.

"How does your friend there stand on all this?" he asked.

"He's my deputy and he stands with me!"

"Shut up and let *him* speak!" Bigelow said. "How about it, Mister?"

"The Marshal's doin' all right," Tom drawled without moving. "I never was much at speakin'."

"I'd learn to be more particular about my company, if I was you," Bigelow went on.

"I already have," Hendley answered. "I'm a lot more particular than I was an hour ago."

A few of the men at the tables glanced at each other and smiled. Bigelow didn't seem to like the joke.

"Think about it, Mister," he said without cracking his face. "Think about it. I can pay you double — triple — what this tinstar marshal offered you."

The men standing around glanced from me to Hendley and back again. The silence ate into me like acid, so I swallowed hard and said,

"Bigelow, you're comin' to jail dead or alive. I'll give you one more chance before I draw on you."

He let out another of his cramped little laughs.

"Drawin' is not my line," he said. "I got a friend, does all my drawin' for me."

And he nodded toward the other side of the room at Ben Turner. Hendley told me later he'd had a brush with "Turner" back in the Texas panhandle. The man's real name was Craigle — Ben Craigle. Apparently he was a professional gun whose services came high. When I heard about this afterwards, I felt damned thankful I hadn't known it that day in Bigelow's bar.

Turner, as we knew him in Paco, didn't live in town — at least not all the time. I'd seen him around pretty often, and I knew he liked people to think he was rough. Lately he'd been hanging around the Blue Chip, drinking, playing cards, and not doing much else as far as I knew. Rumor had it he'd gotten out of more places than one just ahead of a lynch mob. He was tall, stoop-shouldered, and long-armed like a monkey. And he always seemed to be right at the stage where you couldn't tell whether he was raising a beard or just hadn't shaved for a week.

Turner was leaning against the wall opposite Hendley and me. He'd been watching the card game there, and he looked at us and grinned when Jason nodded his way.

Two other men were standing with him, where they'd been watching the same game — or pretending to. On Turner's left was a fellow I never heard called anything but "Tank" — though he claimed to be Turner's brother. Tank had a taste for cheap beer, and a stomach to match. His chief claim to fame around Paco was a foul mouth and a worse temper. God knows why either he or Turner let the other one call him brother. But they stuck together like a pair of snakes.

On Turner's right was a local no-good named Joe Train. He claimed to work for Jason, too; but doing exactly what, nobody ever made out. I'd had to lock him up drunk one night not long before, and I knew he didn't waste any love on me. He eyed me now like a side of beef he wouldn't mind hanging on the nearest meathook.

I looked them all over, trying not to show I was worried. Turner had on two guns and the others wore one apiece. I didn't much care for the idea of looking down four gun barrels at that close range. As I watched the three across from me, I was aware of several persons (including Pim) leaving quietly but losing no time about it. I heard their boots whisper over the floor and the big swinging doors creak behind them.

"Which one's your friend?" Tom asked directly, as he stood up straight. "I wouldn't want to make any mistake."

There were still a number of people in the room, but they kept mighty quiet.

"They're *all* my friends!" Bigelow came back.

"Looks like you got a lot of friends." Tom spoke without looking away from the three across the room.

"Not so many I couldn't use one more!"

By now there was silence in the room like a dead man couldn't have caused. Every eye but mine was fixed on Hendley.

"Well, what do you say, Tom Hendley?" Bigelow asked in his oiliest tone.

Without taking his eyes off Turner, Tom shifted the tobacco in his mouth and spat a thick stream of juice on the floor. (There was a spittoon three feet in front of him, but he didn't even try for it.) It seemed as though you could have heard that tobacco splat from one end of town to the other. And of all the sounds I've heard in my life, few ever made me feel better.

The place broke into a little eruption. Chairs scraped back, people began to mutter and shove, and in about one minute flat the Blue Chip emptied as if Bigelow had dumped a dozen diamond-backs across that mahogany bar. The only ones left besides Tom and me were the three on the far side of the room and Jason standing at the back.

"Think you can handle the one on our left?" Tom asked, under cover of the exodus noise.

"Sure!" I lied.

"Good. I'll take the one in the middle and the fat one."

The swinging doors had stopped swinging, and except for a shout or two in the street you could have heard a chicken sneeze.

"You got a coin, Mr. Bigelow?" Tom asked quietly, without letting his eyes leave Turner for an instant.

"I got lots of coins."

"Just one'll do. Get it out and hold on to it. Make sure you don't reach for a pocket with a gun in it — by mistake."

I was watching Jason out of the corner of my eye, and I saw him reach into the front of his vest and pull out a silver dollar. He was still smiling and trying to look calm, but I noticed he got fouled in his watch chain before he dug up that dollar. I couldn't much blame him. I was nervous myself. They had us four guns to two — odds like I'd never been up against, except fighting Indians, which doesn't really count. I felt the sweat running down my arms, but there wasn't a drop showing on Hendley.

"When I give you the word, Mr. Bigelow," he said, "flip it up in the air. When it hits the floor, your friends can do whatever they're goin' to do to keep us from takin' you in."

Tom paused for a breath.

"All right, Mr. Bigelow — when you're ready," he said.

Jason glanced first at us and then at his gundogs. I guess he thought they were ready as they'd ever be. Turner was giving us his idiot grin while Joe Train and Tank looked grim as hangmen on either side of him.

Suddenly I heard the chunk of Jason's fat finger and the whir of a coin spinning through the air. I never heard it hit. Ben Turner clawed at his guns and as soon as he moved, I reached for mine. Before I pulled clear, I heard that Navy revolver at my elbow. Then came shots from both sides of the room at once. I fired three times myself. Some glasses smashed behind me, and I felt bits of plaster shattered off the wall sting the back of my neck. But it was all over so quick I can hardly remember what happened. The place was full of smoke, I heard somebody fall, and I knew I wasn't hit myself — but that was all I could be sure of.

I *felt* more than *saw* Tom Hendley standing beside me. He was staring straight in front of him with my Colt still smoking in his hand. Aside from drawing it, he hadn't moved a hair.

When the smoke thinned, I could see all three were down on the other side of the room. Ben Turner had pitched forward across the table in front of him, smashing it flat on his way to the floor. Tank lay out full length behind him, and Joe Train hunched sideways against the wall like he was trying to push it down. From somewhere in the room came the sound of Jason's dollar, still rolling. It had happened that quick.

I don't exactly know how, but two of my shots had found their mark in Joe Train. One had nicked his shoulder and the other one caught him just under the throat. (Tom always told me I aimed too high.) But each of the other two bodies had just one bullet apiece in them — and in almost exactly the same place. I looked them over later, and if you'd stood the bodies up one behind the other, you'd have sworn a single shot could have done for the two of them. They were hit almost squarely in the stomach but a little up toward the heart — right where Barney Gilpin got his.

Jason Bigelow hadn't moved. He just gaped at the three bodies like he expected them to get up and do some more shooting.

"You got any more friends, Mr. Bigelow?"

Again, Tom spoke without looking 'round from the three across the room. His voice seemed to come from the other end of town.

Jason didn't say a thing. His jaw hung so far open it didn't seem to belong on his face. After a minute or so he pulled himself together and, straightening his coat, walked out into the street. We walked behind him to the jail and locked him up with no more trouble.

4
Backlash

THE NEWS SPREAD like smallpox. When we got back from locking up Bigelow, every pair of bow-legs in town was out in front of the Blue Chip. They watched like kids who'd just been slapped while we carried out the bodies. I guess they were too dumbfounded to think of helping.

After collecting my gun again from Hendley, I had gotten Gabby Macrae from around at the jail. Together, he and Tom and I carried Bigelow's boys over to McCabe's barber shop. Gus McCabe was a wizened old shaver who had barbered logs before he took to working on people. As a carpenter he could still turn out a respectable coffin, and he seemed to have a corner on the local market. His coffins came high — almost fifteen dollars apiece, depending on the size of the occupant — but I thought getting good ones was the least I could do. None of the three dead men had kinfolk in Paco, so I took the burying money off Bigelow in jail.

When Tom and I got back to my office and sat down to catch breath, the crowd began to break up. I watched them through the window, standing around in little groups, talking low and glancing over at my office every so often. I remember thinking at the time I would have liked to hear what they were saying. I found out all too soon.

In the excitement after the shooting, most people (including me) seemed to have forgotten Pop Maguire. But Cass Cramer didn't. And the next thing I had to do was ride out to Maguire's place with a posse. The word got there ahead of us, though. And when we arrived, Pop Maguire was scarce as last week's pay. I never saw him around town again.

After that, everybody just stood by till Judge Perkins came around on circuit. By then, Bigelow had gotten himself some slick shyster-type down from Denver, and the jury got hung instead of Bigelow.

I was kind of surprised at the face things took. After the trial, opinion shifted Bigelow's way. People felt Maguire, by high-tailing it, admitted undertaking the rustling on his own. And they tended to blame Hendley more than any one else for the shooting. The furor over his killing one drunk was nothing to what came of his shooting two sober men. For days afterward people used to stop me on the street and blister me about making Hendley move on. But Tom had saved my skin that day in the Blue Chip, and I didn't have much patience with people who tore him down.

"Every time that stranger comes to town he kills somebody," Abe Dalt told me one morning. Dalt ran the general store, read almanacs all day, and was superstitious as a Hottentot.

"First time he come here it was *one* man," Dalt whined. "Second time it was twice that many!"

"Well, we better keep him in town," I said. "If he leaves and comes back again, he's liable to kill *four*."

Nate Purvis buttonholed me once and said he could tell Hendley was a no-account gunslick just from looking at him. But Purvis never carried a pistol, or had much to do with people who did; and how he thought he could tell a gunslick from a cowpoke was beyond me.

"As long as there's shooting, innocent people are liable to get hurt," Purvis argued. "I understand those men of Bigelow's were a pretty unsavory lot. But if this sort of thing goes on, you can't tell who might get hit the next time. Why, it might be some one who isn't even wearing a gun!"

"And it might be some one who *is!*" I said before I walked off. "You think I like shooting any more than you do?"

I'm sure I never heard half of what was said. But I heard enough. People thought Tom a killer and Mayor Garvey and me something worse for letting him call himself deputy marshal. Bigelow's money and liquor had evidently made him a few friends around town. But just to remind me that some cats have nine tails, a few people sided with Cass Cramer, who was mad at me for not shooting Bigelow along with the others.

Tom stood up under it pretty well, I thought. Nobody said anything to his face, but he must have known what they were thinking. People went out of their way to avoid him. And most places he went would clam up like a church meeting as soon as he came in. But it didn't seem to bother him. — Maybe he'd been through it all before.

He lived like a real loner, Hendley did. He liked to do things by himself. And it was almost as if he was snubbing Paco instead of vice versa. He started building a little house for himself at the end of town, and I used to give him a hand with it whenever my own work permitted. But though he seemed grateful every time I came, he never asked me to help him. Never asked anybody, so far as I knew. And nobody else ever offered.

Occasionally he and I used to ride out into the hills together to do some practice shooting. He never used any pistol but mine, and he showed me shooting like none I've seen before or since. Sometimes it almost scared me to watch him. He wasn't just a man with a gun when he shot. Every inch of his body became a part of that pistol — *all* gun, nothing human about him. And when he had a bad time — missed a shot or two nobody else would even have tried — he was sullen and moody the rest of the day.

I learned quite a bit from those trips. I was used to thinking I knew how to handle a pistol. But Tom made me feel like a kid learning it all for the first time. I could feel my gunning improve, every session I had with him. And it worried me a little to find out how much I began to like it. As time went by, I could tell that more of me was changing than I thought good.

Of course, he kept after me to sell him the gun. And more than once I felt tempted to let him have the thing and get on out of my life. But I never could. My old .44 had come to mean too much to me. I made up my mind to hang on to it as long as I had any use for life.

I think I was the only one in town Hendley had anything much to do with. As long as he stayed in Paco, neither he nor the town ever made any real attempt to get along. He never went to church or did anything other people did — except drink. But when he drank, he drank hard and alone. He said even less in his cups than out of them, and he had the kind of temper whiskey made worse. Squirrely Gibbs, the bartender who had taken over from Jukes at the Silver Pick, told me about the worst of Tom's bad nights. It was unfortunate for all concerned, but it was something Tom forgot before Paco did.

According to Gibbs, Hendley and Grif Staley had been drinking for an hour or so at opposite ends of the Silver Pick's bar. Grif was tall and heavy-set — strong enough to bend a cold branding iron without much trouble. He liked to sound off, drunk or sober. And he liked to pick fights, whether he won or lost.

He and Tom had been drinking the same brand — as Squirrely said, soaking it up like the Mojave Desert. And toward what he thought was the end of their evening, Gibbs, to keep from opening two bottles at once, had been ferrying the same one up and down the bar between them. They matched each other drink for drink until Grif got tired of asking Gibbs for the bottle.

"Pour that bastard a couple on me," Staley said, in a voice they could have heard across the street. "And leave your Goddamned bottle where I can reach it."

Two or three of the others at the bar smirked to each other. And Gibbs, who had the bottle in his hand at the time, looked over at Tom with a questioning glance. Tom waved his hand casually.

"Let him have it," he smiled. "I don't want to drink with a damned fool who can't hold his liquor."

Staley blinked for a moment while it sank in.

"Maybe you want to fight?" he said finally.

"Maybe."

With that everybody began to move back from the bar and left them facing each other alone from either end. Tom had been leaning on the bar with both elbows, but he stood up now and turned toward Staley. Grif squared himself around in Tom's direction and let his hands drop very slowly to the buckle of his gunbelt.

"You pretty fast with that iron, ain'tcha?" Staley muttered with a dirty smile.

"Pretty fast," Tom said quietly.

By this time Staley had gotten the belt unbuckled. Without taking his eyes off Tom, he threw it down — gun, bullets and all — on top of the bar. It knocked over a bottle and a couple of glasses, but nobody moved a hair.

"I ain't gonna try to outbark no gundog," Staley grinned. "But I'll see can't I learn you some manners barehanded."

Tom didn't budge, but he darted a quick glance around the room at the men who were watching.

"Ain't there anybody here to take care of this damned fool?" he asked.

Gibbs told me there was a little snicker from the crowd, like they were ready to see Staley tear Hendley apart. Grif had plenty of friends in the house, and two or three of them could have gotten him out of there then without much trouble. Nobody raised a finger, though. And Gibbs said the whole thing smelled like a put-up job. So far nobody'd ever seen Hendley do anything but shoot. And if he cut down an unarmed man now with the feeling against him the way it was, that bunch in the Silver Pick would have had him sucking wind at the end of a rope in five minutes.

Gibbs said the sweat came out on Tom's forehead till it shone like a wet melon.

"How 'bout it, Mister Deputy Marshal?" Staley's voice grated. "You gonna take that harpoon off your hip, or am I?"

It was so quiet, Gibbs told me, you wouldn't have thought there could be *two* people in the place, much less the ten or so who were.

Tom reached up slowly to the tin star he was wearing on his vest. Without looking away from Staley, he unpinned it and tossed it onto the bar.

"That's the only thing I'm takin' off for you!" he said.

Grif Staley was feeling his whiskey. He broke into a grin that showed every tooth he had left.

"We'll see!" he laughed.

Tom didn't move an inch as Staley came toward him. Grif moved slowly down the length of the bar, still grinning as he came. He let his left hand slide along the polished surface, his right doubled into the fist most people in Paco would have gone quite a ways to avoid. He got about two feet from Tom and stopped. Then all of a sudden he made that bear-like lunge. He threw his whole body into a swing that seemed to come from the other side of the world. Tom stepped back quickly and caught the blow with his left shoulder. And that punch hurt. Hendley's shoulder was stiff for days, and Doc Hobbs thought the bruise would never go away.

But the blow unbalanced Staley more than it hurt Tom. In the split second while Grif was recovering, Tom drew steel. There was a white flash of shirt sleeve as his arm went up and six inches of pistol barrel came down across Grif Staley's skull. Squirrely said it made a wet sound like a meat cleaver splitting a side of beef.

Staley sank to the floor with a little sigh and boots began to shuffle towards him. Tom didn't even look at him, though. He still had his gun out, and now he turned it on the gang watching.

"Hold it!" he said, as they began to move. The hammer was back now. And Squirrely told me that, when Tom cocked it, a drop of black blood fell off the end of the barrel.

Everybody froze, and one or two instinctively put their hands up. Tom reached across with his left hand and picked up the tin star from where it was lying. He tossed it up lightly and caught it in his open palm as he looked at the hate-filled faces opposite. Then, stepping over Staley, he sidled along the bar, keeping everybody covered as he went. He paused for a moment at the swinging doors, and then he was gone.

Well, it all wouldn't have been so bad except Staley didn't come to for a couple of days. And when he did, it seemed his brain was permanently damaged. Doc Hobbs sewed him up and stayed with him most of the time till he came around. But there wasn't much anybody could do for a man who'd had a blow on the head like that. Some people said it wouldn't have been so bad if Hendley had killed him. I don't know. But there he was: Grif Staley, a man forty-five years old (fortunately unmarried), left an imbecile for the rest of his life and a monument to the hatred people felt for Hendley.

I felt deeply sorry for Tom myself. I've heard that contempt rides the same horse with pity, but I think mine was a feeling of only pity. He was hard to be sorry for, though — and harder to *do* anything for. He kept at such a distance, even from me, that I found myself wondering whether there was anything in him a man *could* feel sorry for.

Once in a while he liked to put distance between himself and the town. He would take off on a hunting or fishing trip and stay away for days. I went with him once or twice. But I had to stick pretty close to town, so the trips we made together were fairly short ones.

When he went off alone, he never let on where he was going. Just packed enough food and ammunition for what looked like two or three weeks' hunting and headed north to the hills. Sometimes he would come back with buffalo skins and dressed feathers and so much Indian stuff that I began to worry how he got it.

We were talking one night about a peace pipe he had showed me, and he launched into one of the few stories I ever heard him tell. He said he'd gotten the pipe off a chief of the Sioux whose favorite hunting ground was a little valley many miles north of Paco. Evidently Tom had been an Indian scout for at least part of the time before he came to Paco. He and this chief had been friends for quite a while. They sometimes met and hunted together still. And shortly after Tom had come to Paco, he told me, the Sioux chieftain had formally adopted him by tribal rite and made Tom his son. I remember thinking at the time it was a good thing Hendley didn't talk any more than he did, feeling against Indians being what it was in Paco.

Since there wasn't much trouble around town after the Bigelow business died down, Tom's trips by himself became more and more frequent. I never realized what they meant to him, though, till he did something that pulled the whole town up short.

He'd been gone for almost three months this time — longer than he had ever stayed away — and I began to wonder whether he was coming back. So did a few other people. At the Silver Pick they were laying nine to five that Paco had seen the last of Hendley. And then one night when I'd come home late after making a last check on the saloons and the bank, I heard a knock at my door. I lived alone and I had no idea who could want to see me at that hour. I put out the lamp and went to the door with my gun drawn and cocked.

"Who is it?" I asked from back of the door.

"It's me — Tom. Open up!"

At the sound of his voice, I did. But I saw the shadowy forms of *two* people standing outside in the dark.

"Where the hell you been all this time?" I grumbled. "And who's that with you?"

The pale gleam of his teeth in the dark told me he was grinning. But I was too surprised to take it so lightly. Tom had never brought a friend to my place before. In fact, I didn't know he had one to bring. But since he'd waited this long, I didn't see why he couldn't have waited till morning.

I walked back to my table and struck a match. When I got the lamp lit, I turned around and almost dropped my teeth. He had a woman with him — an Indian woman! She was tall and proud-looking with a skin the color of sunset.

Tom just stood there. He kept on grinning at me like he'd just played ace on my king.

"What the hell − ?" I asked, without thinking. "Where'd you get the Indian?"

"She's my wife, Sam. Been married three whole weeks now. Just back from a two-hundred-mile, cross-country wedding trip. − Couldn't you tell I had that married look?"

He put his arm around the girl's shoulders with a gentleness I wouldn't have known he had, and smiled down at her.

"What the − ? Are you joking?"

"She's my wife," he repeated, looking at me suddenly. "It's no joke."

"You mean to say − ?"

It damned near floored me. But I recollected myself when I tried to think how I was going to finish the question.

"Well − well, in that case − ," I said lamely. "I mean, congratulations!"

And I put my gun down quickly and walked over to him, holding out my hand.

We shook, and there was an awkward silence. I'd read somewhere you weren't supposed to congratulate a woman under such circumstances, so I just looked over at her and nodded. She was younger than I'd thought at first. She hadn't changed her expression since she came in, and I couldn't figure whether she was afraid or embarrassed or what. She had big, brown eyes, dark as old saddle leather. And she kept staring at me until I began to feel embarrassed myself.

"Well, aren't you going to introduce me to the bride?" I asked finally, turning back to Tom.

"Oh! Sure." He cleared his throat and looked a little sheepish.

"Sam," he said deliberately, "this is − this is Millyanna."

I found out later that her Indian name sounded something like "Millyanna," and Tom had called her that ever since he had first seen her a year or so before. It turned out that her father was the same Sioux chieftain who had adopted Tom. The girl could speak only a little English, and Tom talked to her mostly in her own language.

I held my hand out to her and she grasped it abruptly without taking her eyes off mine.

"This is Sam," Tom told her quietly.

"Sam!" she said in a deep, clear voice. "Sam. You — good — man!"

She didn't change her expression an eyelash, and I must have turned redder than she was.

"I been telling her about you, horse!" Tom grinned and punched me lightly on the shoulder. "Trying to break her in to you, gentle."

"Well, that's more'n you did for me with her!" I managed to grin back. "Who performed the ceremony?"

"Her uncle. Medicine man in her father's tribe."

That almost put me on the floor again.

"*Medicine* man?" I gaped. "You mean it was an Indian wedding?"

"Well, what the hell kind of wedding did you think?" He sounded almost as surprised as I was. "There aren't any Holy Joe types within five hundred miles of where Millyanna was living. — What the hell's wrong with an Indian wedding? A wedding's a wedding, ain't it?"

I blinked but somehow managed to nod:

"Yeah. — Yeah, I guess so."

I tried to make it sound convincing.

"Well, we'll have to celebrate!" I said lightly, to change the subject. "I want to toast the bride. You can join me, Tom. Then we can all three drink to a happy marriage."

I always kept a bottle of the Silver Pick's so-called finest on hand for snake-bite and bad weather. But when I plunked it down on the table next to the lamp, Millyanna let out a little cry.

"What's wrong?" I asked, as I poured three drinks into the cleanest glasses I could find.

She walked slowly over to the table and stared first at the glasses, then at me. Finally, she picked one up and sniffed it.

"Bad! Bad!" she cried and put the glass down as if it was poison.

"No drink, Tom! No drink!" And she turned toward Hendley with a wild, frightened look in her eyes.

They talked Indian back and forth for a minute or so. Then Tom turned to me with a resigned smile.

"She says men in her tribe get in trouble because of this," he explained, nodding toward the whiskey. "She won't touch it herself and doesn't want me to. — Guess you'll have to drink by yourself this time."

In spite of Millyanna's look, I had to laugh. I emptied two of the glasses into the third and tossed it off while Tom just stood there, licking his lips.

"I'll be damned!" I said, wiping my mouth on the back of my hand. "You sure as hell *are* married, Hendley! You sure as hell are!"

5
Late Proposal

WELL, NEXT DAY everybody had a new name for Hendley — though I never heard any one call him "Squaw-man" to his face. Even Jack Diller, who was in jail for sheep stealing, knew about it by noon. How the hell he found out, I never knew. But when Tom came into the office after lunch, Diller walked over to the edge of his cell and leered:

"Well, Mr. Hendley, they tell me you've picked yourself up some Indian stuff."

The cell block was practically in the same room with my office, and Diller was only a couple of feet behind Tom when he said it. He was leaning up against the office end of his cell, with one hand wrapped around a bar, and the other tucked into the top of his pants. Before any of us knew what was happening, Tom drew, slashed around, and bent his gun barrel across Diller's knuckles where they were holding onto the bar. He smashed two of the man's fingers so bad it took Doc Hobbs almost three hours to fix Diller up with casts and splints and what not.

When that story got out, people had it that Tom went into an unarmed prisoner's cell and pistol-whipped the man for saying something bad about Indians.

The short of it was that feeling got pretty high pretty quick against Tom *and* the girl — even higher than it had been against Tom alone. This time the women of Paco got into the act. Men were against the girl because she was Indian, and that was bad enough. But now the mistress of the Paco school and Parson Preble's wife and a few others started referring to Millyanna as a common prostitute. To their way of thinking, she and Tom had never been married and now "the morals of the community were suffering."

I was a bachelor, and all the whispering in the world wouldn't have bothered me. But Mayor Garvey had a wife, and one night he came around to tell me that something had to be done. Neither one of us knew what. Tom wasn't about to leave town now that he'd finished his house. (I think he'd just been waiting till he finished it before he got married.) And under the circumstances I wouldn't have wanted him to leave. Besides, he was a good peace officer and Garvey knew it. He was rough as hell, but people didn't fool around with him.

Garvey and I had quite a hassle. He finally convinced me it might help if Tom and Millyanna got married — *again*, he hastened to add — this time in the Paco church. Together we went to see Parson Preble about it. At first Preble flatly refused to perform the ceremony. But he finally agreed to do it, if Millyanna would become a Christian. This left me with the job of persuading Hendley.

Tom realized something serious was afoot — something worse than any of the ill will he had run into before. He sensed that the women were against him now but exactly why had never occurred to him. Men trying to kill him he could handle. But he didn't know what to do about women with their noses up — women who wouldn't even look him in the eye or speak to him. He was a proud person himself, and that just made it worse. Everything considered, I believe trying to explain this business to Tom was the hardest thing I ever undertook.

I went over to his house a few nights after I'd talked with Preble. I knocked on the door and waited. I didn't hear a thing inside, so I knocked louder. I waited a little longer, and then I opened the door and hollered out who I was. Nobody told me to leave, so I went on in. The house had just been painted, and everything smelled fresh and clean as a new dollar.

I walked into the little parlor where I saw a lamp was burning. And there was Tom in his armchair with Millyanna sitting cross-legged beside him on the floor, her head resting on his knee. He had been drinking, and the tears were still wet on her cheeks. I could see why they didn't want company. But what I had to say wouldn't be any easier tomorrow, so I just stood there facing them. Millyanna looked up at me slowly. When our eyes met, she got up quickly and went into the other room.

Tom stayed where he was. For a minute I wondered whether he could have done anything else. He still had his gun on, and his hair and shirt and the back of his chair were soaked through with perspiration. His eyes looked as glassy as if he was unconscious.

I pulled up a small wicker chair and sat down next to him. As I got closer, I could smell the whiskey through the sweat.

"What the hell you want?" he said, without looking at me.

"I want to talk to you about something personal."

He looked as though he didn't even hear me.

"Sometimes a man gets mighty tired!" he said, almost to himself.

"Tom, – "

"I come here and do the best I can," he went on, as if I wasn't there. "I just don't see what they want. Don't expect 'em to like *me*. But what the hell can they have against her? . . ."

I leaned over and squeezed his leg to try to snap him out
of it.

"Tom, there are some things that some people just can't —
or won't — understand. Maybe it's too hard for 'em."

The glassy look was still there, his eyes seeming to get bigger
every minute.

"Sometimes a man gets mighty tired."

He moved his head slightly as though he wanted to shake
it. I still had my doubts as to whether he knew I was sitting
there beside him. So I tried getting down to cases.

"You're the first person around here who's ever married an
Indian, Tom. People don't know what to make of it."

He swore and shook his head in earnest now.

"Wouldn't do this town any harm if a few *more* of 'em
married Indians. Might learn something. I've known Indians
a damned sight friendlier 'n these people."

He still hadn't moved anything but his head, and I couldn't
make him even look at me.

"I don't doubt that you have. But you won't win these
people over by talking that way."

"So how the hell *should* I talk?"

I sat there stewing to myself for a minute or so, and then I
blurted it out.

"Tom, it might help if you got married."

"Married?"

He cocked his head to one side and glared at me now.

"I *been* married. What the hell you talkin' 'bout? Get
married! What kind of man you think I am?"

"I mean get married *here*. In the church. Have old Preble
do it so's all the town can take note."

He was on his feet in a minute — unsteady but breathing
fast and fighting mad.

"They been *saying* things about my wife! — They been *saying* things, haven't they? — Bastards! Why, she's a chieftain's daughter. Gave up her own people and a hell of a lot to marry me. She'd be a queen anywhere but this place! Those filthy-minded —"

"Tom," I said, getting up and putting my hand on his shoulder, "don't work yourself up. — Hell, I've *fought* Indians in my day, like as not some of Millyanna's own blood. But you're my friend and she's your wife. That's all I need to know. I'm only one man, though. And the rest of this town wouldn't give a damn if she was the best Indian God ever created. She'd still be Indian and different, and they'd hold *that* against her if there wasn't anything else."

He stared at me stupidly while I spoke and then shook my hand off his shoulder.

"Hell!" I said. "You didn't expect it to be easy, did you? You don't *have* to live here, Tom. But if you choose to, dammit, you got to live by the local rules whether you like 'em or not."

He swayed silently on his feet for a moment.

"This is one damned small town!" he muttered. "If I didn't have a house here, I'd give it back to the Bigelows and Ben Craigles and get the hell out."

I shook my head.

"It wouldn't do any good, Tom. You'd have the same trouble anywhere you went out here. Back East it'd be worse."

His eyes flashed at me.

"You call yourself a friend and you come here and tell me this —"

"It's because I'm your friend that I did it."

"I — I got no friend!" he said thickly. "Never had any. Kin and enemies only people I've known ever — ever since I was a kid. — And I got no kin any more."

It hurt me deeper than I thought it could to hear that.

"You're drunk, Tom! — You know that's not so as long as I'm alive."

He stared at me silently for a moment. Then he gave a half smile, punched at my shoulder and missed, and shuffled over to the window. He leaned against the sides of the sill with both arms and stood there, staring out at the dusty black of another night.

I knew he'd done a lot of moving in his time. And I wondered whether he would ever really settle in Paco — or anywhere. I figured the next five minutes might tell. Even now with the whiskey on him he had that crouching-animal look you don't see in men who are used to house-living. I found myself pitying him all over again — the same time I was swearing at him for being so damned independent.

After a minute he wiped his wet forehead against the window glass and turned around quickly.

"All right. I'll play it your way. I'll have a God-damned church wedding!"

I couldn't keep from smiling as he walked back to his chair and flopped down in it.

"Good, Tom!" I assured him. "I think it'll help."

He shrugged and stared down at the floor.

"Hate to drag Millyanna through it," he muttered. "But if it's got to be, I guess the sooner the better. Make it tomorrow at high noon. You lay on the preacher and meet me at the church."

I shifted from one foot to the other, trying to think how to make the rest of it tactful.

"There's just one hitch, Tom. Parson Preble says Millyanna will have to be a Christian before he can perform the ceremony in good conscience."

"*What?*"

He leaped out of his chair like a screaming eagle.

"Well, by Jesus Christ, I draw the line!" he yelled. "Damn Preble for a presumptu'us son of a bitch! When we got married, Millyanna said she wanted to keep the Sioux faith and I told her it was all right by me. I don't mind gettin' pronounced one thing and another by some backwoods baptizer. But I be damned if I make my wife change what she believes. — Before I do, I move out of this hell hole and be a God-damn' Indian myself. Why, I'll take up *her* religion. Got a hell of a sight more charity than anything this town ever believed in. I've never had Indians act toward me like the people here. No! *Hell*, no! I be God damned if I even *ask* her! — You tell Preacher Preble — "

But he never finished. He stopped short and I wondered if he was going to draw on me. I was just standing there like a steer getting butchered when all of a sudden I became aware of Millyanna. I'd almost forgotten she was in the house but, of course, she'd been in the next room and had heard everything. Not that she had to listen very hard, Tom was shouting so.

She had come in behind me, and Tom stopped as soon as he caught sight of her. She moved across the room, quiet as a ghost, till she was standing next to him. She never took her eyes off his but stared at him hard with all the pride and devotion a man ever got from a woman.

"Sam — good man!" she said, struggling to find words in English. "Sam say — we do."

I swallowed hard. At a time like this she used my language out of courtesy to me!

Tom took her by the shoulders very gently and began to talk Indian to her. He didn't shout or rave or anything but just spoke quietly for several minutes. It was such a change from the way he had been talking to me that I couldn't do anything but blink.

Millyanna didn't say a word. But when he'd finished, she took his hand in both of hers and turned toward me.

"Sam say — we do," she murmured.

Tom was dumbfounded. He looked first at me and then at the girl.

"You mean it?" he asked sheepishly.

She nodded.

"Sam say — we do."

Tom looked at me belligerently.

"You satisfied, McCallum?" he growled.

I don't remember ever bowing to any one in my life, but I tried to bow to Mrs. Hendley then. I couldn't think of anything else to do. It was only a slight bow with my head and shoulders, and I felt embarrassed as soon as I'd done it. I guess I looked like the china-shop bull, trying to apologize for what he'd done.

I must have been turning red all over, even as I started for the door. I didn't feel at ease till I reached the Silver Pick, where my nose could catch up with the rest of me and get red itself from a more familiar cause.

6

Wife and Friend

A COUPLE OF WEEKS later Paco duly noted rectification of Hendley's so-called "witch-doctor" wedding. The change of status implied was no doubt least significant to the parties most intimately concerned. But it gave every one else something to talk about. And in a God-forgotten, sand-filled canteen of a town like Paco that *was* something.

Millyanna in the meantime had been through a baptism — "ordeal by water," Hendley called it — and a dozen lectures on religion by Parson Preble — "ordeal by fire," Hendley called that. Apparently Preble liked to think himself something of a missionary. (No preacher would have stayed in Paco if he hadn't, God knows.) And he harangued away at Millyanna as the walking embodiment of his own excuse for being. The funniest part — though you had to watch where you laughed about it — was that Hendley had to sit through the sermonizing with her! And the inside of Preble's church had never seen Hendley's hide before. (The language business was what got him there. Millyanna knew only the simplest English; and since nobody in the town but Tom could speak Sioux, Tom was really indispensable.)

Hendley asked me to be his best man and, of course, I said I'd be honored. But aside from that he never mentioned the wedding to me after our first talk about it. I could tell the whole thing still burned him, though. And so could Preble as the wedding date got closer. I gathered Hendley didn't waste much grace on the job of interpreting. He never even shed gun during the lectures. I don't know whether Preble ever mentioned it to Hendley; but he mentioned it to Garvey, who mentioned it to me. Preble felt mortified, so he said, to see some one translate the verities of Holy Writ with one thumb hooked in his gunbelt and the fingers of the other hand drumming on his pistol butt. I told Garvey I reckoned Preble would have to stay mortified: I wasn't about to tell Tom to shed. So Hendley went on with it, sounding (I guess) like some unwilling martyr who'd be damned if he was going to die forgiving the executioner.

The morning of the wedding dawned clear as a bottle of corn. Hendley showed up shaved, shiny, and on time to the minute of the ten o'clock marrying hour. As best man I was there ahead of time. So was Mayor Garvey, who had agreed to give the bride away. None of Paco's womenfolk deigned to observe the occasion. Of course, Preble was there; and I almost pitied the man. He was shifting about from foot to foot and wiping the sweat off his bald brow as if *he'd* been the one getting married. A few of the town's more curious (and, as far as I was concerned, least welcome) gathered out front in the street. Not one of them ventured inside.

Garvey and Preble and I were waiting up at the far end of the little church in front of the covered altar. At the sound of the latch being lifted, we turned toward the door as one man. I guess Tom must have had trouble with the lock. As it clicked a couple of times before it got unstuck, we could hear him swearing on the other side. Then suddenly the heavy panels winked sunlight as he flung the door back out of the way. It rattled against the wall like a bucket of nails. And there was Hendley, gun and all, with one hand around Millyanna's waist, glaring as if he'd come to fight a dragon. Millyanna clung inside his arm, delicate as a flower at the foot of an oak.

Garvey didn't bat an eye, but Preble turned white as his shirt front. I heard him begin to dither something about "Great merciful Father — !"

"Contain yourself, man!" Garvey snapped under his breath.

Preble contained himself with an effort, and the couple moved deliberately up the narrow aisle. Preble seemed to be realizing it's hot work to brand a heifer while the bull looks on. I almost laughed, but Garvey must have heard it coming. He gave me a look I remember now and sent that laugh back where it came from.

Millyanna struck me as the calmest person in the church that day. She spoke up strong and happy when her time came. Once when Preble in his nervousness omitted a couple of words from the vow he was having her repeat, she supplied the missing words from memory and said the thing as it was supposed to be. Preble blushed back almost to his normal color. When he finally got through, we three followed the newlyweds out to see them off.

Just about the time I thought the worst was over, it happened. We were standing on the church steps, and Tom had taken out some silver dollars to pay Parson Preble the marrying money. I had offered to take care of this for him, but he insisted on doing it himself. He counted out the fee like he was paying for a new coat. And then he announced that the joke was on Preble: nobody had thought to ask whether he, Thomason Hendley, was a holder of the Christian faith!

Preble gave something between a snort and a gasp, but he didn't have time to say a word. Hendley cocked his chin up like he was trying to see the ends of his own moustache and went on:

"I never been baptized, catechized, circumcised nor nothin' — not in any church *anywhere*. And I don't intend to be!"

Whether Tom knew what all those words meant I don't know. But they had their effect on Parson Preble. If his mouth had dropped open any farther, he would never have gotten it closed again.

"What's more," Tom ground out, the ends of that black moustache just twitching, "I don't intend to ever darken the door of *this* place again."

And he jerked his head at the church like he was shaking something off his back. Millyanna couldn't have known what he was saying. But she sensed that something was wrong. She moved closer to her husband and stood there looking at him tensely, as if asking what he wanted her to do. But Hendley never took his eyes off Preble.

"And if you survive me, Mr. Best Man," he continued, turning finally to me, "Just spare my remains the insult of a church funeral! If heaven has in it the likes of what I've seen around here, I'd just as soon be somewhere else."

With that he pulled his black hat tight on his forehead. And taking Millyanna by the arm, he got her into the rig he had borrowed and the two of them drove off down the street toward his house.

The few people who were standing around drew back out of Hendley's way without a word. They'd heard everything, and they turned to each other with nods and whispers as the rig passed out of sight. I remember as I watched it hearing Preble murmur behind me,

"Lord Jesus and God have mercy! Lord Jesus and God and the angels —!"

I took a long breath and looked hard at old Garvey. And he and his mane of white hair looked hard at me.

Well, Tom was as good as his word — or as bad! He never set foot in church again — Preble's or any other, as far as I know. But oddly enough, Millyanna did. In the course of Preble's lectures, punctuated as they were by her husband's homely translations, she must have been truly converted. Winter and summer, rain or shine, she never missed a Sunday after the wedding. It was the closest thing to a miracle Paco had ever seen. It touched us all — all except Hendley. It was so much salt in the wound to him. It made him more bitter, if anything could — made him curl up tighter inside, like a human armadillo.

I thought things might get better after the baby came. For not many days went by before everyone knew Millyanna was pregnant. And the son (for a son it was) arrived just seven months after the church wedding. Tongues wagged as tongues will. But gossip about timing got swallowed up in something else.

Apparently there were complications about the birth. According to Doc Hobbs, Millyanna was lucky to come through it alive. The boy was born in good shape, though — healthy as a wild colt. But there could be no question of other children. The night of the birth, in a mad rage over almost losing Millyanna, Tom cursed Doc Hobbs for a clumsy fool — said he would have liked to shoot him on the spot. Hobbs was pretty cool toward Hendley anyway. I guess he had seen too many men with Hendley's mark on them. But the rift that came between him and Hendley now was one I knew could never be healed. And because Doc Hobbs was generally liked, Paco had something else to hold against Hendley. The man walked completely alone — walked alone and, as they said at the Silver Pick, talked to nobody, not even himself.

I guess we were all surprised when we found out he hadn't always been that way. One day we got a glimpse of somebody he once walked *with*. It was a few months after the birth of little Tommy. (They named the child for his father.) And when it was all over, I felt damned thankful we'd gotten only a glimpse.

I was sitting in my office doing some desk work that morning. I'd almost finished when Jim Potts came running in. His eyes bulged bigger than two fried eggs and he was breathing like a fast freight.

"You better come quick, Mr. McCallum!" he puffed, when he'd caught his breath a little.

"Why, Jim, what's the matter?"

"They's a stranger — over at the Silver Pick."

"Well? There're lots of strangers 'round here."

"Yessir, but not like this one!"

Instead of calming down, the boy seemed to get more excited.

" — from some place back East," Jim went on. "Says he's a friend of Mr. Hendley's. Wants to see him."

I couldn't help laughing.

"What's so awful about that?" I asked.

Jim shook his head.

"Man like Mr. Hendley — he don't have friends."

I got up and walked around my table to where the boy was standing.

"That's no way to talk about my deputy, Jim. Mr. Hendley saved my life once. And as long as I'm alive, he's got *one* friend anyway — you understand me?"

I stared hard into the boy's eyes. He had on an old pair of boots somebody had given him, and he looked down now at them. For a moment he seemed more ashamed than shook up.

"Awww, you could o' done for all three of 'em that day in Bigelow's, Mr. McCallum. Everybody knows that."

I put my hand on the boy's shoulder and squeezed hard.

"No, young fellow," I shook my head at him. "That's *not* something everybody knows. Mr. Hendley saved *my* life that day and maybe the lives of some other people too. This town ought to feel grateful to him for that, if for nothing else."

Jim winced under my hand and looked down at his boots again.

"Yessir. — But just the same, you better come over to the Silver Pick."

"Well, Jim, lad — " I said, releasing his shoulder, "what's wrong with a man coming to look for an old friend?"

Jim looked up quick and blinked at me.

"This feller looks like he don't have friends either."

I looked back at him hard when he said this. But rather than meet my gaze he hung his head and stared down at his feet. I could see toes squinching up and down inside those boots. Then suddenly he looked up at me as wide-eyed as he'd been when he first came in.

"And he's got two of the biggest guns I ever see in my life! They're hard to get a look at, though — under that long black coat. — They're all shiny like they been polished to death!"

"What's his name, Jim?"

"He didn't let on. Jest said to tell Mr. Hendley 'the Doc' wanted to see him."

"'The Doc'?"

Jim nodded.

Long coat, shiny pistols, Easterner — it all rang a bad bell with me somehow.

I told Jim to go find Hendley and deliver the stranger's message. The boy took off with another ear-to-ear grin while I was buckling on my Navy Colt. I left my office and headed for the Silver Pick in a far from cheerful mood.

As I walked I remembered ugly stories I'd heard in Dodge and the Kansas cow towns. I kept reminding myself Hendley had never mentioned *Doc Holliday* to me — if that's who the stranger really was. But why the hell should he? Why should anybody mention Holliday? Stories were all over the West about him. He wasn't good to *have* in your past — though better there than in your present. And yet this *couldn't* be Holliday. In spite of the trademarks — pistols, black coat, "Doc" for a nickname — it couldn't be Holliday. My luck just wasn't that bad.

I was still telling myself all this as I entered the Silver Pick. But the words quit coming as soon as I cleared the doors. Everything was as usual — almost. Squirrely Gibbs was back of the bar and the inevitable game was going on at the front table. But the stranger seemed to darken the whole dingy room from the spot where he sat in the back, playing cards by himself.

He was facing the door, and he didn't look up when I came in. But I could tell he saw me. You get so you can, after you've worn a badge long enough. He kept on laying out cards in front of him, but he knew I was there.

He was leaning back in his chair, a low-crowned black felt hat shoved up on his forehead — long legs stretched out under the table. A bottle of whiskey and a couple of glasses, one of them half full, stood by the cards. He must not have been sitting down when Jim saw him, because now he had his coat pulled back behind his pistol butts. Anybody who looked could see them. And I knew there was only one "Doc" in the West who carried a pair of nickel-plated beauties like that.

I had never seen Holliday, but I'd heard a lot about him. And the descriptions had been pretty accurate. He was about forty years old, neatly dressed and thin, with black-brown hair. His mouth, proud and ugly, looked as though it had been cut

in his face with a dull knife. And he was paler than I thought
any living man could be. People said he was sick, and maybe
that's why he was pale. But it didn't keep him from making
other men sick — "sick unto death," as the Bible puts it.

I didn't like the idea of tangling with Holliday. (He seemed
to tangle with the law wherever he went.) I didn't even like the
thought of having him around. In fact, there wasn't anything
about him I *did* like, as I stood there watching him.

After a moment, I walked slowly back to his table.

"Mind if I sit down?" I asked.

"Would it matter if I did?" he muttered.

He glanced up quickly from the dirty brown cards on the
table. I saw him look me over from badge to boot, rest his eye
on my gun a moment, and then motion me to an empty chair
with the deck in his hand. He moved his eyes so fast I could
hardly be sure they'd stopped on my gun.

He went ahead with his playing, and I sat down to the
regular click-click of cards being snapped out on the table.

"Have a drink," he said, without looking up from his game.
"I find it's in the best interest of all concerned to keep the
machinery of law and order well oiled."

I passed up the drink and just watched. He kept on laying
out cards, and I noticed his hands were almost as white as his
face.

"That a Navy Colt you got?" he asked, turning up the third
ace in a row.

I nodded.

"If it's a good one, it's a *damned* good one," he said. "Does
a lot for a man."

He went on laying out cards, one on top of the other.

"What do you want with Tom Hendley?" I asked suddenly.

He stopped and looked at me hard.

"Did *he* send you?"

I shook my head.

"I found out you were here before he did. — What do you want with him?"

He smiled and went back to laying out cards.

"Oh, he and I used to be friends."

"So did Judas and Jesus Christ."

He laid down the cards and poured himself a drink. Then he eyed me sharply.

"To tell you the truth, I heard he's wearing a badge and I thought I'd have to see it to believe it."

I leaned an elbow on the table and turned my back toward the others in the room.

"Let me tell you something," I said, quietly. "I know who you are, and I'm going to be here when Hendley comes through that door. I won't call your name because I don't want the whole town to know who they have the dubious pleasure of entertaining."

He grinned as I cast a quick glance over my shoulder. Every eye in the house was on us.

"But it doesn't matter to me who the hell you are," I went on in the same tone. "If you're looking for trouble, some of it'll come from me. Hendley saved my skin once, and I don't plan to sit by and watch him get cut up by a travelling gunslick."

He quit grinning long enough to throw down his drink. Then he grunted and rolled the glass between his fingers.

"Spoke real good, Marshal," he said evenly. "Spoke like a true son of the old frontier — or something worse, if there *is* such. — It's a social call I'm making. If I want somebody the other way, I don't wait around for him to come to me. If you know me like you claim, you ought to know that."

He poured himself another drink.

"Saved your skin, huh?" he said. "Well, you might say he saved *mine* once — saved it from a girl I was kind o' sweet on. Now, they tell me, some Indian has saved his from *her*."

He cleared his throat with a rattling cough and reached for the cards again. He hardly had them in his hand when the swinging doors banged back against the wall and Tom pranced in with a grin I thought would split his face. Holliday jumped up to meet him. If each had been trying to grab the other's gun hand before he could draw, they couldn't have caught hold sooner.

"Doc Holliday," Tom laughed. "You beat-up old bastard —!"

I had meant to warn Tom to name no names, but it was too late now. Squirrely Gibbs, who was drying glasses, dropped the one he had in his hand and stared at us across the bar. Jim Potts had followed Tom to the Silver Pick, and I saw him peep over the swinging doors right after Hendley came in. As soon as he heard Doc Holliday's name, Jim disappeared in a flash of white eyes and teeth. And the poker game at the front of the room broke off short like the cards had cholera. Soon we three and Squirrely (who was still staring) had the saloon to ourselves.

When Tom and Holliday got through back-slapping and calling each other salty names, Tom recollected himself enough to introduce me.

"We've already met," Holliday said, without offering his hand.

I said something about leaving the two of them alone, but Tom insisted that the three of us have a drink together first. Squirrely came to, finally, and set us up passable whiskey in response to Tom's demand for the best in the house. Tom poured us a shot apiece and held up his glass.

"To whiskey or blood, whichever's thicker!" Holliday rapped out before Tom could say a word.

Tom laughed:

"You haven't learned a new toast in all these years!"

We emptied our glasses, and I was about to take my leave when Tom sang out,

"Say! You still got them chrome cannons?"

He grabbed Holliday's coattail and jerked it back to look at the guns. Holliday grinned.

"By God, you do! Look at 'em!" Tom said.

He snatched the one nearest him out of its holster and began playing with it.

"Just be damn' sure you wipe it off when you're through," Holliday said.

Tom didn't even hear him. He was stroking that pistol like it was part of a woman.

"Most beautiful thing I ever saw!" he said in a whisper.

It was the first time I'd heard him use the word "beautiful." It *was* a nice gun, though. A Colt .45, single six, with the most perfect job of nickel-plating I ever came across. It had a barrel longer than most .45's, and the front sight had been filed off clean. Except for the white horn handle plates the whole thing gleamed like a piece of silver.

"Not a gun in the West can touch it!" Tom went on, as if he was talking to himself. Then he looked up at me. "Not even yours, McCallum," he said. "Not even yours."

I shrugged and did my best to smile. He was right, but I was damned if I felt like admitting it. He looked at me with a kind of disdain in his eye, like he didn't need me *or* my gun any more and wanted us both to know it. But he didn't look long at me: that gun was just too much for him. He went on playing with it and spinning it on his finger as if there was nobody else around.

Holliday watched him for a while and then winked at me. Suddenly he reached out and grabbed the pistol.

"Gimme that thing!" he said. "You know what it looks like. God damn, you haven't changed a bit!"

And he rammed the pistol into its holster.

"You still mean to keep 'em?" Tom asked. "I got some money saved up by now."

"I sure as hell do!" Holliday growled. "They're mother and wife to me, man. Only things I could ever count on. — Which makes 'em *better* than a woman, wouldn't you say?"

Tom smiled and punched him lightly on the shoulder.

"We agreed not to mention that, didn't we? Anyhow, since she ran off and left me, too, we can call it square."

Holliday made a face:

"*You* call it square. *I* won't mention it."

"Dammit, how about letting *me* forget it if *you* can't? I've forgotten everything else. — And there was one hell of a lot *to* forget —!"

"Well, have another drink and un-forget," Holliday said. "I came to talk over old times."

He gave me a sidelong glance that said he wanted it to be a two-man talk. I'd finished my drink by then, so I thanked Tom for it and took off. I felt a little funny about the way I'd acted before Hendley got there. I was glad enough to move out.

As I walked back to my office, I noticed people in little knots on the street, whispering and nodding at each other. They stopped and just looked at me when I got near them, but I knew what they were talking about. News travels fast where there *isn't* much. And I wasn't surprised when a little later, Mayor Garvey and a few people who liked to think they were the town's "responsible citizens" came into my office.

Garvey said hello and smiled affably, but the rest of them didn't give him a chance to speak.

"Mr. McCallum," Abe Dalt began, "we're all of us worried about having that outlaw in town —"

"I beg your pardon, but Doc Holliday is not an outlaw," I interrupted. "Nobody wants him for any crime that I know of."

I felt pretty funny defending a man I had so little liking for. But I resented having that gang descend on me. Garvey was welcome any time. But some of the others I disliked almost as much as I did Holliday — though for different reasons.

"Since when isn't killing a crime?" Nate Purvis asked. Purvis's bank had recently been designated a western depository for Wells Fargo funds; and rumor had it Purvis was too tight to install the bigger safe which by all rights he needed. I guess he sweated the departure of every disreputable character in town.

"The only people I ever heard of him killing," I told Purvis, "had guns in their hands and were trying to kill him first. That may not cut any ice with you, but it does with juries in these parts."

"But Doc Holliday is no good — he's wound up in a shooting everywhere he's been," Henry Beeman said. Beeman ran the *Paco Gazette,* and I remembered reading a lurid story once in his paper about some of Holliday's escapades.

"He's a gambler, Mr. Beeman. In his business you don't make many friends."

"Well, we want to make damn' sure he doesn't do business here!" Beeman snapped.

"It's a free country," I said. "How're you going to stop him?"

"It ain't that free."

"That's your problem, Marshal."

"One gunslinger is enough for this town."

All kinds of remarks came out then, everybody talking at once, until all of a sudden Mayor Garvey asked, above the rest of the noise,

"Mr. Purvis, ain't that your child down yonder at the Silver Pick?"

They all stopped muttering and turned to look out the window. It was a few minutes after the noon hour by this time, and the kids had been let out of school for lunch. But instead of going home, most of them had gone to the Silver Pick to sneak a look at Doc Holliday. They had crowded up to the big front window and were shoving at each other to get a peek under the swinging doors. I guess Jim Potts must have had a few friends his own age that he liked to keep informed.

"By God, it is!" Purvis gasped. "He ought to be home at dinner."

"Why, there's all three of your'n, Ezra," somebody else said.

"Surer 'n hell!"

"Pesky children! Haven't they got anything to do?"

"I licked mine this morning, but I'll damn' well thrash him again for this!"

In thirty seconds my office was clear of everybody except Mayor Garvey and one or two others who didn't have children. We just watched as Purvis and company swooped down on the youngsters. When things had quieted a bit outside, Garvey turned to me with a sigh.

"Sam, I'm sorry about this," he said. "Most of us simply feel there's been enough violence around here. And having Doc Holliday in town is just asking for more. I don't know what his connection with Hendley is, but there ain't room in any town I been in for two such men as that. Some of them who were here just now said they wouldn't mind seeing Hendley and Holliday kill each other — but, be that as it may, somebody else might get caught in the storm."

He pulled out a cigar, bit the end off, and shook his head.

"It's no good, Sam," he said. "Doc Holliday's got to leave town. We figured you were the one to tell him. But now that I think about it, I believe it's me."

I reached out and put my hand on the old man's shoulder.

"I'll tell him, Mr. Garvey," I said.

"Thanks, Sam," he smiled. "But I know how you must feel if he's a friend of Hendley's. I think it'll be better all around if I tell him."

"Do what you think best, Mr. Garvey," I nodded. "I'm coming with you, though. If you want me to do the telling, just say the word."

He looked at me with an expression I couldn't fathom. Just as I saw something sad in his eyes trying to make its way out through the crow's feet, he wrinkled his forehead like a wind-whipped dune and turned for the door, scowling.

I left the others standing in my office and followed him out. He was walking the way he always did, like a general at the head of his troops.

I couldn't help marvelling at him as we walked that street together. He wasn't even wearing a gun. In fact, I'd never known him to wear one. He didn't have to, I suppose. He could squint down a lit cigar fierce enough to make you think it was a loaded Winchester. He was looking straight ahead of him as we went, grinding that cigar like the bullet doctors give a man before they take off an arm or leg. Behind him he left a thin rope of smoke that tried to hunch its way free to the upper air before getting swallowed in Paco's dust. Gray hair and guts on the end of a stick of tobacco — that's all he was. Old enough to be the father of Hendley and me and Holliday, too. And young enough to think he could lick hell's host with a pair of bare hands. — Well, if he couldn't, I remember thinking, I didn't figure on surviving the effort.

When we reached the saloon, Tom and Doc Holliday were still sitting at the same table. Garvey and I walked over to them, and Tom got up to introduce the Mayor. Holliday nodded without rising. Tom glanced at me uneasily and sat down, inviting Garvey and me to join them. We did, and Tom poured drinks all around.

We passed the time of day for a while, Holliday all the time giving Garvey the hard eye. And Garvey was kind of uneasy under it, I thought. He didn't look back at Holliday but kept staring down at his glass.

Tom sensed something was up. He darted his eyes back and forth between Holliday and Garvey and suddenly quit talking. I felt it wasn't up to me to do anything till the Mayor spoke his piece. So I kept quiet, too, and watched Garvey for a sign.

Nobody said anything for a minute or so, and I could hear Squirrely Gibbs at the bar, giving the inside of a glass hell with his towel. Finally the Mayor looked straight into Holliday's face and took a deep breath.

"Mr. Holliday —" he began.

But before he could get started, Holliday cut him off:

"Save it, for Christ's sake."

Holliday finished his whiskey and brought the glass down on the table with a clump.

"Save it. I'm just goin'."

Hendley leaned forward and looked hard at his friend.

"Doc! Doc, you mean you're lettin' 'em run you out o' town? Is that it?"

Suddenly Tom got an ugly look on his face. He turned to Garvey without giving Holliday time to answer.

"He's a friend of mine!" Tom said. "Ain't a deputy's word that his friend will keep the peace good enough around this town?"

Holliday smiled and poured himself another drink.

"No, Tom," he shook his head, "don't fight it. I'm not worth it, I promise you. I been down this road before. I haven't gotten respectable like you — but I'm not a God damn' dog in the manger — such as the manger is."

The sneer in his voice seemed to make Tom all the madder.

"Are you trying to run my friend out of Paco?" he asked, never taking his eyes off the Mayor.

Old Garvey looked right back at him.

"If he's leaving town already," Garvey said steadily, "there ain't any need to *ask* him to."

Holliday reached out and put his hand on Hendley's arm.

"Take it easy, boy," he said. "I don't want to hang around here. This kind of life doesn't suit me — even for a day, even for a night. No, not worth a *God*-damn."

He took a long swallow of whiskey.

"Trouble with us, Tom, we got only two choices — either settle for life or keep on moving. You say you're gonna play the hand you've dealt yourself. Well, I'm not ready to gather moss yet. And sure as hell not here!"

He gave Hendley a reassuring pat on the shoulder.

"Don't worry. I wouldn't be leaving if I didn't want to."

He finished off his drink and poured himself another. None of the rest of us said anything.

"Yessir," he chuckled, "when the kids sneak a look at you through the window and get skinned for it, you can tell you're not exactly welcome."

He threw down his last drink and stood up. He must have put away a stomachful. And notwithstanding his legendary capacity, I thought he was beginning to show it.

"It's like when a friend gets married," he went on. "The girl he picks may be the damnedest slut that ever crawled out of a gutter — may be the whore you slept with last night. — But since she's married your friend, all you can do when you see her is tip your God-damn' hat."

And he tipped his hat at Mayor Garvey.

"Nothing personal, Tom," he added. "Nothing personal."

Hendley got up slowly and looked hard at Garvey and me.

"I'll ride along a ways," he said.

They left without another word. When they were out the door, Squirrely Gibbs came over to the table where Garvey and I were still sitting.

"Who's gonna pay for all the whiskey, Marshal?" he asked. "That was the best bottle in town and it's damn' near gone!"

Garvey reached in his pocket and pulled out a five-dollar gold piece. He slapped it down on the table and left without waiting for change.

"Cheap at twice the price!" I heard him mutter as he went.

We both stared after him till the doors stopped swinging. I finished my drink in one gulp, and when I opened my eyes Squirrely was fixing to pour what was left in the Mayor's glass back in the bottle.

"Squirrely!" I roared, getting up.

He jumped like a shot buck, spilling some of the whiskey.

"That's paid for!"

I grabbed the glass out of his hand and threw down what was left. Then I up-ended the glass on top of the bottle, which Squirrely was still holding. His hand shook like a mustang's mane, and I could still hear the chatter of glass-on-bottle as I left.

I went back to my office and sat down to the work Jim Potts had interrupted that morning. I hadn't been at it long when Hendley came busting in looking about as wide-eyed as Jim had earlier. He was out of breath like he'd been running, and he had something hidden behind his back.

"What on earth's eating you, man?" I asked, getting up.

"I wanted to show you first, Sam!" he smiled. "Look! Look what Doc gave me!"

And from behind his back he pulled one of Doc Holliday's shiny pistols. He shoved the thing into my hands, and against my will (though I don't exactly know why), I found myself going over it just as I had seen Tom do. The chamber and bore were in almost perfect condition. Without a doubt, it was the finest handgun I'd seen in my life. It made me feel almost ashamed of my own, and it was the only gun I *ever* knew to do that.

"Does it shoot like it looks?" I asked him.

"Better! It'll outshoot anything but a Winchester!"

"How the devil did you get it off him?"

"He *gave* it to me — farewell present!" Tom grinned. "Just before he took off, he asked me one more time to come with him on — on some business he had in mind. I told him I couldn't, with a wife and kid in tow. So he said he wouldn't be seeing me again and all of a sudden gave me this."

Tom stopped for a moment and his grin got wider.

"Told me, since he wouldn't be meeting *me* again, he wouldn't need but *one* anymore!"

"Well, I guess you'd have 'em both if you'd shot him for 'em," I laughed. "Congratulations. That gun's quite a handful. — And Tom — I'm mighty glad you decided to stay."

I offered him my hand.

"Thanks, Sam," he said, as we shook. "Maybe I wouldn't have if it hadn't been for you."

He turned to leave but stopped when he reached the door. "By the way," he asked, "who paid Gibbs for all that liquor?" I told him Garvey had.

"Hell," Tom grinned, "I'll pay him again. It was worth it!"

After he'd gone, I couldn't help wondering whether it was. But I didn't find out till a long time afterwards.

7

A Home for the Gun

WITH HOLLIDAY'S PISTOL in his hands Hendley was like a man inspired — not so much a kid with a new toy as an adolescent with a new love. After Holliday gave it to him, I never saw Tom without the thing until he quit wearing it forever. It came to seem so much a part of him that some of the jokesters in town wondered whether he took it off when he went to bed. But nobody ever asked him.

He had no use for my gun any more. He would sit in my office sometimes, cleaning his gun or burnishing that silver barrel on his sleeve, and talk to the damned thing like it was alive.

"Shine up! Shine up, ol' baby!" he would say as he worked on the bore. I would just swear to myself and go on reading a newspaper as though my life depended on it.

Actually, he didn't have that much real use for the gun after Holliday gave it to him. Paco mellowed as it got more prosperous. There was plenty of grazing room in the hills to the north, and that and a little farmland south of town seemed good enough to attract a fairly sober sort of settler. Indians began to give the place a wider berth as cattle and farms pushed the game farther off — and most people in Paco liked it that way. Aside from corralling drunks and one or two cattle thieves, Tom and I had little to do in a professional way till the Graysons took a crack at Nate Purvis's bank.

But that didn't come for a number of years. Meanwhile, I invested most of my savings and spare time in a few acres and some cattle, which I hoped would keep me from begging in my old age. The place was several miles from town and it had just about everything I needed — a small stream and a house not fit for a family but adequate for me.

Hendley kept busy with his hunting and fishing and — when he was around — raising his son. He always used to like to go by himself when he went off hunting. But as the years went by and little Tommy got old enough to ride, he used to take the boy with him on some of the shorter trips.

I found myself feeling sorrier for Millyanna now. She had planted a small vegetable garden out back of Tom's house. And what with looking after it and the house and the child, she usually found plenty to do. But she needed to. Paco never got used to an Indian in its midst, and none of the women in town made any real effort to take her in. Even her church-going and her willingness to send little Tommy to the town school never made Paco do much more than tolerate the girl.

Yet this didn't seem to bother Millyanna as much as it did Tom. She was a tough, proud spirit — deeply sensitive, but willing to put up with anything as long as she had him. Tom could never exactly understand their situation, though. And he knew he couldn't do much about it anyway. So it just got to him, deeper and deeper. Hell, it got to me. About all I could do was stand by and watch as the knots got tighter inside him.

I think Millyanna's resignation may have made it even harder on Tom. The fact that she didn't show resentment for snubs she got from the Paco women made him show his all the more. His temper hadn't improved with age, and people stayed careful of what they said about Indians when he was around. But he knew he couldn't stop all the talk. And he couldn't keep little Tommy from getting his share. "That half-breed bastard" I heard the boy called, one time. (Some few took it on themselves to condemn the child because he was conceived before Parson Preble had said it was all right with him and God.) Like I said, I heard the boy called that name just once. But what I didn't hear held its own.

Tommy learned fast when it came to riding and hunting. He had dark hair and bright, quick eyes that made his swarthy little face appealing. As a youngster he looked more like his father than Millyanna, and he favored Tom all the more as he grew. He hated to spend time indoors, and he liked nothing better than scrapping with the town kids who tried to bully him. He liked to shoot, and handling his father's Winchester came as naturally to him as handling a horse.

But learning rifles is one thing and learning pistols another. I told Tom so the time I came to visit and found him showing Doc Holliday's gun to Tommy when the boy was only nine. I think Hendley was a little embarrassed at being discovered, and he should have been. I told him you couldn't hunt much except human beings with a pistol and nine was too damned young to start.

Tom didn't take very kindly to my butting in. Anyway it didn't change his mind about what he taught the boy. Pistolling came to take almost first priority on the kid's out-of-school curriculum.

But the town itself was partly to blame. On the one hand, Paco had strict rules against selling liquor or guns to an Indian. And on the other, Hendley never got over his bitterness at the way Paco had treated his wife. I think he felt he was striking a blow at the town somehow by teaching his half-Indian kid the pistol.

One afternoon I remember sitting in Hendley's parlor when
he and Millyanna and little Tommy were all there, and the talk
got onto Indians and how few we saw around Paco any more.
(Tommy couldn't have been much more than seventeen at the
time.) Hendley was silent for a moment and then he stood up
abruptly. He looked hard at Tommy, who was watching him
like a cat. Tom jerked his head slightly toward the door. And
before I got over my surprise, the two of them were out of the
house, riding for the hills, where they always went to practice.
I can still see the tense light in the boy's eyes — almost like he
was seeing a vision — and his old man, solemn as a chieftain,
looking like he was going out to preside over some heathen
sacrifice.

I wasn't the only one who didn't like the boy's learning old
tricks too young. Father and son were hardly out the door that
time when I heard Millyanna's voice cut through the sense of
helplessness that rooted me down.

"You stop 'em!" she said, coming over to me and squeezing
my arm with a strength that surprised me.

"Why, what are you talking about?" I asked. I tried to
seem casual for my own sake as well as hers.

"No good! No good, Sam!"

She closed her eyes and shook her head quietly.

"No good, young boy learn bad life!" she continued, when
she opened her eyes again.

"You stop 'em, Sam. You only one who can!"

She still had a wild, rough beauty about her that hadn't
grown old. She was fighting to hold back the tears now, and I
felt her hand tremble just before she let go of my arm. My
heart went out to her then as I don't believe it ever has to any
one. — But then the old feeling of helplessness closed in on me
again.

"Have you ever tried to stop *him* from doing something?" I asked.

"Many time!" she said, looking hard at me. "Many time! — Have you?"

That put a different burr under my saddle. I tried to laugh it off.

"I got more sense!" I smiled at her.

But it was a bad joke, and I wiped the smile off quick. I told her I had said something to Tom about it and that I would again, when an opportunity came. I tried to convince her, too, that she was getting worked up over nothing. But I didn't believe that myself. I left feeling like a tired old man and went down to the Silver Pick for some liquid rejuvenation.

I would have liked to talk to Mayor Garvey about the whole thing. But Garvey was getting old now, and lately he'd been so ill he couldn't get out of bed. The only other thing I could think to do was to talk to the boy himself. And I got my chance a couple of weeks later.

Tommy came into my office one day about noon to walk home for lunch with his father. Hendley wasn't there, but I expected him shortly. So I asked Tommy to sit down and wait. He did, and we got to talking about horses and hunting and the usual things.

He was a cheerful boy with a head full of sense, I thought. Some of his mother's dark beauty hovered around the corners of his face, though his chin, nose and overhanging brow were like his father's.

"Tommy," I asked finally, "have you given any thought to your future — what you want to do, or be, in life?"

He looked at me blankly.

"Why do you ask me that?" he said.

"Well, you're growing up, boy," I told him. "You're almost a man. You'll have to do more than think about these things pretty soon."

"I have thought about it — often," he answered, turning his eyes on me seriously. "I want to go and do something for my people."

That caught me altogether unprepared.

"Your — people?" I said quietly.

"My people," he nodded. "My mother's people — the Sioux. I feel I couldn't spend my life here — here in Paco. — Indians have many problems now. I think I could help them."

I stared at him in amazement. I knew he couldn't have gotten that idea from but one person.

"Well, Tommy, *we're* your people, too!" I said. "You are your father's son as much as your mother's."

He looked at me silently for a moment.

"But I can do nothing for you — for white men — for my father's people. Nothing that one of yours couldn't do just as well — or better. — For my own people I think I can do something."

All his mother's proud nobility shone through his eyes as he said this. I wondered, and yet I could understand — or thought I could.

"Does your father know this — what you plan to do?" I asked after a while.

He shook his head.

"He's never asked me."

I reflected that Hendley would have been more likely to tell than ask.

"You — er — you *plan* to discuss it with him, I guess?"

The boy glanced down at the floor and then looked up at me quickly.

"I plan to tell him when I must leave."

"Well, when do you think that'll be — your leaving?"

He shook his head.

"I don't know. I must learn what he can teach me before I go. — He is a good teacher, and I love him."

I cleared my throat and tried to look as solemn as I could.

"Well, Tommy, I don't deny that your father knows a lot — hunting, fishing, trapping, scouting. But this business with the pistol — that big silver one that belonged to Doc Holliday — do you think that's something you ought to be learning? Something that'll help you 'help your people,' as you say?"

He grinned all over.

"That's the best part!"

"The best part? What do you mean, 'the best part'?"

He shrugged.

"It's what he knows best. It's what I want most to learn."

"No, dammit, it's not the best part!" I insisted. "You shouldn't be learning that unless you're going to be a peace officer. — Why, Indians don't have any use for pistols!"

"Indians don't," he admitted. "But this one will."

"*What*, then? What use will you have for a pistol?"

He was quiet a moment.

"I don't know," he told me frankly. "But I'll find one."

While I was trying to think how to answer that, I saw the boy glance out the window and then suddenly get up.

"My father's coming," he said. "Mr. McCallum, my mother always told me you were a man I could trust. Can I trust you to keep what I told you a secret — to let *me* tell my plans to my father first?"

"Certainly. Certainly, boy," I assured him, getting up. "I hope I never live to disappoint your mother — or you — in anything. — Just keep what I said about the pistol between ourselves, too. All right?"

And I held out my hand, smiling.

"All right!" he replied and shook.

I liked his grip much better than I liked his father's the first time Hendley and I shook hands. I guess the care and keeping of the gunhand was something Tommy had yet to learn.

I stood at the window and watched him and his father walk down the street together, going home. They both had the same easy, stalking slouch. Except for the round stoop of Hendley's shoulders, you might have thought they were the same man, doubled by a mirage on the sandy street. — I couldn't help wondering then what sort of a hard-nosed little bugger *I* might have had, if I had ever let myself.

I never spoke to the boy again about his plans or the pistol. He and his father just kept on with their hunting and fishing and practicing together, riding around the countryside like the pair of wild Indians they almost were.

8
Red-handed Robbery

NOT LONG AFTER my talk with Tommy, Hendley himself
brought up the subject of the boy's learning to shoot. I knew
he was proud of Tommy's skill; and I had figured that the next
time he gloated about it in front of me, I would come down on
him with all four feet. He gave me a good opportunity.

It was a Friday in June — oddly enough, the very day the
Grayson gang knocked over Nate Purvis's bank. I remember it
well. I was sitting alone in my office nursing the wrenched
right shoulder I had suffered when my mare put her foot in a
gopher hole two days before. She'd thrown me cleaner than
horse or human ever had. And Doc Hobbs had strapped up
my arm and chest so tight it almost hurt to swallow whiskey. I
knew I wouldn't be much good to anybody till I got out of that
damned cocoon. And I was just waiting to turn over some last
minute matters to Hendley before I went back to my ranch for
a rest.

It was late in the afternoon when Tom came in. He'd been
sweating hard. His hair, already graying, was matted together
in a tight little ring where his hat had mashed it down. On
somebody else it might have looked like a halo.

"That kid of mine learns fast!" he grinned at me, wiping
his forehead on the sleeve of his shirt. "I couldn't have shot
any better myself when I was Tommy's age. — Won't be long
now before he's man enough to handle Doc Holliday's gun."

"Don't you think there are some other things he ought to learn first?" I asked, watching him from my chair.

The grin disappeared so fast it was as if his face had made a mistake to ever grin.

"No!" he grunted. "No, I don't. That's the thing I learned first and the thing I'm thankfulest for. Once he's learned that, he can go on and learn what else he wants to."

"Suppose he won't want to learn anything else?"

"Then that's *his* business."

"Maybe that's the business he'll want to go into."

"So? — *You* seem to think it's good enough to spend some time in."

I shook my head.

"There are two sides to this business," I said. "You know that as well as I do. And I was a long time getting on the side I'm on."

He almost sneered:

"Are you so happy with the side you're on?"

I'd never heard him talk like that before.

"I'm damned sure it's better than the other," I told him. I let that sink in on us both for a moment.

"But we're not talking about me," I went on. "I'm getting old and close to useless. — If you teach a kid the gun before he's got control of *himself*, you're doing the kid — and maybe a lot of other people — one hell of a disservice. Don't you think you may be making a mistake to start the boy gunning too young?"

"No," he said quietly, walking over to my desk. "No. *You're* making the mistake. That boy's mine. He's my flesh and my blood, and I'll teach him what I damned well want. — You try to come between him and me, and you're in trouble, Mister."

"Tom," I said, getting up with an effort and walking around to where he stood, "don't get me wrong —"

"Nobody's gettin' you wrong," he snapped. "We been together too long for that. — I know when you're trying to get to me, and I'm telling you to quit. You been after me about that kid ever since I can remember. And if you don't stop, I'll stop you."

"Tom, we're too old to be fighting —"

"As long as I live," he cut me off, glaring as if he wanted to stab me with his eyes, "as long as I live I'm not too old to be fighting anybody."

I don't know what I would have said to that, but I never got the chance even to think it. We were both cut off by an explosion that sounded like the Almighty had finally run out of patience. The windows rattled, and the teeth I had left danced in my head like warpath Indians. For a moment I was stunned, till the yells and commotion outside brought me around.

"Tom!" I said recollecting myself: "get uptown and see what that's all about. I'll send Gabby Macrae after you and be along myself, soon as I can make it."

He took off without a word just as Gabby came running in from the jail. We had no customers at the time, so I sent Gabby after Tom.

I thought the noise had come from the Silver Pick. Everybody in town who could move must have been in the street, running that way and yelling to beat hell. I made it as fast as I could, but the pain in my shoulder slowed me quite a bit.

Before I reached the saloon, I could see smoke coming from the shattered front window of Nate Purvis's bank a few doors farther down. A single shot sounded from somewhere out back, and I saw Hendley up ahead of me cut down a side street to circle the building. I followed his lead and cut behind the saloon, trying not to let the smell of garbage and horse-dung make me gag. I reached the rear of the bank with a handful of others in time to see some shooting I guess they're still talking about in Paco.

Three men with face bandanas were scrambling onto horses a fourth was holding. I saw two more come running out of the bank carrying a heavy leather bag between them. They slung the bag across one of the horses and mounted up. I almost thought they were playing some game until they started shooting.

The first four were already heading away when they got off a couple of shots that stopped us where we were. Hendley was the closest one to them by then, but there was a good sixty feet between him and the last rider. I was too far back to worry much about getting hit, but the men nearest Tom dove for cover when the dirt started jumping in front of them.

Not, Hendley, though. I saw him stand right where he was and take aim with both hands. The late sun on that long gun barrel made it seem on fire even before he pulled the trigger.

The nearest rider must have been eighty-odd feet from him now, the next one ninety or a hundred. He fired twice — one shot at each of them, no more. I can see him now, standing there while the bullets licked at his toes, aiming that silver cannon as if nothing else mattered or ever would.

And he got the last rider.

"Christ! Did you see that?" an out-of-breath voice sputtered behind me.

"Hell, yes! And I *still* don't believe it!"

People stepped out of doorways now, and from behind trees and fences. They passed me and swarmed on beyond Hendley to where the rider was lying, crumpled like an old saddle against the outhouse that got in his way when he fell.

"Looked to me like he winged the other one, too!" somebody said.

"Yeah! I seen him stiffen like he felt a brand on his butt!"

"I never even *heard* of shootin' like that!"

The empty horse and the rest of the riders were out of range in a matter of seconds. Hendley stood where he'd shot from, the gun still smoking in his hand as he squinted after them. When I got up to him, I put my good hand on his shoulder and looked him in the eye without a word. He glanced at me quickly and then looked down to reload.

"Ought to have *had* that other man!" he muttered, shaking his head.

By this time several people had gotten to the fallen rider. For lack of a better place, they carried him back into Purvis's bank. They laid him on the floor in the little room behind the cashier's cage. Some scattered papers and the contents of an up-ended spittoon shared the floor with him.

Nate Purvis entered from the front office just as they brought in the shot rider. Evidently the gang had man-handled Purvis and tied him to a chair before they blew his safe. By now, somebody had released him and he was running around fit to be tied — again. I sent Gabby Macrae to round up a posse as I pushed my way over to get a look at the man on the floor.

They'd pulled his face cover off by the time I got alongside. He may still have been breathing then, but he was dead when Doc Hobbs arrived a minute or two later. Dead or alive, though, the blood and dirt couldn't keep us from recognizing a familiar face — that of one Rufus Grayson. As soon as we knew for sure he was dead, Hendley rolled the body over on its stomach to see where the bullet had struck.

All the time Nate Purvis was hopping around like a young bull that had just made steer. He hadn't seen the shooting in the alley. All he knew was that his safe had been blown, but everybody was talking about some crazy shot Hendley had made.

"Why the hell'd you have to *kill* him?" Purvis beefed at Hendley. "God-damn' trigger happy tin-star! If we'd gotten him to talk, he might have given us a lead on the gang and the money."

All of a sudden Hendley's face went livid. I never saw him get so mad so fast.

"Why didn't you have something besides a two-bit cheesebox for people to keep their money in?" he spat back. "Maybe no one would have tried a thing like this if *you'd* been doing your job. Some of *my* savings were in this place."

I thought for a minute he might swing on Purvis. I reached out and put my hand on Hendley's arm.

"We've got a lead on the gang, Mr. Purvis," I interrupted. "The dead man there is Rufus Grayson. He and his two brothers live north of here up in the Granite Hills. They have a shack near where the old Creel Mine used to be. None of 'em ever did anything they didn't all do together. That gang'll stop somewhere to split up the take. They were heading north out of town, so Creel Mine might be a good place to start looking for 'em. Soon as we get together a posse, I'll send some of 'em to the Graysons' shack. The rest can follow the gang on the north road in case they split before they get into the hills."

"Well, what the hell are you waiting for?" Purvis asked. "Why aren't you organizing a posse?"

"The posse ought to be in front of the bank right now," I went on evenly. "This kind of news spreads fast. There's a lot of depositors who'll want that money back as much as you."

Some of those in the room spoke up to agree. Several said they were ready to ride then.

"Good!" I said, turning to Hendley. "Tom, you know those hills pretty well. Take five men and head for the Grayson shack. And you — Charlie Currus —"

Charlie had done some special-deputy work for me before, and he'd been one of the first to reach the bank after the explosion.

"Charlie, you take the rest and follow the gang on the road north. I wish I could ride along, but I'm in no shape for it. As soon as Gabby gets more men together, I'll send 'em after you. But get going now while the trail's fresh."

"Take 'em *all*, Charlie!" Tom said suddenly. He never shifted his glance from Purvis's wizened little face.

"I work best alone," he went on. "I know those hills better than some people know their own office. I could find Rufe Grayson's shack on a moonless midnight. And I'll get there quicker by myself."

Nate Purvis and Charlie and the rest all looked at me. It would have been a waste of time to argue with Tom, and I wanted somebody to move.

"Take 'em all, Charlie," I nodded. "But get going. We're wasting high time."

Charlie took off without a word, and twelve men with him. As they left, Purvis turned to me, his eyes wide as silver dollars.

"Marshal!" he said. "Are you going to allow this? The only clue we have to a robbery by six bandits and you're letting *one* man run it down — alone ?"

There were still quite a few of us left in the back room of the bank, including Hendley, who was about to go. When he heard the question, he stopped and bristled like a cactus. I waited a moment till the room got quiet.

"He's a hell of a *good* man," I told Purvis.

"Not every one shares your opinion, Marshal!"

Purvis spoke like he was spitting, and he didn't so much as glance in Hendley's direction. Some of those who were just outside in the alley pushed back in to hear what was coming. A couple of the boys who had picked up Rufus Grayson's body let it drop and stared at me.

"You leave the marshalling to me, Mr. Purvis, and stick to running your bank."

"If you've got one left!"

Hendley was close to the door and his remark snapped from across the room like a whip. It was too true to be funny.

"Tom, you better horse-up," I said quickly. "I'll take care of things here."

"I got lots of time," Hendley muttered, looking darkly at Purvis. "Speak up, Mr. *ex*-Banker. What's on your mind?"

Purvis turned toward Hendley, his clenched fists showing white across the knuckles.

"I know you," he said, "and I know your way. A shot in the gut and *your* job's done. But your way isn't the right way, this time. I don't want two or three men killed up in those hills. If the Graysons are all in on this thing, I want 'em here for questioning. I want my money back. And I don't want any God-damned hangman going off to butcher my prime witnesses!"

No one had talked that way to Hendley since he'd been in Paco. He was absolutely white with rage, and I could see the muscles hopping around under the skin of his cheeks. I walked over and stood next to him.

"I've got every confidence in my deputy, Mr. Purvis," I said, looking Hendley straight in the eye. "I trust him to use only what force is necessary to bring in the Graysons for questioning."

"I trust him to give 'em some of that quick silver!" Purvis snapped, glancing down at Hendley's pistol. "That's all he ever does with a man he's after — goads 'im into drawing and then cuts 'im down like ripe wheat — all the time knowing the fellow has no chance against a professional gunslick like him."

"Maybe you want to go after 'em yourself?" Hendley cracked.

"That's not my job!"

"It sure as hell isn't!" Hendley said. "Maybe you want me to check my gun with you — go after 'em barehanded?"

Purvis seemed to have nothing to say. And all of a sudden Hendley reached for the buckle of his gun belt. He whipped the belt off, took the gun in his hand, and then threw the belt and holster both on the floor at Purvis's feet. They fell with a sound like thunder in that hushed room. He broke the pistol and emptied four of the six chambers into the palm of his left hand.

"There's two more Graysons — right, Mr. Purvis?" Hendley asked with a sour smile. Everybody was too surprised to move, much less say anything. Purvis just blinked his puffy eyes.

"Well, this'll make it just one bullet apiece — *if* they ask for it," Hendley went on.

He stuck the pistol into the top of his pants and flung the four bullets at Purvis's feet.

"Maybe that'll help you to sleep better, Mr. Purvis."

Without another word to any one Hendley turned and stalked out of the bank. By this time Gabby Macrae had brought our horses over from my office, and Hendley was up before any one could stop him.

I followed him out to the alley and called to him.

"Tom! Tom, are you out of your mind?"

He looked down at me for only a moment. His white teeth gleamed like lightning under the black cloud of that tired moustache.

"Don't send anybody after me, Sam."

Then he gave his horse both heels hard and went.

I stood there in the alley, watching till the dust had swallowed him up. I was still fighting down the sick feeling that churned inside me when Purvis came out, huffing and puffing, and stood beside me.

"Well, I — I didn't mean for him to do anything like that!" he whimpered.

"No?" I said, without looking at him. "Just what the hell *did* you mean?"

I didn't wait for an answer — if he had one.

9
Rich Return

SOME OF THE BOYS took Rufus Grayson by McCabe's to get measured, and I went to see Millyanna. She and Tommy had just found out about the hold-up. I figured they would hear the whole story sooner or later, so I went ahead and gave them the facts – all except that Tom had taken only two bullets with him when he left. Young Tommy seemed as excited as if I'd been talking about buried treasure. But Millyanna just looked a little sadder when I finished. I couldn't tell whether she knew I was keeping something from her or not. I didn't stay to find out. I hoped she wouldn't realize how much the whole thing bothered *me*.

At the Silver Pick people were talking about nothing else. The fight between Hendley and Purvis got even bigger play than the robbery itself. And I was surprised at how many people seemed to agree with Purvis. They quieted down a little when I came in, but not enough to keep me from knowing how they felt. I even heard a few toasts to Nate Purvis! To him and his "speedy recovery" – of their money and his. There may not have been much love spilled over Hendley in Paco, but there was one hell of a lot of whiskey.

Charlie Currus and the posse came back next morning – Saturday – with bad news. They had ridden hard on the fugitives all the preceding afternoon. Then about dark they had come on a deserted ranch house up in the Granite Hills. The bandits had hidden some fresh horses there and taken off on them in different directions. Charlie and his men were pretty tired by that time; but more important, so were their horses. And the bandits — with night coming on and fresh mounts under them — had managed to lose the posse altogether.

Tom didn't show up all that Saturday. And come evening, I began to get worried. If I'd been in shape to ride, I would have gone out after him myself. But I decided to give him till Sunday noon before I sent somebody else. Charlie Currus volunteered to go; and I told him, if Hendley wasn't back by midday, to take five men and see what he could find up at the Grayson shack. To complicate matters further, young Tommy had gotten into the act. Millyanna came by my office on her way to church that Sunday and told me the boy had taken a rifle and left town alone at sun-up to look for his father.

I got more and more edgy as that Sunday morning went by with no sign of Hendley. I didn't feel like waiting out the last hour till noon by myself. It was too early to be drinking, so I decided to follow Millyanna. I was in church trying to sing it off when Gabby Macrae came tip-toeing down the aisle to whisper in my ear that Hendley was back. I racked my book, trying to look as casual as I could. And Gabby and I walked out together. Just as we cleared the door, I caught a glimpse of Millyanna following us out.

"Is Tommy with him?" I asked Gabby quickly.

"Not a living soul's with him!" Gabby said.

"Where the hell is he?" I asked.

Gabby nodded toward the street.

"Yonder. Headin' uptown for Nate Purvis's house."

I took off for Purvis's at the closest I could come to a run. Millyanna was not far behind me. The little crowd that had gathered in the street slowed us both. They were shoving each other and trying to run, one or two carrying bottles that had somehow survived Saturday night.

Up ahead I could make out what they were following. Hendley's round shoulders were bobbing up and down like a snake's back in time to the slow walk of his horse. He was leading two other horses behind him, each with a body slung over it like a broken sack.

I followed along, pushing my way through the press as best I could. The crowd wasn't so heavy as the smell of sweat and cheap whiskey that clung like creditors everywhere. I elbowed, cursed and shoved, but Hendley had reached Nate Purvis's before I caught up with him.

He must have known he was being followed — and had been, since he passed the Blue Chip on his way into town. He rode on without looking back, though — as if there wasn't another soul in the world.

When he got to the white picket fence in front of Purvis's, he dismounted. The gate was latched, and he had some trouble undoing it. Suddenly he quit trying. With one kick he knocked it off its hinges and walked into the yard, leading the horses after him. The crowd formed in a little circle outside the fence. They were quiet now, with the silence that comes just before a chopped-through tree cracks and falls.

"Come the hell out of there, Purvis!" Hendley bellowed.

He led the two pack horses up to the porch. Purvis couldn't have helped but know that mob was in front of his house, but he wouldn't show his face.

"Come out, damn you, Purvis!" Hendley yelled. "I know you're not in church either."

We all knew Nate Purvis wasn't any more of a churchgoer than Hendley. Since coming to Paco, Purvis had been to church only once that I knew of, and that was to bury his wife. He had been so thankful to get shed of her that everybody figured it might make a Christian of him. Everybody was wrong. And

I could see a few faces in the crowd exchanging winks at Hendley's remark. I had reached the kicked-in gate long since. But there I stopped. I just stood now with the rest to see what Hendley was going to do.

Purvis still didn't show, so Hendley turned to his own horse and removed a leather bag he'd been carrying across the saddle. He threw it onto the porch and it landed with the ring of heavy metal.

"There's your gold back, Purvis. Or part of it."

Tom spat and turned to the pack horses. Drawing his sheath knife, he began to cut loose the two bodies.

Meanwhile Purvis appeared at the front door. He just stood there for a moment, his beady little eyes glowering.

"What's the meaning of this?" he asked hoarsely.

"I *thought* that gold would bring you," Hendley said over his shoulder. He had gotten one of the bodies free by then. Hefting it on his back, he turned and flung it down on the porch in front of Purvis.

"Thought you might like to talk to Kurt Grayson," he said. "You better talk fast. He was alive when I started back, but not by much."

Purvis stooped quickly to look at what was left of Kurt Grayson. In a minute Hendley had the other body free. And just as Purvis stood up again, Tom flung what turned out to be the third Grayson onto the little porch at Purvis's feet. The body rolled over with a rattle of chaps and spurs.

"You might have trouble makin' Rory there understand you," Hendley nodded at the second body. "I think he was gone when I hitched him up."

Purvis glanced quickly at the body. Then he reached down and rolled it face-up.

"Why, they're dead! They're both of 'em *dead*, man!" he said, straightening up and staring at Hendley.

"Then let that bag there speak for 'em," Hendley grunted, nodding at the black coil of leather he'd thrown down first. "It's their share of the loot. — That's all the talk you're interested in."

He didn't wait for a reply. Taking his horse by the bridle, he started walking back out to the street. Purvis just stood there looking after him like a school kid. The crowd had been as still as death till then. But when Hendley reached the gate, they started to murmur and jostle each other to get back out of his way. I was in the front rank, and I didn't move back.

"Hi, Marshal," he nodded to me with a sick grin.

I could see that his face was a terrible white in spite of its burn by the wind and sun — the saddle-leather tan that made one of the jokers in town say he'd like to skin Hendley for horse-harness when he died. In spite of that ghost of a grin there was something ominous in Hendley's face. And I'd never heard him call me "Marshal" in all the years I'd known him.

He stopped in front of me and dropped the bridle from his hand. I said nothing, and the crowd quieted down again to hear what was coming. Very deliberately, never taking his eyes from mine, he pulled that gun out of the top of his pants. He broke it smartly with a click that fell on us like the sound of a bone breaking. He held the pistol out by the barrel.

"Can you spare me six fingers, Marshal?" he asked. "I'm dry as hell."

I took the gun, its nickel gleaming dully through a coating of sweat and dust. The cylinder had two empty cartridges in it, and there was black powder in two of the other chambers. The remaining two were clean as Monday's wash except for the dust that would have collected in a couple days' ride. Four shots had left that gun since it was last cleaned. And I had seen two of them fired the day of the robbery. I glanced over to Purvis's porch where I knew the two other bullets were. Purvis was still staring at us like a fish out of water, and the sight of him brought me back to my senses.

I was about to swear like a heathen when all of a sudden Hendley went down on his face in the street. One shoulder tucked under him as he fell. His legs, sprawling out behind, made him look like the twisted wishbone of a chicken. He went almost without a sound. I heard only the flop of one leg as he dropped.

For a moment I was too surprised to ask myself why. But then we all saw. His left boot had been full to the brim with blood. And with his leg out flat behind him now, it all came out in a rush, turning the dust under him a rusty yellow as the ground drank him up.

With a little gasp I stooped to turn him over. I heard a murmur from the crowd as it shuffled nearer, but I didn't turn around. For the first time I noticed the ugly stain at the top of Tom's black pants and the heavy trail leading down along his left leg. I ripped open his clothes and saw the compress of a handkerchief soaked in whiskey he'd applied to the wound himself. Sure as hell, there was the bullet hole, just south of the belt line. And there wasn't any hole in his back. The Grayson's weren't the only ones carrying lead that morning.

I threw aside Tom's bloody handkerchief and replaced it with a clean one of my own. I was trying to pull his clothes back together when something happened that stunned me. I felt a hand reach around me from behind and grab my left wrist. I turned my head. I was eye to eye with Millyanna, only she wasn't looking at me. She'd shoved her way through to the front of the crowd by now and she was kneeling beside me, staring at the closed eyes and white face of her husband.

The crowd had been muttering, but it wasn't till then that I found myself hearing what they said.

"The God-damn squaw!"

"For Christ' sake, look at *her*!"

"Where's her feathers?"

Millyanna couldn't have heard them. Or if she did, she didn't show it. But then she seldom showed anything before the town.

I stood up quickly and shoved Tom's gun in my belt.

"You, Hendricks!" I nodded at the first friendly face I saw in the crowd. Will Hendricks had helped me with some work on my ranch, and I knew I could count on him.

"Go find Doc Hobbs," I said. "Tell him to get over to Hendley's house right away. I'll be there with Hendley by the time Doc arrives."

Hendricks left on the double and I turned to Gabby Macrae.

"Pick up that saddlebag, Gabby," I told him. "And get some one to take those bodies to McCabe's."

Then I turned to the crowd.

"Some of you men bear a hand with my deputy. We've got to get him home fast."

Gabby secured the saddlebag (which Purvis didn't want to part with, at first) and then detailed a few of the boys to take care of Kurt and Rory Grayson. Meanwhile, Millyanna had pulled Tom's clothes together and had gotten one arm around his back and the other under his legs as if she was going to try to move him herself. I put my hand on her arm quickly.

"Millyanna! Don't try to lift him. We'll get him home all right —"

But she shook my hand off her arm, still without looking at me. She just kept staring into Hendley's face as though it might be for the last time. The perspiration that was breaking on her face made it shine like sunrise. Her eyes grew wide for a moment and her nostrils flared as her breath came faster. Then she gathered him to her and got him off the ground with an effort that made her stagger. She looked half his size as she held him. The crowd hushed as if somebody had given a slap to every one of its faces. They parted silently for her when she started home, cradling Hendley in her arms like a sick child.

I stood dumbstruck with the rest as I watched her move off. Even Nate Purvis quit jabbering about his sack of money. He just stared after her like a cow in the slaughter 'chute after that hammer-tap between the ears.

Maybe we'd all be standing there now if Herm Cromwell hadn't said something. Herm used to drink with Rory Grayson whenever Rory made it to town. I guess he must have felt bereaved or something, with Rory catching flies over on Purvis's porch.

"Looks like a woman took the job off your hands, Marshal," he sneered. He was standing just behind me, but he spoke loud enough for the crowd to hear.

"'Woman', hell!" he added quickly. "God-damn' squaw, I meant to say."

I whipped around before the general snicker I heard could get bigger. My good hand caught a fistful of Crowell's shirt front and pulled him off balance. I saw his right hand make a move toward his holster so I flung him to the ground on his gun side. I had my own gun out and covering him with my left hand before he could roll over.

"Get up, Crowell!" I said. "Get out of my sight before I take iron to that thing you call your head."

He got up and dusted himself deliberately without saying a word. He never even glanced at my revolver, but he gave *me* the hardest look I'll get this side of Judgment.

He slunk off down the street and most of the crowd went with him. I felt the sweat-soaked back of my shirt go cold as I watched them. Nobody said anything, but one by one they gave me the eye as they walked away. Crowell was trash and every one knew it. So this wasn't a vote of confidence in him. It *was* in what he said, though. Millyanna would always be a 'squaw' to them – something less than human, to make bad jokes about.

After a minute I turned and put up my gun. I wiped the sweat or whatever it was out of my eyes and started after her. I was a minute or so catching her up, but she didn't seem to know I was there even when I got alongside. It was almost a quarter of a mile to their house, and Tom must have outweighed her forty or fifty pounds. But she didn't seem to hear me when I offered to help. She made it all the way without even stopping. And I walked along beside her, feeling strangely proud to be there – feeling a lot of things.

The heavy gun in my gut nudged me uncomfortably as I walked. But part of the time it helped to keep my mind off the black ooze that dripped from the heel of Tom's left boot.

10
Recovery and Retreat

HOBBS GOT THE bullet out before Tom came around. I stayed and watched till the Doc was finished, though there wasn't much I could do to help. Of course, Millyanna stood by the whole time. But it was a one-man job as long as Tom stayed out, and mercifully he did till after that probing.

I knew Hobbs wasn't happy to be treating Tom. I watched him frown and grunt and make faces like a monkey while he poked around for that slug. It was close in Hendley's little bedroom. Even the walls seemed to be perspiring. And every now and then Hobbs would wipe off on his shirttail in an effort to keep sweat from falling on Hendley. Sometimes the effort was successful.

"Never thought I'd be taking a bullet out of *him*!" Hobbs snapped at me when Millyanna had to leave the room for a moment. Though sandy-haired, the Doc had a red-headed temper. I think he would almost have preferred Hendley conscious for the treatment he was getting.

"Got innards of iron, though," Hobbs went on. "And a hell of a lot of luck. It's only a flesh wound, as these things go. The bullet didn't lodge in anything vital. — Lost plenty of blood, but he ought to be all right, once he gets his strength back. — Frankly, I'm glad to get a look inside him. I wouldn't have believed he had bowels at all."

Hendley's strength was long coming back. Some thought it never did come — though something else came in its place.

Ever since he rode back from the Granite Hills with a bullet aboard and the Graysons in tow, he was known as "Granite Hendley" — "Old Granite." The name wasn't meant as a compliment; but it stuck, as such names do.

More than ever, people were afraid of him now. The few wild ones we still had around town gave him as wide a berth as the stunted streets of Paco would allow. And news of the incident spread so fast that most of the gamblers and saddle-sores in the territory steered clear of Paco. But putting aside what the ne'er-do-wells thought, the town's attitude in general took a turn for the worse. Fear, hatred, resentment — whatever it was, like a scared rat it just went underground.

The money Tom got back from the Graysons came to about a third of the total Purvis claimed to have lost. Nothing was ever heard of the other bandits, and most people thought Purvis was lucky to get back as much as he did. Not Purvis, though. He kept on saying we might have gotten a line on the rest of the gang if the Graysons had been brought in alive. (I couldn't help but agree with that.) And since there were no other witnesses, we were left with what Tom might have to say about the shooting — which was easier for me to take than it was for the rest of Paco.

Hendley's boy returned late that same Sunday afternoon. He headed straight for the Grayson cabin, taking the difficult shortcut he thought his father must have used. Hendley had evidently taken the longer (but easier) trail back with the bodies and hadn't run into the boy. Tommy found the cabin torn up inside and empty — except for the body of a woman lying on the floor. He had picked up the trail of the three horses outside (knowing the lead horse was his father's) and followed it back to town. For more than that we had to wait on Hendley himself.

While we waited, Doc Hobbs and I had a look at Kurt and Rory Grayson in the back room at McCabe's. Hobbs got one bullet out of each of their stomachs. Both bullets had come from a distance, too — no burn marks on the clothes or the bodies — and from Hendley's gun. The Doc and several people besides me knew the extra heavy slug on a hand load that Hendley's .45 threw. And each bullet came from the spot in the gut where Hendley always placed his shots.

The next day — Monday — Tommy went with Charlie Currus and some of the boys back up to the Grayson cabin for a look at the dead woman. She was white and about thirty, and she'd been shot in the neck at close range with a Winchester. Nobody knew her, and most of the posse agreed she couldn't have been much to look at even when she was alive. The so-called cabin was more like a line shack, and a pretty flimsy one at that. It had seen one hell of a hassle not long since, and Charlie Currus told me he couldn't understand why the whole thing hadn't come down in the process. The place was almost a foot deep in broken bottles, rusty cookpots, and pieces of homemade furniture.

Charlie and his party buried the woman and came back to town without much light to shed. It wasn't until the following Wednesday that Tom was enough himself to tell us what had happened.

Apparently he had reached the cabin Friday evening (the night of the hold-up) and discovered there was a woman inside. Figuring she was waiting for some one, he had hidden and waited all the next day. Toward night-fall Saturday two riders (who turned out to be Kurt and Rory Grayson) came in from the northwest. Since he didn't have but the two bullets, Tom decided to wait till daylight before making his move. But that night Kurt and Rory got tired of punishing their supply of whiskey and started in on each other. During the uproar somebody got to the woman with a rifle. Tom knew from the voices that the two men had survived. The shooting sobered them a little; and after they quieted down for some sleep, Tom moved in against the cabin wall to be ready for them in the morning. He positioned himself at the corner nearest the cabin's one door, not far from where the horses were tied. That way the rising sun would be at his back and he could get a clear line on both men as they came out to load the animals. When they finally showed, they came together and Rory was carrying the Winchester. Tom said the sight of that rifle made him hesitate. But he thought that they might spot him first if he delayed; so he made his play at once and called out to them to drop their guns. He was covering them from the back and to one side, and as they turned, Rory gave Kurt some sort of signal. They both tried to fire on Tom simultaneously. Tom figured he must have taken too long over his first shot, trying to make sure that the Winchester was out of the picture. Kurt Grayson had time to get off one of his own just as Tom fired the second time. Tom said he saw Kurt go down on top of Rory. And at the same time he felt "a kick in the gut like from a mule I couldn't see." It spun him around against the cabin and almost dropped him. He remembered standing there, leaning on the wall for a minute, just to see whether he could. As he sucked what he thought might be his last breath, he could feel his pants getting warm with blood.

After a bit he made it around into the cabin, where he said he found whiskey enough "to clean a cannon-ball hole" — and to wet down an all-night thirst besides. Thanks to the strong stuff the Graysons had left, he was able to keep that little date with Nate Purvis. Since the woman had been dead for several hours already, he left her where she lay, just hoping he had the strength to get himself and the other two back to town.

We never found out about the woman — who or whose she was, and whether the bullet that killed her had really been meant for her. She was the one loose end to Hendley's story, and she gave his enemies (that is, practically all in town) something else to gossip about. I didn't doubt his story, though. And nobody I knew of questioned it to Hendley's face.

Tom was flat on his back for close to three weeks — almost a corpse himself. Some one at the Silver Pick remarked we ought to bury Hendley now, while he seemed amenable. But if that fellow had ever entered the room where Hendley lay, he would have remarked to another tune. All of Tom's old fire still lived, even if some of his strength was gone.

As soon as he got force enough to talk, the first thing he asked was whether the bullet was out of him. Millyanna and I were both there at the time, and I told him it was.

"Who did it?" he asked with a groggy stare. "You, Sam?"

I *had* taken bullets out of people before, and Tom knew it. I told him this had been a difficult job and Doc Hobbs had done the honors.

"Jesus!" he groaned. "Would've died in front of Purvis's before I let that son of a bitch touch me. Don't want him back here again. Tell him I'll kill him if he sets foot in my house."

I knew Hendley's feelings about the man, but Hobbs wasn't bad as frontier doctors go. I thought he'd done a good job on Tom, and I said so.

"Don't give a damn!" Tom ground out. "'Drather've had *you* do a lousy job than *him* do the best in the world. Don't even call him if I'm dying. I don't want his face to be the last thing I see."

Next on his mind was the pistol. He wanted to know where it was, and Millyanna glanced quickly at me before she answered.

"Where the hell's my gun?" he said. "You people deaf?"

Millyanna told him she had hung it and the belt in the closet with his clothes.

"Get it!" he grunted without looking at either of us. "Nobody but the man who kills me has the right to take my gun. — Hate to think that bastard Hobbs might have had the right."

I smiled because I could see the life coming back, but I felt deeply sad that it wasn't somehow filtered by what it had come through.

Very deliberately Millyanna went to the closet across from his bed and got out the heavy gun and belt. She laid them on the bed in a dark heap beside him. I could see the shiny barrel nosing out of its black coil like lightning sniffing through a storm cloud.

"Put it in my hand."

Suddenly Millyanna looked up at me with a helpless stare. Any one who didn't know her would have thought she was afraid to touch the thing. I figured it might do Tom some good at this point, so I reached over and unwound the black belt. The gun felt cold as something dead when I shoved it into his hand. I couldn't look back at Millyanna. Yet out of the corner of my eye I could see both of hers get full and shiny, though not a drop ran over.

A sort of lump came in my own throat as I watched Tom clutch that pistol. He barely had the strength to lift it. If he'd been dying, it would have seemed pitiful; but as it was, I felt something close to horror come over me.

"'S not loaded!" he said after a moment. He could tell just by weighing it in his hand that the cylinder was empty.

"Load it. — Load it for me."

I glanced at Millyanna. Her lip was trembling. And all the courage that kept back her tears couldn't keep back the rest.

Her whole being oozed out of those brown eyes in a wave more intense than tears could ever have been. With a sharp breath that was almost a groan she ran from the room.

"Tom —," I began when she had gone.

"God damn it, will you load it for me?"

I looked hard at him for a moment and then grabbed the gun from his hand and began loading it from his belt. I couldn't help noticing even then what a beautiful piece of machinery that pistol was. Tommy must have cleaned it for him since the morning I brought it home. I knew Millyanna wouldn't have touched it. It shone now like a new dollar that had forgotten it was only money. It had a heavy but comfortably solid feel. And I marvelled anew at its workmanship, at the way the parts moved and fit together.

I re-seated the cylinder and laid it loaded beside him on the bed. He covered it with his hand, letting his fingers play slowly over the gleaming barrel. He smiled faintly, still without looking at me.

"Tell him!" he murmured, finally. "Tell that damn' horse doctor what I said."

I left without a word and was glad to feel fresh air inside me when I reached the street. I lost no time passing the word to Doc Hobbs. And he understood me perfectly. He allowed that Hendley was one patient he felt damned glad to lose, no matter how.

I went by to see Tom every day while he was recovering. I think Gabby Macrae and I were just about his only visitors. But a lack of interest on the part of the town didn't seem to bother him. He was moving around his room after about a month. And though he had as little to say as ever, I could see the old restlessness coming again. Once he got clear of the bed, I usually found him sitting by one of the small windows in his room — not reading or anything, but just looking out, wondering (I suppose) how long it would be before he was out there again where his thoughts were.

"You seem to be recovering fast," I told him during one of my last visits. "I envy you."

"I'll make it!" he nodded with a confident smile. "But what are you envying me for?"

I sniffed and tried not to look as grim as I felt.

"The shoulder I got thrown on — it doesn't want to loosen up," I said. "Guess I'm just older than I thought."

My arm was out of the sling and strapping now. But it felt as though it was just nailed on, and I could hardly lift it above head level.

"I'm sorry, Sam. Are you taking care of it?"

Doc Hobbs was looking in on me regularly, but I didn't like to tell Tom that.

"Soaking it!" I smiled. "Every day I soak it — from the inside out."

Tom smiled back.

"The best medicine," he nodded. "That and time."

"Well, time is something I haven't much of. Besides, it's my gun arm that's gone. And a marshal without that is going to be out of a job one way or another pretty damned soon. When you're able to work again, I aim to turn the whole business over to you. What time I've got left I plan to spend on that piece of gravel I own, trying to whip it into a passable ranch."

"You gonna quit marshallin'?"

He looked at me like he didn't believe it.

"That's right. You've been doing most of the work anyhow. I figured you can handle the job — if you want it."

He grinned.

"I think I can handle it. But I'm sorry you're leaving, Sam. It'll be kind of funny, not having somebody around to give me hell about how much I like my work."

I took a deep breath.

"I never gave you hell about that and you know it. — It was about insisting that other people like your work — little Tommy, for instance."

His face clouded.

"Little Tommy ain't so little any more. He's old enough to know his own mind."

"He wasn't six years ago."

Tom was silent for a moment, that moustache a-tremble with more than his breath.

"I'm thinkin' —," he began slowly, "I'm thinkin' it's a good thing you got a bad arm — Mr. Marshal McCallum."

I stared back with what was left in a pair of old eyes that had seen better days, if not better men.

"Maybe it is," I said. "But I'm not just sure who for."

After a moment he broke into a smile that even lifted the ends of that drooping moustache.

"I'm sorry you're leaving, Sam. I'll miss you. And that's a fact."

He held out his hand. We shook for the first time in twenty-odd years, and I left.

I don't know whether what I had said made him get well faster or not. But he was out and walking the town in another two weeks. After that it wasn't long till he was on his horse again, doing just about whatever he felt like.

An awed silence followed him now wherever he went. The Silver Pick quieted down like a Sunday school when he walked in. And people who used to look the other way when they saw him coming quit their talking and watched him now till he got past. Sometimes they even flicked a hat brim his way if they thought he was looking. A ghost walking Paco's main street in daylight couldn't have had a more sobering effect. Some even said he *was* a ghost — that he'd left whatever flesh and blood was his up there in the Granite Hills with the Graysons' woman. It was amazing how the stories grew. I even heard that he'd made some deal with the devil — in the form of an Indian medicine man — and that as long as he stayed true to Satan, no bullet on earth could kill him! How much of it anybody believed, I never could be sure. But people believed in that silver cannon strapped to his leg. It was enough. That and the sight of him, Granite Hendley, hard as flint and liking it fine.

Not long after Tom got back on his feet, something else happened that Paco noticed. Mayor Garvey died one night of whatever it was that had plagued him for a long time already. He had some ailment Doc Hobbs didn't even know what to call, much less how to cure.

Garvey never had any children, and his wife was his only survivor. She was a funny, frail little woman with pale features and lemon-yellow hair. She looked even littler now that her husband was dead. But after that most people in town looked littler to me.

We laid him under the finest tombstone the territory could afford. Practically every one in town contributed to the price of it. Mrs. Garvey at first wouldn't hear of anybody else paying for her husband's rock. But we all knew the Mayor had nothing and that she would be needing whatever he'd left her. We told her we had already collected the price and that we couldn't give it back because we didn't know who had given how much.

Old Garvey got a good funeral, too — if such a thing can ever be considered good. The service was short, and the weather held cool and comforting as the place Parson Preble said Garvey had gone. The Paco graveyard was small in those days, and there wasn't even room in it for all the living who wanted to pay their last respects. Lots of people sat on the wood fence that went around outside while Preble made with some of the best burying words I think I ever heard. The hymn-singing was strong, and nobody looked drunk.

Garvey's passing was hard to take. I had missed him already — ever since he went into that last long illness. He had been the only old man I ever felt like talking with about the things that bothered me. In fact, by the time he died, he was just about the only man older than I in Paco. And *that* was hard to take, too.

If I could have, I would have gone to Garvey about turning over my badge to Tom. Maybe I should have talked to *somebody* anyway. But I didn't care much for the younger heads that seemed to have taken over running Paco — shopkeepers, saloon owners, and city types who centered around Nate Purvis and his money. "Stability" they talked about, and "respectability." But they had notions of those things a damned sight different from mine. The more I heard them talk, the prettier my own scrubby acres used to seem. I found myself wishing they were just a little farther from town.

As I look back now, I think, if I had cared more for Paco, I might have been able to do more for Tom. Anyway, if I'd known what was going to happen, I never would have left town. But I guess most of us, if we'd known what was coming, would have chosen to miss this world altogether — if we'd ever been given the choice.

11

Call of the Civilized

NOT LONG AFTER I'd given up marshalling, Nate Purvis of all people paid me a visit at the ranch. I don't know now exactly what he wanted; but that was (in part, at least) my fault.

I'd always thought Purvis was slick as eel guts; but I had other reasons for not being happy to see him. Frankly, I was having trouble with the ranch. My right arm and shoulder were still quite stiff, and getting around wasn't as easy as it had been. The water supply turned out unreliable, and clearing the worst of my land was slow and costly. I thought that in the next year or two I might have to borrow on the place, and I hated to have Purvis see the shape it was in.

I was saddling my horse out behind the house when he drove up in that shiny two-wheeled rig he'd brought back with him one time from Denver. I cinched up the girth and leaned over my horse with one arm around the pommel, watching him. He got down, huffing and puffing like he'd done a day's work, and walked over to where I was.

"Howdy, Mr. McCallum."

I nodded without saying anything.

"Well, aren't you going to ask me in?"

"No."

"No? Well, that's not very hospitable of you, to a man who's come all this way."

"No," I repeated.

"Meaning, no, it ain't very hospitable?"

"Meaning 'no' to whatever you came out here to ask."

"Well," he grunted, "you *are* a deep one, McCallum."

He paused and looked around at my house and land, wiping his forehead with a gleaming white handkerchief that must have come from a better place than Denver.

"Mighty hot out here," he went on, folding the handkerchief carefully and stuffing it back in his coat pocket.

"Mighty hot — and dry!" he added, looking at me sharply. "Hardly enough water to keep a *man* wet down, much less a herd."

"There's enough," I lied.

"Well," he went on, as if he hadn't heard. "I guess, if you stay out here long enough, you get used to it. — Me, I haven't been here long and the place seems dryer 'n a hundred hells."

"You can always leave."

He chose to ignore the remark and suddenly grinned at me.

"You want to talk out here in the sun, McCallum?"

"No."

"Meaning you want to talk somewhere else?"

"Meaning I don't want to talk. I got things to do."

"Well, I'm sure. I'm sure we all do," Purvis mumbled in an effort to sound good-natured. "But aren't you curious about why I came to see you?"

"Being curious never helped a man run a ranch."

"'*Ranch?*' You call this a ranch?" He waved his hand out at the dry sage that was almost crackling in the sun. "Looks more like a sodbuster's last stand!"

I made as if to get on my horse, and he walked over a step closer.

"McCallum!" he said quickly, "I think you'll be interested in what I've got to tell you."

He took a deep breath and tried to look sincere.

"Some of us in town feel we need a new mayor, now that old Garvey's left us. Seems to be some difference of opinion on who it should be."

Here he pulled a cigar from under his coat and looked at it as if it was too good to give away. I shook my head before he half-offered it to me.

"Some of my friends and I are going to put up a candidate," he went on. "We want you to be our man. What do you say?"

"I've already answered you."

He blinked at me a moment.

"Well, if you won't run —." He bit the end off his cigar. "Well, we hope to enlist your sympathies, if not your services. Will you support our man?"

"I've got a full-time job supporting myself," I muttered.

He lit his cigar and puffed at it, watching me closely all the time.

"You'll find some of the most substantial men in town on our side," he continued. "Men whose interests, I believe, are ultimately the same as yours. I think you'll find it worth your while, McCallum. — Will you give us your promise at least not to work for the opposition?"

I spat across my saddle without taking an eye off Purvis.

"I work for nobody but myself now," I told him, "and I make no promise I don't have to."

I wondered as I said it where else I might be able to borrow some money.

"Is that so?" Purvis spouted cigar smoke through a few irregular teeth. "Well, if you stay out of this business altogether, I guess that'll make us as happy as if you came in on our side."

"I'm doing it to make myself happy."

"Is that so? Well, — may you live to be happy!"

And with a flourish of his cigar and a crooked smile, Purvis turned to walk back to his rig. About that time my mare let fly with a noise I never hope to hear a human better.

"Well said, old girl!" I remarked loud enough for Purvis to hear.

He turned around with a sour grin:

"And goodbye to you, Mr. McCallum!"

I watched till he and his rig were off my land — as I hoped, forever.

I went to town no oftener than I had to now, since my shoulder didn't enjoy the trip. I knew little and cared less about any election in Paco. A couple of weeks later when Charlie Currus rode out to see me, I figured he had come about the same thing — though I knew he wouldn't have been on Purvis's side. (Charlie and I had talked Paco politics before.)

It was shortly after noon when Charlie arrived, and this time I was *unsaddling* after a morning's ride around my acres. I asked him in for the noon meal and offered him one of the two chairs I had to my name. We talked about the heat and what beef might bring and then I saw him squint one eye and suck in his breath the way he always did before coming to something important.

"No!" I grinned, waving my hand.

Charlie's gray eyes stared at me blankly.

"What the hell you mean, 'no'?" he said.

"I mean you've got my sympathy, but I'm not going to run for mayor or fight anybody else's campaign for 'em. I hope you beat that bank bastard, and I'll come to town to vote for you. But aside from that, — well, I'm a broken down cowman with a herd of my own to work. It's damned small but it's all mine, and it's a sight easier to handle than that gang in town."

Charlie picked up his hat and began playing with it.

"I knew you weren't interested in *that*," he said slowly. "I told 'em so — a few of my friends who wanted you for the job. — Anyway, Purvis and some of the 'city fathers' have put the election off for a while. I came out about something else."

"Something else going on?"

"Quite a bit," he nodded. "You ought to come to town more often, Sam. Or maybe you shouldn't have left."

"Why? What's that got to do with anything?"

"Maybe some of what's going on wouldn't be."

"Such as?"

"Such as — do you know who Marshal Hendley's new deputy is?"

"Can't say I much care. — But do *you* know how hard it is to find a good deputy around here?"

Charlie shook his head, though I knew it wasn't in response to my question.

"Sam," he said, looking at me suddenly, "it's young Tommy — his own *boy*."

The breath went out of me as though I'd been hit. Charlie was talking about a man, a full-grown twenty-year-old, who I knew was better able to take care of himself than most people seven or eight years his senior. But he scored the word "boy," thinking it would have an effect on me. It did.

"Charlie — Charlie, you can't mean it!"

He nodded slowly without taking his eyes off mine. My throat went dry as the hot breath blowing in my face through the door.

"How long — ," I swallowed hard — "how long's this been?"

Charlie shrugged.

"Couple weeks – maybe a month. Since not long after you left for good – or maybe I should say, 'for better or worse.'"

"What do you mean by that? – You think I could have stopped it?"

"I think you could've, if anybody could."

"That's just it. – *Could* anybody? What did Millyanna – Tom's wife – say?"

"From what I heard, she said plenty," Charlie went on. "I understand they had one hell of a fight about it – she and Hendley. But it didn't do any good. Hendley wanted it. And young Tommy wanted it. There wasn't much she could do."

I took a long breath and seemed to have trouble getting rid of it.

"Has the kid had to do anything yet?"

Charlie shrugged again.

"Hauled in a couple of drunks once. And broke up a fight the other night. He's handled himself pretty well for such a damned colt. Doesn't say much. Just mighty steady, and all business. In fact, I've got some admiration for the kid."

Charlie hesitated and twirled his hat half a turn on his hand.

"But –?" I suggested.

"'But,' hell!" Charlie growled. "You know how people in Paco are. Indian for a peace officer! Hell fire, man – most of 'em take it as a personal insult. If it wasn't for the boy's father, the kid would have gotten a free ride out of town two weeks ago – with a bucket of tar to cool his pride."

"He's *not* an Indian!" I snapped. "At least, he's only *half* Indian. And, I'm beginning to think, the better half. – What do they want in that damned town – a man who keeps the peace or a peace that's not worth keeping?"

"*You* know what they want, Sam. — If God Almighty came to Paco as an Indian, they'd run him to hell out! — And if young Tommy doesn't *look* that much like an Indian, there are some who claim a bucket of tar might remind him what color he *is*. Like a young snake on his back, they say — just needs to be turned over so he can crawl away."

"Who've you heard talk like that?" I glared at him. Charlie threw up his hat and his free hand and leaned back in his chair.

"Talk's cheap, Sam. You can hear worse than that if you're close enough."

"Thank God I'm not close enough," I muttered.

Charlie gave me a sour little laugh.

"That's not the worst of it!" He shook his head deliberately. "It's past the talking stage. Now they're going to *do* something about it."

"*Do* something? You mean they're going to lynch him?"

"No, no, Sam!" Charlie shook his head again. "There isn't a lynch mob in the territory that would stand up to Granite Hendley. They know what to expect from him. And they know they'd have to deal with him, if they went for the boy. — No, this is something a lot more subtle."

He paused and rumpled his yellow hair with the hand that wasn't holding his hat.

"Something with a mind behind it," he went on. "A mind and some money. A way to get the kid and at the same time strike at the old man *through* him. Wrap it all up neat and quick."

"What the hell you talking about?"

"You ever hear of Lafe Colber?" he asked quickly.

"Lafe Colber — Lafe Colber. — I remember circulars on him from the days when I was marshal. Wanted in connection with a shooting in Dodge City. As I recall, they tried and hanged some other body for the murder."

Charlie nodded.

"They shouldn't have. Lafe's no good. A drifter who hires his gun out when he can't make a living any easier way. He's a pretty good gun, too, from what I've heard. But he usually plays where the stakes are high — Dodge, Abilene, Silver City. Doesn't fool around with towns in the butt end of a moth-eaten territory like ours."

Charlie stopped and scratched his chin.

"But you know something? He's in Paco right now. I saw him this morning before I came here."

I swallowed hard.

"Must have taken a lot of money to make Lafe Colber come to Paco," Charlie went on. "A lot of money."

"Whose money?" I swallowed again.

"Whose do you think? Only one person I know of in Paco with money enough to count on buying a bath at the end of the week. — And from what I hear, *he's* got a tub right in his own damned house."

I couldn't do anything but sit there for a moment.

"What do you think's going to happen, Charlie?"

He took a deep breath.

"Well, I've *heard* Lafe Colber came down here just to take on the kid. He didn't want to tangle with Hendley, but would if he had to — for twice what he's getting to fight the kid. He came by himself, which means he won't make his play as long as Hendley and the boy are together. It's my guess that, if and when he ever gets 'em apart, he'll jump the kid and then try to get the hell out before Hendley can catch him."

Charlie stopped and fixed his cool, gray eyes on me.

"That is," he went on, from under that gray stare, "unless somebody makes Colber get the hell out first."

That look came from a long way back. It was the way I remembered he used to look after he and I had had some disagreement back in our range-riding days, when I was foreman over him. It almost made me afraid now, but somehow thankful, too.

12

To Satan's Gates

I SAT AND STARED at Charlie Currus for a long minute or two. Lines had come in both our faces since we looked at each other for the first time, on horseback, across that lifelong red sea of cattle. I'd respected him then as a man who tried to do an honest day's work, and now I thought how little he had changed in spite of his lines. I found myself hoping he felt the same about me.

"I guess it's harder than I thought to retire," I told him. "What are we waiting for?"

I was still pretty spry for an old man, and I was almost out the door before Charlie realized it. He was after me in an instant, though. And as I went through the door, I heard his voice right behind me:

"Sam!"

I turned and he was holding out his hand. I grabbed it. And if it had been Lafe Colber's throat, we wouldn't have had to go any farther.

"Lend me that damned horny hand saddlin' up, and we'll be on the road a lot quicker!" I said.

My mare and I were ready to ride in a matter of minutes. I was about to swing myself up when Charlie hollered:

"You look naked, for Christ's sake! Where the hell's your iron?"

I noticed Charlie had a Winchester alongside his saddle, in addition to the .44 he always carried on his gunbelt. But many things had gone through my mind while he was talking to me. I remembered old Garvey and how he had seemed to get things done without ever carrying a gun in his life. — "Gray hair and guts on the end of a black cigar!" — I smiled as I thought about him. My hair was gray enough by now, and against my right arm I could feel the reassuring nudge of a lone cigar through the front of my open vest. — About the rest of the formula I wasn't so sure. But I'd made up my mind about the gun.

"I'm leavin' it home, Charlie."

"Are you out of your head?" he gasped. "Lafe Colber's no damned Sunday-school kid!"

"I'm leavin' it home," I repeated.

"For Christ's sake! — Colber's knocked over some good men in his day. Been known to shoot at least one in the back. And that's the same as shooting a man who hasn't a gun. If you get in his way, don't expect him to hold back just because you're unarmed."

"When a man gets to be my age," I said, "it's time he learned to count on something better than a gun."

I turned my mare's head toward Paco and gave her the spur.

"Of all the damned fools —!" I heard Charlie growl as he got under way beside me. I believe I even chuckled, though I had a sick feeling he was probably right.

We made it to town without a word, harsh or otherwise. I remember thinking then, maybe for the first time, that the country around us even looked beautiful in a thoughtless, sun-baked way. The dirty white of the rock hills back of Paco faded up into tawny sky that was just beginning to show the red of a dying day. And the flats and rolls of earth that stretched away to the south bunched up brown and crusty like half-baked loaves in an open oven. I had seen it all a thousand times and thought God couldn't have made it uglier, even if he'd put his mind to it. Why it looked better to me then, I had no idea. Maybe toward the end of his day a man feels more content with where he is.

When we reached Paco, my watch showed a quarter to five. Hendley's house was on the way into town, and I decided to make that our first stop. We reined up and I asked Charlie to wait outside. He was more than willing.

I don't know whom I had expected to find there – Millyanna for sure, Tom maybe. The boy was the only one I wasn't prepared to see. He was there, though. And when I saw him, I felt glad at least to know where he was.

It sounded like Tom and Millyanna were both talking at once when I walked up on the low front porch. They stopped when my boot hit the first step. Tom knew my knock – and my walk, too, I guess. He hollered me in without moving to meet me and didn't even turn around as I entered.

Before I had time to say hello, I could feel the tension. Tom was standing by the front door, his fists on his hips, tight-lipped and hard-faced as ever. The boy was across the room from him, standing with thumbs stuck in the top of his gunbelt. And he had a wild-eyed, expectant look about him that the grim set of his mouth couldn't hide. But Millyanna! One look at her would have seared the soul of a statue – or given it one to sear. She stood between them, proud and straight as a spearshaft, fists clenched and her eyes hot as two live coals.

"What are *you* doin' in town this side of Saturday night?" Tom said without looking at me.

I glanced first at Millyanna and then at the boy. But they both had their eyes fixed on Tom.

"I came to talk to you," I said, licking the dust from my lips.

No one moved or said a word, and I could hear a lazy fly buzz against the screen door in back of me.

"Then talk — and talk fast," Tom said.

I looked again at the others, but their faces showed no change.

"Could we — could we step outside for a minute?"

"That's about all we can step outside for," Tom muttered. "Go ahead."

I turned and opened the door. Tom hadn't moved, and I glanced back at him as I stepped onto the porch.

"Look to your mother, boy," he said and followed me out.

"What the hell's goin' on?" I asked in a low voice, when we were facing each other.

"You think it's your business?"

He tilted his chin at me; and the evening sun, catching the gray ends of his moustache, made them look almost white.

"In view of how long I've known you — the *three* of you — I think it is."

He turned away from the sun and glanced at the door of his house.

"Lafe Colber's in town," he said, turning back to me suddenly.

"Charlie Currus told me," I nodded. "So?"

"So I sent my boy — my deputy — to tell him to get to hell out."

"Did Colber leave?"

Hendley laughed silently in spite of himself.

"You know who Lafe Colber is?" he asked.

"I know he's no good — for you, Tommy, Paco — anybody. I'm damned glad you moved him on."

Tom looked serious.

"He's good for something. He's a son of a bitch, I know — but a damned good gun. Not so good that Tommy can't take him. But a damned good gun."

"So? Has he left town or not?"

Hendley laughed again — this time out loud.

"*Hell*, no, he hasn't left town! — If he'd left as soon as the kid told him, he wouldn't be *worth* the takin'!"

"What do you mean? What's happened?"

"Tommy told him to get out by five this afternoon — or get ridden out on the end of a .44. He was goin' uptown to finish the job when *you* showed up."

"Tom, don't let him!" I burst out. "Can't you see, you're playing right into their hands! They *want* Tommy to face off with Colber. They *want* him to go out there and get killed —"

"Who the hell's 'they'?" Tom interrupted.

I took a deep breath.

"Everybody around here who hates Indians," I said quietly, " — and who hates half-breeds maybe worse."

His whole body down to the ends of his moustache seemed to stiffen.

"Watch what you say to me, McCallum!" he got out between his teeth.

"Tom, I wouldn't have said it if I thought there was any other way. — Why else would Lafe Colber come here? A gambler and a paid killer! There aren't any high stakes in Paco — nothing for a hired gun to do. Charlie Currus is convinced — and so am I — that they've paid Colber to come down here and pick a fight with Tommy — because they don't want an Indian marshal. And you're just makin' it easier for 'em."

"Well, damn their eyes!" Tom came back at me hard. "My kid can take ten of Lafe Colber. — I hope to hell they paid him in advance!"

He turned and spat over the end of the porch.

"I figured before, and I still do," he went on, "it's a good opportunity for the boy to show his stuff. I taught him myself and I'm damned proud of him. I'll be there to see he doesn't get jumped by somebody else. And if it's a fight Lafe Colber wants, why, he'll sure as hell get it."

"Tom, you can't lick a whole town that way."

"The hell I can't. I know this town. It hasn't got the backbone of a cream puff."

"Tom, even if the boy *does* knock off Colber, they'll just get somebody else."

"Let 'em."

"Tom, there doesn't have to *be* a fight. Let *me* go and get that gunner to leave. There won't *be* any blood on the streets or on your boy's hands. This whole business can be settled without shooting."

He cut me off with a quiet little laugh.

"What the hell?" he chuckled, glancing down at where my pistol usually hung. "Bare as a baby's ass! You turned preacher or somethin'?"

The front door opened and young Tommy stepped out before I could answer his father. Millyanna followed him. She came over and stood behind Tom, who was still looking at me with that damned smug smile.

"It's time I went," the boy said, quietly.

"Don't take my boy from me!" she murmured. "My boy — only a boy!"

All of a sudden I felt almost dizzy with fear.

"She's right, Tom," I told him quickly. "If you won't let me handle it, go yourself. Leave the boy here. Lafe Colber's been a killer since almost before your son was born. Leave the kid at home. — There'll be other opportunities."

Tom looked at Millyanna a moment, then turned back to me. It was almost a smile that crossed his face then, but it froze the sweat-soaked shirt to my back.

"Hell!" he grinned, "you and me are both too old, Sam. It's a young man's game, this keeping the peace. — And as for my son, well, you've got him wrong. He's not a kid — not any more! *Are* you?"

He turned quickly toward the boy, who was standing six or eight feet from us on the other side of the porch. Before I knew what was happening, Tom had whipped out his plated .45 and tossed it across the intervening space at Tommy. The boy didn't flinch or even move — except for his right hand, which swung up nimbly from the elbow and caught the heavy pistol just where it would have struck him in the stomach. I thought I heard a little cry escape Millyanna, but I forgot it as I watched the slow, deep smile that broke on the face of the boy.

"You're a man now," his father went on, "so it's time you put away childish things. — Leave me yours, and then go do your duty."

Still smiling, the boy broke the shiny .45 to check its load. Then he tossed his own .44 to his father. I found I couldn't take my eyes off the youngster! I watched him spin the .45 and move it up and down with his wrist, feeling that easy balance against the heel of his hand. It was almost the way his father had looked that night when I first put my Navy Colt in his hands, all those years ago.

The boy turned and started down the steps. I watched him, unable to move, as he passed Charlie Currus and the horses and headed for the center of town. I don't think I heard Tom's footsteps as he left the porch to follow his son, but I was aware of his going. I felt as though in a dream, or like a drowning man watching his whole life pass before him in an agonized moment of time.

I came to with a jolt as I felt Millyanna's grip on my arm. And then I heard Charlie Currus holler at me, wanting to know what the hell was happening. Millyanna's grip, desperate on my arm, tightened beyond even what I thought her strength could be. I looked at her helplessly as her lips trembled.

"Sam — you good — brave man!" she said slowly. "Stop this gunfight. Bring back my boy!"

I remember being enough myself to marvel at how well she had learned to speak English. I glanced down at my arm, wondering if she was trying to squeeze it in two. Immediately she relaxed her grip and dropped the hand to her side. I glanced away at Hendley's back, and farther off at his son's. A thousand thoughts must have gone through my mind then. I could feel a hot wave of something I'd better call anger well up inside and throw itself against the wall of my brain.

"It's gone too far!" I shook my head at her. "Nobody can stop this thing now."

And then it struck me like a cold-water dousing.

"Except *you!*" I added. "You might have a chance!"

"Me?" She stepped back and looked at me strangely. "Me — what — how?"

"The boy loves you," I said. "You can get out there and put yourself between the two of 'em before the shooting starts. If Tommy saw you in front of him, he wouldn't go through with it. I *know* he wouldn't! Once you get him out of this, your husband and I can send that gunslinger on his way. — And it's this time or never, Millyanna. If you don't stop *this* fight, you'll never be able to keep the boy from it as long as he lives."

She stood there and looked at me for a moment — proud, beautiful, impassive. And through those dark cheeks framed in night-black hair she blushed like the evening above her.

"Well — what do you say?" I asked her.

She said nothing. Instead, without taking her eyes off mine, she began tucking up her skirt. And the next thing I knew, with hardly a sound from her moccasined feet, she was off the porch, out the yard gate, and running down the street after her husband.

I took off after her, making the best time I could, till a cry from Charlie Currus stopped me. I had my eye and mind on Millyanna, and I'd almost passed him without realizing it.

"Sam!" he yelled, damned near in my ear, "what the hell's going on?"

"The kid wants to shoot it out with Colber, and his mother's gone to stop it. Come on! We're late."

I was running by then, trying to catch Millyanna and feeling my age with every step.

"Do we need the horses?" Charlie hollered.

"Hell, no!" I called over my shoulder. I had trouble enough without my mare picking up a stray bullet.

Millyanna was only eight or ten yards ahead of me now, and I was gaining on her. The town was awfully quiet around us, but I kept thinking it just seemed that way because of what I was almost afraid to hear. And then we turned the last corner.

I felt suddenly sick as I looked up the dusty little wagon track we called main street. Tom was standing not far in front of us against a corner of the post office. Millyanna was almost up to him. And young Tommy was out in the middle of the street, walking deliberately toward the solitary figure standing in front of the Blue Chip, waiting.

Not another living thing was in sight. Horses, and even dogs, had been cleared off the street. Doors were closed, store windows boarded up, shades drawn. The very dust in the street seemed to be lying low for a reason. In a white flash it hit me. Everybody in town must have known this was coming! And to have known about it and done nothing meant to have had a hand in it. I felt sick and mad and so helpless I almost forgot to breathe.

Tom heard my heavy step, I'm sure, before he heard Millyanna. He turned and stared at us, absolutely amazed.

"What the hell — ?" he began.

Millyanna had almost passed him without stopping, but he reached out and grabbed her on the run. He pulled her to him and stepped back quickly behind the corner of the building.

"You out of your mind, woman?" he hissed. "Go home! This is no place for you!"

"No!" she shook her head. "I go home with my boy."

Tom glanced at me.

"Get her the hell home, Sam," he snapped. "She's got no business here."

"She *does!*" I told him, stopping to catch my wind. I was still at the corner of the building where I could keep an eye on the street. She and Tom were little more than a foot away, he holding her to him with her head pushed up against his shoulder and glaring at me like I was to blame for her being there. In that split second I thanked God I was.

"She *does*. She's the only one who can talk sense into that fool kid of yours. Let her do it before it's too late."

By now Tommy was about forty yards from the silent figure in front of the Blue Chip. The boy was still walking. He had the same deliberate gait his father used. And all the time, as if without any effort at all, his right hand never moved more than an inch from the white handle of that silver gun.

Hendley looked as though he wanted to bite me in half. In an instant he had pinned Millyanna so she couldn't move. Her right arm was immobile against his chest and her left, caught below the elbow by his own left hand and arm that circled her narrow body. With his right he shoved the muzzle of Tommy's pistol against my chest, under my left armpit. I hadn't even seen him draw!

"Now you listen to me," he ground out. "If you so much as make a move, I'll lay you in the dirt till this thing is over. I won't kill you, Sam, but I'll put a slug where it'll salt you down good. If you can't learn it any other way, by God I'll teach you like that: anybody coming between me and what I think good for my son is in trouble."

I knew he meant it even before I heard the hammer go back. As I looked into those stone-colored eyes, I knew I'd never been closer to taking on lead. I just stood there — turned my head away and concentrated on the two men in the street. In a moment I heard Tom, still holding Millyanna, move around behind me to the other side where he could see, too. In the process he shifted his gun to the small of my back. I waited, anxious to hear him drop that hammer down. He never did.

By now, Tommy was about thirty yards from Lafe Colber. He stopped a moment and looked over the tall, thin man standing in the street before him. Colber had on dark gray pants and a double-breasted vest to match. The ends of a string bowtie hung down over it. His hat was lighter — gravestone gray, you might call it. And he was wearing two guns in a wide black belt slung low on his hips. All in all, he could have passed for a Paco fashion plate — right down to the couple days' growth on his face. He grinned when Tommy asked if he was about to leave town.

"Not for you, squaw-boy!" Colber belted back.

Whether this rattled the kid, I couldn't tell. His voice came out clear and firm:

"Then look out for yourself. I mean to make you."

I saw Tommy square his shoulders and shift his weight to move in on his man. Colber suddenly stuck out his chin like a snapping turtle looking for flies.

"Just a minute, kid!" he called.

Tommy stood his ground.

"That's fancy artillery you got on!" Colber said. "I like to bet when I draw cards. Something to make the draw interesting. Maybe you'd like a little bet on this one. Say, my guns — both of 'em — against that shiny one you got on. — Winner take all."

The boy hesitated. I was afraid for a minute he was going to take his eyes off Colber long enough to turn and look at his old man. In my heart I cursed that silver pistol. Everybody in the territory must have heard about it by now. And here was this cheap gundog, trying to trick a green youngster into looking away for that fraction of a second that would mean getting in the first shot. Colber must have known Hendley was watching — had probably seen him standing down by the post office before I got there. I ground my teeth helplessly, but the noise in my head didn't drown the whisper I heard from Millyanna — from wherever her lips were, muffled behind me against Tom's heavy shoulder.

"Jesus forgive us!" she murmured.

I must have made some movement — whether to go toward Tommy or just to turn and look at the face of his father, I don't rightly know. But I felt that pistol stab me like a knife. I groaned and stood there, my eyes fixed on the two still figures in front of me.

"What do you say?" Colber went on. "Tell you what: I'll throw in my horse — sorrel gelding 'round at Thompson's stable. If I lose, I figure I won't be needing him."

Tommy hadn't moved, but still he said no word. I held my breath for fear he would turn around. I knew Hendley was too proud to open his mouth to the boy now. I hoped the kid would have sense enough to say nothing and go for his man. But I ought to have figured — as Colber must have — that young Tommy had some pride of his own.

"You're on, Colber!" he snapped suddenly, and started walking.

The sun was almost directly behind Tommy, but it had gone down far enough to let cool shadows take over the street. And Colber looked almost like one of them — thin, dark, biding his time. As Tommy got closer, I saw Colber slowly turn half-sideways, his right hip slightly forward. It looked so casual you could hardly tell he was trying to make a knife-edge of himself.

And then it happened. Tommy was within twenty yards of him, and I couldn't tell who drew first. But as I watched, I remember thinking Lafe Colber had a rattlesnake for a right arm. He whipped that gun up in one black blur of motion with a little red dot of fire in the middle. And he dropped to one knee as he fired.

I didn't hear but one discharge and it was all over. They'd both fired together, and but for the smoke from the silver pistol I could hardly tell that Tommy had fired. He had stopped when he drew, and now he swayed forward a little as though he was going to keep on walking. But the gun slipped from his fingers, hitting the street in a little puff of dust quiet as a raindrop. And almost before the pistol struck, the kid followed it down. His hat rolled forward as his head hit, and his legs in their loose black pants bunched under him like a coil of rope.

Lafe Colber, gun still in hand, was on his feet walking toward the boy before any of us could believe what had happened. I heard something hit the ground behind me, and right away the ache was gone from my back. I turned quickly and looked at Hendley. His face was like snow and his eyes seemed to be coming out of his head. Young Tommy's pistol with the hammer still back was lying by Hendley's foot. He'd been holding Millyanna so she couldn't see the shooting, but now his arms were limp as if they'd been broken. Millyanna turned and looked down the street. I heard her catch her breath sharply, but she didn't scream.

I looked back at Colber. He was holding that gleaming gun in his hand by now. He had holstered his own, and I saw him grin down like a goat as he turned the big pistol over in his hands.

I had just started toward him when I heard something between a scream and a tortured sigh behind me. But it came from Hendley, not Millyanna. I turned in time to see him drop like a sack and clutch at the dirt with his fists before he lost consciousness. Millyanna couldn't have helped but hear him, yet her eyes were fixed on the twisted body in the street.

She left Hendley without a glance and ran to her boy. I followed her, but she was kneeling in the dust beside him, cradling his head on her breast, long before I got there. Colber simply stood and watched her, still with that goat-grin on his face. I don't think she even knew he was there. She didn't even know I was. And as she had lifted the father, she lifted the son in her own strong arms and started slowly home.

I saw her face as she passed me, the immortal face of woman in pain. Her dark eyes were cast down into the form at her breast; and out of the corner of one of them the tears she had held for this boy, this moment, came in a slow and silent stream.

13
Mourning

AS I WALKED toward Lafe Colber, I heard doors opening around me. Here and there boots began to slither along the board sidewalks. And the low mutter of voices came to me as the town began to put out its head. I didn't look to the right or left. I just kept on walking.

Colber watched me uneasily as I approached. He glanced down at the silver pistol when I stopped in front of him. Almost compulsively he shoved it into the top of his pants. I looked him up and down and noticed then for the first time the ragged slash across the left front of his vest. Tommy's bullet went a little wide, and I wondered whether Colber had felt it—whether he realized even now just how lucky he'd been.

"Get out of town, Colber!" I said. "Get out fast and get out far before that boy's father cuts you up like you deserve."

Colber grinned at me.

"Who the hell are you?" he grunted. "You're not wearing a star. Don't even have a gun."

"I got something better."

I even managed a grin of my own before I swung.

It was the last punch I ever threw — the last good thing I did with my old right arm. It caught Lafe Colber just above the mouth. I felt his teeth slice into my knuckles at the same time the shock swept down from my shoulder. It was as if the pain came up my spine and strapped the whole right side of me in a thong of fire.

Colber went down on his back and writhed there with his hands across his face. In a moment he rolled away from me and managed to get on his feet again. His nose was twisted to one side and he was spitting blood as he reached for his gun.

I was too far from him now and in too much pain to jump him. I just stood there and watched, my right arm hanging on me like the dead limb of a tree. Except for the pain in my arm and side I felt nothing but a desperate calm. For the first time in my life I didn't care what happened to me. I wasn't even sure I was still alive.

Colber must have been dazed from the blow. He wasn't so fast getting his gun up. It was one of his own — the one he'd shot young Tommy with. Why he didn't use Hendley's, I don't know. But the one he pulled was good enough. He'd already proved that.

It came up slowly like he wanted to make sure he didn't miss. His hand was shaking as I saw him cock the thing. And then I heard a roar that sounded as though it came from all around me. I blinked. And when my eyes opened, I saw Lafe Colber's gun spinning out of his hand. He clutched the hand to him in a tight little fist, and I saw he was bleeding from that now as well as his mouth and nose.

I turned around and there behind me was Charlie Currus, his Winchester still smoking. He had led his horse a pace or two into the street by the post office and was steadying his rifle across the saddlebow. I don't know why, considering the way I had felt a second before, but I was never happier to see a friend in all my lorn, born days!

Charlie walked around his horse, still holding the rifle on Colber, and came slowly toward us.

"Get to hell out, you and your God-damned guns!" he said. "Don't come back here even for your funeral."

Colber looked first at me and then at Charlie. He was breathing hard, and he tried to swallow. But the blood and the pain must have gagged him. He retched on the ground at his side.

"I'm goin'!" he said finally, wiping his mouth with the back of his good hand. "I'm goin'."

He backed a couple of steps away from us, looking wild as an animal out of a trap. He didn't even stop to pick up his hat or the pistol Charlie had shot from his hand. He backed until his boot hit the sidewalk in front of the Blue Chip. Then he turned and went quickly up the steps inside. I never saw him or Hendley's pistol again.

As soon as Colber was out of my sight, I became aware of the faces hovering in doors and windows and on the sidewalk around me — the same faces who had lived there, watching me grow old as marshal. Not one of them had lifted a finger when Lafe Colber was about to kill me in the street before their eyes. I looked about me into some of the faces I thought I'd known better than others. Eyes dropped and boots shuffled as an occasional head tried to slip behind its neighbor.

Nobody said a word to me, and God knows I said nothing to them. There was absolute silence in that street — except that the blood of Tommy Hendley cried from where it was turning black. But nobody seemed to hear it.

The faces suddenly began to blur as I felt the first tears I had known since childhood rise inside me. Tears, not from an aching arm, but from an old man who didn't have any more strength to fight. I breathed deep and kept them down. I don't think even Charlie Currus knew they were there. Though maybe he did.

"We better go, Sam," I heard him say, quietly. He was standing behind me to the right, still holding his Winchester

ready with one hand. The other he placed lightly on my
shoulder. I almost fainted from the pain!

I turned away, stepping from under that hand, trying not
to let him see how much it hurt. I took one final look around
at what were no more than ghosts to me now. I looked till I
spotted the puffy gray mask I knew as the face of Nathan Purvis.
He stared back at me from the verandah of the Blue Chip,
blank-looking but unashamed. And without taking my eyes off
his, I spat in the street in front of me.

I turned my back then and started away from that wilderness
of white faces. Charlie Currus came with me, the black snout
of his Winchester poking along between us like the muzzle of a
faithful dog. When we got to the corner of the post office, I
almost stumbled over Hendley. God, there he was, flat on the
ground where he'd fallen! Nobody had done a thing about
him.

With my left hand I picked up the cocked pistol that was
still lying next to his foot. I eased the hammer down and
shoved the gun into Tom's holster.

"You'll have to heft him, Charlie," I said. "My right arm's
gone."

"Christ!" Charlie swore. "That *was* your bad arm you hit
him with! How's it feel?"

"Like hell. But my left is all right. Let's get him onto your
horse."

Between us we got Hendley home and laid him in his own
bed. He was still out cold, short of breath, and I didn't have
any idea what was wrong with him. I thought Doc Hobbs
ought to see him, in spite of what Hendley had told me before.
So I sent Charlie Currus to get him.

"Hobbs is probably at the Blue Chip, if he's in town," I
told Charlie. "Drop over to the jail and get Gabby Macrae to
fetch him."

Charlie left, and I took Tom's gunbelt off and hung it in the closet. When I went to have a look at young Tommy, the house was so quiet I couldn't help expecting the worst. Millyanna was waiting for me at the door of his room. When I asked whether I could help her with the boy, she looked quickly at the floor.

"Millyanna," I said when she didn't answer, "I've taken bullets out of people before. Let me look at him."

"Nothing — nothing to do!" She looked up at me with suddenly dry eyes. "No one can help my boy."

"He's dead?"

She didn't answer but opened the narrow door behind her. A single lamp was burning in the room, its dim light warming the rough wood bed I remembered watching Hendley make a short lifetime ago. And on it — the too-still figure with its up-turned boots and the blanket stretching to cover the pillowed head.

"He died quickly!" Her voice came gentle through tears that were no more. "A hateful death, but he died quickly. — For me now is to save the life that is left. How is my husband?"

I stumbled back from the lamplit room and was glad to hear her pull the door to behind me. I had to tell her I didn't know what was wrong with Tom but that I had sent for Doc Hobbs. She looked at me sharply when I mentioned that name.

"You know the thing that is best," she said deliberately and then vanished noiselessly into Tom's room.

Charlie Currus came back shortly and told me Gabby had gone for the doctor. To ease my arm in the meantime, he helped me make a sling for it out of one of Hendley's old bandanas. Charlie had gotten himself something to eat while he was out, but I wasn't hungry and just had a pull from the bottle he'd picked up over at the jail. It was probably mine anyway. Millyanna wanted nothing to eat. She remained alone at Tom's bedside.

It was late before Doc Hobbs arrived. He looked at me hard but didn't say a word when I met him at the door. I took him into the bedroom, and Millyanna and I both stayed while he looked at Tom. He took his time about it and gave Tom as complete a going-over as I guess he ever had — even looked into his unopened eyes.

"Must have had a stroke or a heart attack from the shock," he told us, when he'd finished. "Still seems paralyzed. I have a hard time even feeling a pulse."

Hobbs stood up from the bedside and wiped off on his shirtsleeve. The little bedroom was hell-hinge hot with two kerosene lamps and the four of us burning away.

"There's not much I can do," he said in a tired voice. "His throat's clear and I can give him the strongest restorative I've got. He may wake up, and then again he may not."

Millyanna looked questioningly at me.

"Do what you can," I told him.

Hobbs dug a small vial of red liquid out of the beat-up black bag he carried. And with Millyanna supporting Tom in the bed, he succeeded in pouring a little of it on Tom's tongue. Millyanna let his head go back on the heavy pillow, and Hobbs packed his medical gear without another word. He had a quick look at my arm and, after strapping it up as he had before, took off.

"Colber is gone," he told me, as he was leaving. "And just between you and me, I think Hendley'll be gone by sun-up."

It must have been half an hour before Tom showed any effect from the medicine. Millyanna and I had both stayed by the bedside, and at the end of that time we saw his eyes begin to move. When he got them open, they rolled over like a couple of pendulums, fixing first on Millyanna, then on me. His jaw dropped down and I heard his throat click a couple of times as he tried to speak.

"Rest. Rest!" I told him, as I saw he was having trouble forming words.

He acted as though he hadn't heard. He kept on moving his mouth, though no sound came. He was trying to say something, his eyes fixed now on Millyanna. But neither of us could make out what it was. The lips moved again and again in the same way, and the Adam's apple kept bobbing down and back between the strings of his throat. Millyanna glanced at me and then put her face down close to his lips.

"What is it? What is it?" she whispered.

His eyes came alive with a new strength as her troubled face approached his own. The lips continued to work and suddenly I heard a hoarse whisper that seemed to fill the room:

"My gun — my gun — my gun —!"

Millyanna drew back with a look of helpless horror. I heard her gasp as the same two words kept coming from the moving mouth on the pillow. She had been sitting on the bed beside him but she got up now, almost involuntarily. Unable to look away from him, she took one faltering step backward and then another till she hit the wall. With the back of one hand to her lips she struggled to suppress the low groan that wracked her whole body.

I was on the other side of the bed, and God knows it was hard enough for *me* to look at those cavernous eyes and listen to him ask for the gun. I leaned over close to his face myself and said — probably louder than I should have:

"Rest. *Rest*, for Christ's sake!"

The noise must have shocked him. His mouth stopped moving and the eyes rolled over to burn themselves out on me. But they closed before they could, and his breathing became almost regular for a change.

I stood up and glanced at Millyanna. She was still leaning back against the wall. The hand was down from in front of her face, and she looked as though she almost had hold of herself. She took a deep breath, which I saw made her shiver in spite of the heat. And when the knock came at the door, she looked to me to answer it.

I walked over and opened the door on Charlie Currus. I'd almost forgotten about him! He had insisted on sticking around as long as I did, and he'd heard me holler from out on the front porch where he was sitting. I told him nothing was wrong, and he went back out on the porch.

As he walked away, I suddenly realized how tired I was. My arm felt a little better, thanks to a drink or two and Doc Hobbs's strapping. But the pain had spread to my head by now, and I told Millyanna I would have to go in the parlor and lie down for a while. I asked her to call me if anything happened. Hendley's couch was too short for me, so I stretched on the floor with a rolled-up coat beneath my head. It wasn't very comfortable, but I wasn't used to comfort. And at that point I could have slept in a frying pan.

I was out almost as soon as my head touched that coat, but my sleep couldn't have lasted more than an hour or two. It was deep, though. Millyanna had to shake me out of it. I remember lying there on my back, sensing a pain that I thought would tear me apart. When I cracked my eyes, I caught a glimpse of Millyanna, squatting on the floor beside me. She was tugging very gently at my good arm, but the movement made me feel it in the other and I almost screamed.

"All right. All right!" I groaned, and she stopped.

She was holding one of the lamps, and the light wouldn't let me look at her.

"My husband sleeps no more!"

Her voice came quivering at me from behind that blinding light.

"He asks for his gun. — Over and over he asks!"

I began to be aware of a faint noise from the other room. In spite of the pain I was still half asleep.

"Go to him," I mumbled. "Go to him. I'll be there as soon as I can."

She went without a sound, taking the lamp with her.

I rolled over on my good side and tried to sit up. The pain came back on me, and another wave of sleep in spite of it. I staggered to my feet finally and groped around in the half-light from the bedroom for the bottle Charlie had brought. I found it and drained off enough to wake me the rest of the way.

Tom sure as hell did sleep no more. His eyes looked hotter than the whiskey I had inside. The skin stretched tight across the bones of his face and shone in the lamplight, white as the sheet he was lying on. His moustache lay along his lip like a wisp of black smoke.

He stopped his moaning when I walked in. I went around to the far side of his bed and stood there opposite Millyanna. His eyes rolled with me as I walked. Rage, fear — I don't know what was in them. But they looked as though they never *had* slept — and certainly would no more.

"What's the matter, Tom?" I asked quietly. "What is it?"

I heard the clicking in his throat again, but his voice came through strong and clear this time:

"My gun — my gun!"

I glanced quickly at Millyanna.

"For many times — many times — that is all he says."

She was looking down at him quietly now. And as I watched, a single tear made its way over her long-lashed eyelid. The lamplight caught it as it travelled down across her copper cheek. It looked like a running seam of gold against the earth-colored flesh.

I could hardly make myself look back at Hendley. He was still staring at me, his trembling lips hoarsely framing the words,

"My gun — my *gun* . . . !"

I took a deep breath and started for the closet.

"Maybe I can quiet him," I told Millyanna. But she never took her eyes off Hendley.

With my back to the bed, I opened the door and reached in for the pistol of Tommy's that I had hung there earlier. It was clumsy, trying to do it with one hand; but I broke it and managed to empty the cartridges onto a shelf. I left them there and turned back to the bed. He was still watching me as I walked back with the pistol and stood beside him. It was an old .44 — nothing like his own. But I thought it might calm him to feel it.

"Here," I said. "In your right hand."

And I reached across him and shoved it into his fist. His fingers closed around it, but he never took his eyes off mine. I'll remember that look as long as I live. It went right through me — as though he felt I had betrayed him somehow and was laughing at him now in his extremity.

His hand trembled as he tried to lift the pistol. And then with what must have been the last of his strength, he heaved himself upright in the bed. With a little cry of horror Millyanna shrank back against the wall. I was too surprised to do anything but watch as he uttered some inarticulate shriek and flung the pistol from him. It cleared my side of the bed, and I heard it clatter along the floor till the wall stopped it.

The effort of slinging that pistol carried him halfway out of the bed. He dangled over the edge like an old ragdoll, his head motionless against the bedframe. By the time Millyanna and I had laid him back on his pillow, he was dead.

14

Burial and Blue Water

I DON'T THINK Preble would have prayed over Hendley,
though he might have over the boy. But Millyanna wouldn't
even let me ask. She wanted everything done quickly with as
little fuss as possible. So the next day we took them out of
town and buried the boy and his father together, both in the
same grave. I wanted to buy them each a coffin – I knew
Millyanna had no money – but she insisted on burying them
Indian style, just sewed up in a couple of blankets.

There was a place not far from Paco where a little stream
from the Granite Hills stopped to breathe and lazed itself into
a tiny lake. Hendley and the boy used to camp there when the
two of them went out fishing together. We drove to the spot in
a wagon I had borrowed and there committed them to the
earth. Charlie Currus came with us. In fact, it was he who
dug the grave. Millyanna handled the shovel herself whenever
Charlie stopped to rest. But I wasn't able to do any more than
watch the two of them work.

After the grave was covered, Millyanna started us off and
we said together, "Our Father who art in heaven." I think she
would have welcomed some burying words from me – or even
from Charlie. But there we couldn't help her. Both of us had
been to church in our time, but neither of us ever learned
much by heart. The rest of the praying we did like Quakers –
every man for himself – and I guess Millyanna did most of
that. When it got time to leave, she shook hands with each of

us and thanked us for what we had done. She shook mine last; and before she climbed back into the wagon, she told me quietly,

"I am happy some one pray for my husband. — If he had called the name of my son only once last night, I would be able to call *his* name now. — But all my prayer today is for my son."

Millyanna left Paco that afternoon. She took Tom's horse and young Tommy's, and what few personal things of her own she had in the house. I asked her what she wanted done with the house and the furnishings and she said she didn't care.

"No use to me where I go," she told me, shaking her head.

"Well, where *are* you going?" I asked her.

She turned her face up at me with the same proud determination I had seen there the first night I met her. She looked much older now, worn thin and tortured over the coals of twenty years — but still strong and still of her own mind.

"To my people!" she said simply.

We were standing in the parlor of their house at the time, I with an armful of age and agony and she with it all in her heart.

"Is there — is there nothing I can do to make you believe *we* are your people now?" I asked her.

She looked at me and smiled for the first time since the day before.

"No — no!" she said gently. "But I always remember you try!"

I was the only one who saw her off.

Hendley's house and effects went to pay the debts he had in town. I stuck around till things got settled and did my best to see that nobody got more than was coming to him. I wound up with a few dollars to spare, which I put together with some of my own to buy a stone for the common grave. It was a simple stone, with only the names and the death date.

I got back to my ranch as soon as I could. But when I got there I didn't feel like working. I began to be very old very quickly. It all seemed futile to me now — the ranch I'd spent my life saving for and dreaming about. Nothing seemed to make any difference any more — whether the cattle got fat or my stream got cleared, or whether the sun went down and stayed there.

Charlie Currus and Doc Hobbs thought it was because my arm had died and I couldn't work the place myself any more. But there were other things, things that came in the night and stole my sleep and flayed me in the daytime when I remembered them — things that guns and Paco and the people of Paco couldn't begin to let me forget.

I sold my place, eventually — sold it before I let it run down any more. Charlie Currus paid me what I thought was more than fair. I left my spread and Paco, too, without a regret in my heart. I had come from the East, so I travelled the other way now and wound up at an almost decent hotel in San Francisco. — I needed a town that would swallow me up without rubbing its stomach or scratching its head.

I have enough money to last me, if I don't hang on too long. And from where I live, I can walk out a short way and look at the sea. No one expects anything from all that water; maybe that's why it seems so beautiful. I buried my pistol there one day. I had carried that Navy Colt with me all the way from Paco. But one day I walked down to the shore and, as the water came up and washed my boots, I flung it out into the waves as far as my left arm could send it.

I hear from Charlie Currus occasionally. He seems to have made a go of my spread — married the new school mistress and took to raising a family. Had a son and a daughter last I heard. He drilled himself a new well finally, put in a garden for his wife, and sold the herd down to where he could manage it without any help. I always thought well of Charlie. I believe he'll come along fine.

What I don't get from letters, I usually hear. That's one nice thing about a good-sized town. Sooner or later most of the news will catch you up. I heard a story once — some men were talking in the bar where I usually have my supper — about a Sioux Indian woman two of the men claimed to have seen. She had lived a long time among white people and had gone back finally to her own kind. But she hadn't gone empty-handed. She had learned the white man's language and some of his ways, to boot. She had taken his God back with her in a black book which she taught to her tribesmen — all who would take the trouble to learn.

The men were seated at a table behind me, and I got up at once and turned to face them.

"What was her *name?*" I asked them.

They all looked at me as though I belonged in some asylum.

"Prob'ly drunk!"

"Harmless old bastard — "

I heard their whispers go 'round the table.

"Whose name?" one of them asked at last.

"The Sioux — the Indian woman!" I said.

The speaker looked at the others and winked.

"Didn't know Indian women *had* names!" he said.

And the whole table dissolved in laughter. I felt too old to even get mad.

I didn't want any more supper. They were still laughing as I turned and left the room. But it was enough to have heard that story. It gave me a warm moment as I walked down to the shore to look at the sea in the dark.

Author's Afterword

SOME YEARS AGO, while studying English at New College, Oxford, I came across one of those grand literary pronouncements which compel action if not belief. A critic, whose name I have long since forgotten, referred to "Wandering Willie's Tale" by Sir Walter Scott as the finest short story in the English language. As I knew a little about Sir Walter but nothing of "Wandering Willie," I felt I should cure my ignorance forthwith. At that time the shelves of Blackwell's Bookstore were more familiar to me than those of my college library. I therefore made for Blackwell's during a mid-day break for lunch. I knew exactly where the works of Scott were kept; and I hoped that — if I could just *find* "Wandering Willie's Tale," and find it not too long — I might be able to read it "standing up." My economic soul was already mortgaged unto Blackwell's: I felt only a modicum of guilt at the thought of mooching a small "free read."

I discovered the tale to be a discrete chapter in the novel, *Redgauntlet*. Written in broad Scots dialect, the story was far too difficult to be gotten through "standing up." I had heard of *Redgauntlet* but had never laid eyes on it. I knew it was not thought to be one of Sir Walter's best, and I hardly wanted to buy it now for the sake of "Wandering Willie." What a dilemma! Should I try the college library, which might not have a complete set of Scott? — or the Bodleian itself, perhaps to find *Redgauntlet* pre-empted by another reader? In one of those rare moments that ever after seem providential, I noticed on the Scott shelf at Blackwell's a small volume entitled *Short Stories*. Did it contain "Wandering Willie's Tale"? It did! – and besides that, an introduction by Lord David Cecil, the senior English tutor at New College. The price (three shillings and sixpence – then almost seventy-five cents) would show as a pittance on my Blackwell's bill. With even my modicum of guilt allayed, I bought the little book and left to read "Wandering Willie's Tale" sitting down.

That purchase had many repercussions. First, of course, I read the famous "Tale." I found it fascinating. Though comic (in the highest sense), it remains a ghost story in spite of its final, more-or-less reasonable explanation of events. Its supernatural "loose ends" are almost all tied neatly up. The great exception is a certain rent receipt, presented in a dream to the hard-pressed tenant-hero by none other than the devil himself. The whole tale is richly colorful. Its narrator, Wandering Willie, is as picturesque as the characters he describes: he brings out all their craft and quaintness, their humor and superstition, together with his own. Moreover, in its twenty-six short pages, the tale gives a vivid impression of the politics and religion of the period. It is quite a *tour de force* – a fine short story by any standard. In its mood, color, and narrative thrust it may well be Sir Walter's best. But does it deserve the accolade of "finest in the language"?

My own preference is for stories with deeper emotional impact. "Wandering Willie's Tale," with its pat end to an evocation of romantic diablerie, seems a bit too cannily conclusive. It satisfies; it does not disturb. Admittedly, judgments of literary quality are all highly subjective. But as I looked through the rest of Sir Walter's little collection, I found two other stories which struck in me a deeper chord. Each is of the kind that provokes and disturbs — that somehow does not satisfy. Neither has the polish or panache of "Wandering Willie's Tale." And neither is a ghost story: both are all too terribly human. They are simple, violent tales of living and dying — of "joust" and justice — on or near the Scottish border. And both have haunted me over the years as few ghost stories have.

The second of the two will be referred to later. The first (and shorter) is the one to which I responded more profoundly. It is a brief sketch, eight pages long, entitled "Death of the Laird's Jock" — that is, the death of the Laird's son Jock, or Jack, who was so-called during his father's day to distinguish him from the Laird himself. (In this case, the eponomous hero, the Laird's Jock, has so glorified his nickname that it clings to him even after the death of his father.) Aside from its immediate impact, this sketch later moved me to write a novel of my own. The novel, which I wanted to call *The Death of Granite Hendley*, was published earlier in slightly different form by Doubleday & Company as *The Gun and Glory of Granite Hendley*. (It was feared that "death" in the title might inhibit sales: when, all unwillingly, I suggested "Gun and Glory" as an alternative, Doubleday leaped on it like a kid on a carousel.)

What sort of thing is this sketch, "Death of the Laird's Jock"? A slight one, by most accounts. In his introduction to Scott's *Short Stories*, Lord David Cecil refers to it as "not a story at all, only a note for one," and dismisses it as "an embryo," not interesting "save to the specialist student of Scott's artistic method."[1] Needless to say, this mere "note" or "embryo" struck me as an uncut gem.

---

[1]*Short Stories by Sir Walter Scott*, with an Introduction by Lord David Cecil, Oxford University Press (World Classics Edition), London, 1934 and 1952, p. xi. This book will be hereafter cited as *Scott*.

Its action is laid in Liddesdale (just north of the Scottish border) during the wild, old days of clanship and claymores. For many years the Laird's Jock has ruled his Scots roost with the aid of an awesome two-handed sword. This weapon was bequeathed him by an English outlaw, one Hobbie Noble, who, on fleeing the authorities south of the border, was hospitably received by the Laird's Jock. In the fullness of time, an English duellist crosses the border to challenge the best swordsman in Liddesdale. To the joy of his aged father, the only son of the Laird's Jock accepts this daring challenge. And the old man, having never allowed another to wield the redoubtable sword, now gives it to his son for use in the fight. With his retainers and his only other child, a daughter, the old man goes out to watch. Wrapped in his plaids, he seats himself on a great stone overlooking the lists.

Had the duel resulted otherwise, Sir Walter, no doubt, would have waxed eloquent for pages. Instead, he writes, "It is needless to describe the struggle: the Scottish champion fell."[2] Not only does the Laird's Jock see his son cut down: he sees the English challenger wave on high as a trophy the great two-handed sword torn from the grasp of his fallen foe. So seeing, the old man leaps up from his stone, utters an inarticulate shriek, and falls insensible to the ground. He is borne back to his castle, where he lingers on the verge of death, attended by his faithful daughter. He dies at the end of three days, never once having mentioned the name of his son, but uttering "unintermitted lamentations for the loss of his sword."[3]

The entire sketch is couched in the form of a letter from Sir Walter to an artist who had requested a subject from Scottish

[2]*Scott*, pp. 337-338.
[3]*Scott*, p. 338.

history for graphic representation. Scott tells the story and then suggests, as proper matter for a painting, the moment when the old man leaps up from his stone to utter his fearful cry. What use the artist made of this advice, I do not know. But for me the sketch became the germ of the *Hendley* novel.

Transferring the action from Elizabethan Scotland to the West of the 1870's seemed only logical. I could think of no other place where such a novel might be laid. Swords were "beaten into" pistols, Doc Holliday assumed the role of Hobbie Noble, a narrator was interpolated, and a chorus of townsfolk, thrown in.

Meanwhile, a further source materialized. Mark Twain, in *Roughing It*, had written of (among other things) a virtually lawless lawman named Slade, who was at last done in by a mob of his incensed fellow citizens. Twain's account inspired an unspectacular movie (no doubt, a "B-picture") entitled *Jack Slade*. The ending of the movie is different from that of Twain's account and, in a crude way, attempts to show Slade's judgment on himself. It was the first "psychological" Western I had seen. Its protagonist, together with the Laird's Jock, helped provide me a model of sorts for Marshal Hendley. Importantly, the movie concentrated more on the *effects* of Slade's brutality — upon himself and those closest to him — than it did on the man's violence toward offenders. I tried to do the same in *Hendley*. The effects of the town's hatred for its heavy-handed marshal became for me the focus of the story.

The redemptive figure of Millyanna was, of course, suggested by the faithful daughter of the Laird's Jock, although in Sir Walter's sketch she is little more than a shadow. In one way Millyanna proved as elusive as her model. While writing *Hendley*, I thought of it in visual terms as a film. Most of the principals were with me from the start. In the role of Marshal

Hendley I imagined Gregory Peck as he appeared in *The Gunfighter*; for Sam McCallum I chose Gary Cooper of *High Noon* fame; and for Mayor Garvey I thought of Frank Morgan as he played *The Vanishing Virginian*. Any one of a number of actors, I felt, could be young Tommy, the marshal's son. But I was never able to cast the difficult role of Millyanna. I hope this lapse says more of her ideality than of my own imperfect vision!

The chorus of townsfolk — the little community of Paco itself — perhaps fares worse at my hands than it did at those of its marshal. When I thought of writing another novel, the town came to my aid as perhaps I did not deserve. In spite (or indeed because) of its human smallness, I thought little Paco might be "taken to the well" again. Since its more colorful denizens are all dead at the end of *Hendley*, I had to go back in time and write a pre-sequel, or "pre-quel," to it.

For a plot I turned once more to "the Wizard of the North" — specifically, to the second of the two short stories by Sir Walter Scott that had lingered with me over the years. This second story, "The Two Drovers," is a relatively straightforward tale of how "a drover [i.e., a driver of cattle to market] may be touched on a point of honour . . ."[4] It is short (thirty-seven pages) but far from being sweet. And it is vintage Scott. As Lord David Cecil remarks, it is the only other short piece by Scott which deserves to be ranked with "Wandering Willie's Tale." Even so, Lord David writes, " . . . 'Wandering Willie's Tale' is not such an achievement as 'The Two Drovers.' Not that 'The Two Drovers' is more perfect. But it triumphs on a higher plane . . . . [I]t is a heroic tragedy . . ."[5] The story tells

[4]*Scott*, p. 221.

[5]*Scott*, p. xvii.

of a fight between two erstwhile friends, a subsequent killing
to avenge lost honor, a trial for murder that ends in a court-
directed "guilty" verdict, and (ultimately) a hanging. Such was
the germ of A *Woman, a Dog, and a Hanging Tree*. For Scott's
two friends and their falling-out I substituted the perennial
love triangle. The relationship of the three principals would
force the town of Paco to an overdue appraisal of its crude ideas
of justice.

With regard to the justice theme, Walter Van Tilburg Clark's
The Ox-Bow Incident gave my mind an interesting jog. Clark's
novel deals with the lynching of several innocent men who are
thought to be cattle thieves. I reversed Clark's situation and
wrote, not of a lynching, but of a legal hanging which the people
of Paco wanted to prevent. I envisioned a protagonist who,
though of the "weaker" sex, might teach the *macho* little town
a lesson in personal honor — a woman stronger in her own
way than those who did and did not judge her.

Of course, the two novels here presented have more in
common than the same general setting. Both are filtered
through the mind of the same narrator. This narrator, Sam
McCallum, is hardly my alter ego, though some have seen him
so. To me he is first and foremost a character in the story — a
man, not inarticulate, but of limited perception and sensibility.
Only such a person could tell and take part in both of the
stories as I envisioned them. McCallum sees and feels much
that he does not, for one reason or another, understand. Many
a thought, proportioned or "unproportion'd," he gives neither
act nor utterance. I hoped his limitations would appear
emblematic of those of his peers.

Odd as it may sound, even Shakespeare had an effect on A
Woman, a Dog, and a Hanging Tree. Two scenes by the bard

underlay the final confrontation between my heroine, Sadie
Magrath, and her wretched husband. In *Othello* the jealous
moor strikes Desdemona and calls her a whore in front of the
noble embassy from Venice. In *Much Ado About Nothing* the
misled Claudio similarly denounces his virtuous fiancée, Hero,
to her own father at what was to have been the lovers' wedding.
Both are brutal scenes. Desdemona and Hero are altogether
innocent; yet the one retires submissively, and the other falls
into a convenient swoon. In the final bar-room scene between
Sadie and her spouse, Sadie's vicious reaction to his taunt
reverses that of Shakespeare's docile ladies. In part, at least,
her deed comes by way of reprisal for the blindness of the
moor and of Claudio, if not of others who may have so abused
their women.

When all is said and read, this afterword may not be of
even passing interest to the reader. Worse, it may sound utterly
pretentious. But, as has elsewhere been observed, all art is a
coöperative endeavor. Literary debts are to be repaid, even
rejoiced in. To the great Scott, more than to any other, I
acknowledge my inspiration. Without his short stories there
would have been no Hendley, no Paco, no Sadie Magrath. I
hope I have not belittled his achievement. Indeed, I write to
praise Sir Walter, not to bury him. And if I have brought to
others *half* the pleasure Scott brought me, my efforts will have
been very well worthwhile.